CONTEMPORARY AMERICAN FICTION

FAMILY ATTRACTIONS

Judith Freeman was born in 1946 and raised in a Mormon family in Ogden, Utah. She lives in Los Angeles with her husband, artist-photographer Anthony Hernandez, and frequently reviews books for the *Los Angeles Times*. Her next work, *The Chinchilla Farm*, is a novel.

FAMILY ATTRACTIONS

STORIES BY

Judith Freeman

PENGUIN BOOKS

PENGUIN BOOKS
Published by the Penguin Group
Viking Penguin Inc., 40 West 23rd Street,
New York, New York 10010, U.S.A.
Penguin Books Ltd, 27 Wrights Lane,
London W8 5TZ, England
Penguin Books Australia Ltd, Ringwood,
Victoria, Australia
Penguin Books Canada Ltd, 2801 John Street,
Markham, Ontario, Canada L3R 1B4
Penguin Books (N.Z.) Ltd, 182–190 Wairau Road,
Auckland 10, New Zealand

Penguin Books Ltd, Registered Offices:
Harmondsworth, Middlesex, England

First published in the United States of America
by Viking Penguin Inc. 1988
Published in Penguin Books 1989

1 3 5 7 9 10 8 6 4 2

"Family Attractions" first appeared in *Zyzzyva* magazine, and
"The Joan Crawford Letter" in *The Berkeley Fiction Review*.

Grateful acknowledgment is made for permission to reprint an
excerpt from "East Coker" from *Four Quartets* by T. S. Eliot.
Copyright 1943 by T. S. Eliot; renewed 1971 by Esme Valerie Eliot.
Reprinted by permission of Harcourt Brace Jovanovich, Inc. and Faber and Faber Ltd.

LIBRARY OF CONGRESS CATALOGING IN PUBLICATION DATA
Freeman, Judith, 1946–
Family attractions: stories/ by Judith Freeman.
p.   cm—(Contemporary American fiction)
ISBN 0 14 01.0533 6
I. Title. II. Series.
[PS3556.R3915F36   1989]
813'.54–dc19   88–7976

Printed in the United States of America
Set in Primer
Designed by Ann Gold

For my parents, Roy and Alice

and

in memory of my brother, Bob

◆ ——————————— ◆

On a summer midnight, you can hear the music
Of the weak pipe and the little drum
And see them dancing around the bonfire
The association of man and woman
In daunsinge, signifying matrimonie—
A dignified and commodiois sacrament.
Two and two, necessarye coniunction,
Holding eche other by the hand or the arm
Whiche betokeneth concorde. Round and round the fire
Leaping through the flames, or joined in circles,
Rustically solemn or in rustic laughter
Lifting heavy feet in clumsy shoes,
Earth feet, loam feet, lifted in country mirth
Mirth of those long since under earth
Nourishing the corn. Keeping time,
Keeping the rhythm in their dancing
As in their living in the living season
The time of the seasons and the constellations
The time of milking and the time of harvest
The time of the coupling of man and woman

T.S. Eliot, from
The Four Quartets

All my life I have been fascinated by the moment of
change. Between waking and sleeping, for example.
Once, when I was a child, someone walked into the
room at the moment I was falling asleep. That made
me very happy.   Eva Zeisel

CONTENTS

FAMILY
ATTRACTIONS

FAMILY ATTRACTIONS

Evelyn sat in the kitchen, trying to figure out what to do for the twins' birthday. She was going through the "Family Attractions" column in the newspaper.

"How does Magic Mountain sound?"

"Bor-innng," Lois said. Linda didn't respond. She was lost to the music coming through her headphones.

"Hollywood Wax Museum . . . ?"

Lois shook her head. "Why don't we get George in here? He might have an idea."

"Don't ask George what he wants to do because he won't have an answer," Evelyn said. George wasn't the father of the girls, although he'd accepted that role as well as he could, given the fact he was a lifelong bachelor and over sixty when he met and married their mother, several months ago. The girls' real father had died in a fiery collision near Barstow.

"Cabrillo Marine Museum?"

"Dead fish," Lois said. "I can open a can of tuna if I want to see that." She stuck her thumb in her mouth.

"What's that thumb doing in your mouth?"

"I can't answer, I've got a thumb in my mouth," Lois said.

"And you're turning nine tomorrow." Evelyn shook her head. "I rue the day I gave you binkies."

Linda took her headphones off. "Are we going to have lunch or what?"

"Or what," said Evelyn. "It's not even noon."

"We could go to McDonald's."

"Wait till George finishes what he's doing and we'll eat. But we're not going to McDonald's. There's leftover meatloaf from last night. We'll make sandwiches."

Linda put her finger in her mouth and bent over the table, pretending to gag. Evelyn looked hard at her.

"You know, there are lots of starving kids in the world who would be very happy to get meatloaf."

"Name two," Linda said.

"Very funny. I don't know why I'm going to all this trouble here. You two are ingrates."

When George came in from the yard, they were still sitting at the table.

"Ugh," Evelyn said. "You're tracking something here."

George looked at his shoes, then tiptoed back through the door and reentered moments later.

"I hope that wasn't what I think it was," Evelyn said, looking up from her newspaper.

"Just mud," George said.

"The girls haven't been picking up after the dog this week. In fact, they've been very lazy about their chores. I don't know what we're going to do about it." She looked at her daughters severely.

"How about we string them up by their toes and put goose feathers under their noses?" George laid a finger lightly on the end of Lois's nose. She squealed happily.

"George!" she yelled, twisting away from him.

From the beginning, during those first awkward days after the wedding when tests of various kinds were common and the twins saw to it that George remained unassimilated, everyone had agreed that the girls should call him George, and not Dad, as a means of letting them guard their familial territory until such time when they could accept him naturally. For weeks, they kept him outside their circle, sometimes refusing to talk to him at all, other times being intentionally rude. Unkind reminders of his age were used to distance themselves from him: "George is old enough to be our grandfather," Lois said one day in front of him. "George is older than our grandfather," Linda added. Quite recently, however, something had happened. The tide had turned. More and more, they warmed up to him, sensing, old or not, George was the kind of person who, without striving for it, was a source of marvelous fun.

"So how are the plans coming?" George asked.

"Mom doesn't know what we're going to do," Lois said wearily.

"There's the Stuntman Hall of Fame," Evelyn said, still reading from the newspaper. "Or the Museum of World Wars, Sea World, the Pasadena Flea Market. Hey, how about the flea market? That might be fun."

"Fun for you," Lois said.

George spoke up from the sink where he was scrubbing his hands.

"When I was a boy," he said, "I took my mother rowing on Lake Larson every year for her birthday. Lake Larson is in Minnesota," he added.

Evelyn, who harbored a low opinion of George's athletic abilities, said, "I didn't know you could row, George."

"They had the prettiest little boats that you could rent," George said. "That was Mom's idea of heaven." He was about to tell them what color the boats were, a bright blue, and how his mother liked to row to a monastery on the far side of the lake where, near a statue of Christ, they sat on a marble bench and ate their picnic lunch, but Evelyn spoke up first.

"Why don't we take a picnic to Lake Sherwood tomorrow and George can row us around the lake?"

"I don't know this Lake Sherwood," George said. "Is it near?"

Lois, taking her thumb out of her mouth, brightened and said, "Can Barky go?"

"I'm sure they don't allow dogs," Evelyn said. She wanted to slap her daughter's hand away from her mouth. Ignore it, the shrink said, but it was easier said than done. Evelyn turned to her other daughter. "What do you think, Linda?"

Linda held up her hand to indicate that her mother should not, at this crucial moment, interrupt her musical concentration.

"I'm talking to you," Evelyn said.

"She can't hear you," George explained, pointing to his ears.

Evelyn yelled, "I'm trying to plan something here!"

"Sounds good to me," George said happily. "Rowing, a picnic. Great. I could use a day in the sun. Sometimes I think this job is killing me. It's bad enough during an ordinary week, but when it's hot, people get crazy and they'd like to kill you. You go into people's houses and they're filthy, especially under the sinks. I had to crawl under a house yesterday because a rat died between a wall and the bathtub and the smell was coming up through the pipes. There wasn't anything I could do to get that rat out of there. 'You're going to just have to wait until Mother Nature does her work,' I said. 'Dust to dust.' But the woman didn't want to hear that. They don't want to pay you if you can't fix everything, but you've got to charge them for trying."

"What about Barky?" Lois said.

"Take that thumb out of your mouth, you're nine years old."

"Technically, I'm still eight," Lois said.

"I think Barky could go," George said. He stood behind Evelyn and put his hands on her shoulders. As he spoke, he softly kneaded her flesh. "We'll sneak him in."

Evelyn felt a sudden annoyance. Everything was working against her. The whole family was like a wave shoving her back to shore when she was trying to make a little headway here. She waved a hand in front of Linda's face. "Hey you," she said. She waved again.

Linda took her headphones off and stared at her mother. "You just interrupted the best part of 'Material Girl.' Like the very part I've been waiting for."

"What the hell have I done wrong," Evelyn said, and walked out of the kitchen.

George and the girls were watching TV when Evelyn came down later and apologized for being short-tempered. "I'm getting my period," she whispered to George, settling down beside him on the couch. "I haven't actually started bleeding yet but I feel awful. Edgy, you know."

"Oh," George said. He was still unused to a woman confiding in him about her cycles.

They were watching a program on vampire bats on the public television station. The bats were shown flying through the air in slow motion, undulating like swimmers, and although their faces were terrifying, Evelyn thought their bodies quite beautiful. Lit from behind, they had a human shape—legs and arms—with wings of the thinnest membranes, translucent as fine pink silk, stretching from the arms to the body like some sort of see-through garment.

The narrator said that in a small town in Mexico, bats were posing a problem for livestock raisers who annually lost hundreds of animals to anemia as a result of bats preying on them.

In the next scene, two bats were shown sneaking up on a tethered horse that was so gaunt its bones protruded like the spikes of a broken umbrella pushing against the fabric. The bats moved along the ground, hopping like quick little monkeys.

"How do they get these pictures at night?" Evelyn asked.

"Infrared photography, I guess," George replied.

"Ssshhh, you guys," Lois said.

A bat hopped onto the horse's hind leg and bit it just above the hock. The horse stamped its foot and the bat scurried away. But it was too late, the narrator said. The bat had already done its work, injecting a numbing agent, secreted in its saliva, into the horse's leg. Now the bat would wait until it could return to the site and feed without the horse feeling anything. The bats hopped around the horse like mischievous fairies. A few moments later, one of the bats jumped onto the horse's leg and began drawing blood. Afterward, the bats returned to their cave and were shown feeding regurgitated blood to their babies and mates, who hung upside down from the cave's ceiling.

"I just don't see how they get these close-up shots in a cave," Evelyn said. "How come the bats let somebody in there to take pictures?"

"They're using a hidden camera," George said.

"God," Linda said in disgust. "Look at those things."

"I've told you not to use God like that."

"You do."

"You're not old enough. Can it."

Since the farmers were losing livestock, the narrator said, it was decided the bats must be controlled. The same gaunt horse that had appeared in previous scenes was injected with a slow-working poison. When the bats returned to attack it that night, they filled up on poisoned blood and returned and fed it to the others. In the last scene, helmeted men with flashlights were examining a cave littered with bat corpses.

"I don't know how we can eat dinner after that," Evelyn said when the program was over. She puckered her mouth and squinted at George.

George laughed. "It's just nature, Evelyn."

"We could go to Chuck E. Cheese," Lois said. She stretched, yawned sleepily, and rolled over onto her stomach, lying on the carpet in front of the TV. Linda put her feet on Lois's back.

"Get your dirty socks off me," Lois said, and twisted away from her, rolling over and over across the the floor.

"That stuff in the fridge is going to spoil if we don't eat it."

"What are these?" Lois said. She was looking at George's hand.

"Age spots," George said.

"Oooo," Lois said, and fell back on the floor in a slump, as if she'd just fainted. "How disgusting."

Linda took off her socks and stuffed them into one big ball and lobbed it across the room at Lois. Lois ducked, then picked up the sock-ball and threw it back.

"Tell you what," George said. "Since you only turn nine once in your life, we'll go out tonight. How does that sound?"

In five minutes, they were ready to leave. But as they stood at the door, Evelyn looked wistfully back toward the kitchen and said, "I just hate to waste food." She sighed. "All that stuff rotting in the refrigerator."

That night George said, "You have so many nice nightgowns, why don't you ever wear them?" Evelyn, wearing a gray sweatshirt, had just gotten into bed.

"I'm cold," she said. "I just want to be warm."

George slipped his arm under her neck and tried to roll her closer to him.

"It's all right, George."

"I thought I'd get you warm."

He smiled. Evelyn looked closely at his mouth and thought, If he went to a hygienist now, it would be a big, unpleasant job to clean his teeth. He had let it go too long.

She turned out the light. Cars sped past the house, the sound building and fading, like waves. A motorcycle roared by, followed by a car with rock and roll blaring from its radio. It was silent for a while; then, because the light up the street changed, more cars went by.

George said, "What time should we plan on leaving tomorrow?"

"Oh, whenever we get away."

George imagined rowing his family over the water, pulling the boat across the smooth surface of a lake, balancing the weight of his passengers, shifting to counter their movements.

Evelyn, feeling his hips move beside her on the mattress said, "It's the wrong time for that, George."

At first he didn't understand what she meant, and then he did, and he wanted to say something, how he was thinking about something else. Sometimes he didn't know where things came from, why they didn't understand each other better. How could she think he had wanted that, when he had only been thinking about rowing and steadying the load of his passengers?

"It's lunchtime at McDonald's," Lois said as they were loading blankets and food into the back of the truck, which had the name of George's company, LAYTON HEATING AND PLUMBING, painted on the doors.

Evelyn frowned at the picnic basket she held. Catsup had oozed from the bottle and soiled a napkin. She tightened the lid.

"Ooo, bat blood!" Linda said, staring at the thin line of catsup on Evelyn's hand.

"Bat blood!" the girls shrieked, feigning horror, and backing away from their mother. Evelyn held her hands up to scare them and the girls grabbed for each other and ran behind the *Pittosporum* bush.

"Help us, George," they squealed, "save us please!"

"Coming to get you," Evelyn said. She held her hands up and pulled a face.

"Ha ha ha," she said gruffly, and chased the twins around the bush and back to the truck, where George stood ready to catch them and lift them up into the truck bed. They all stood looking at one another, the girls excited and still acting like they were frightened, Evelyn flushed from running, George calmly smiling.

"Now promise me you won't stand up or move around if I let you ride back here," he said to them.

As they pulled away from the house and drove down the street lined with flowering acacia, George checked the rearview mirror to be certain the children were safe and still in their places.

Under a sky that was gray, they drove west on the Ventura Freeway. By the time they reached Calabasas, openings appeared in the clouds and big holes of blue showed through. As they were passing the pet cemetery, Evelyn said, "I wonder where we'll bury Barky when he dies."

This upset George. It seemed unnecessarily morbid since Barky was only three and a vigorous, happy animal.

"Don't think about it," he said.

"I'm trying to think about something other than the damned thumb sucking," she said.

George looked in the rearview mirror. The girls were waving at an older couple in a Cadillac who were following them. The couple weren't waving back.

"Marla tells me to ignore it and I try, Lord I try, but every time one of them sticks a thumb in her mouth I think, where have I failed here? It's like a picture of my failure. I didn't give them something. I didn't do something right."

George could not think of who Marla was. The counselor at school? The psychiatrist Evelyn went to before the one she had now?

He said, "How do you know those twins wouldn't have sucked their thumbs if they'd been born to somebody else?"

"Well, you can't ever know something like that."

"Everybody does the best they can," George said. "If they could do better, they would."

"Maybe this is over your head. Or out of your ballpark or something."

"What do you mean?"

"Maybe you've got to have kids to know what I'm talking about."

"I've got kids now," he said. He waited for her to say something but she didn't.

The Cadillac pulled into the next lane and began passing. As it went by, the girls waved again. He could see their fluttering hands and wished the people would wave back, but they kept their eyes straight ahead, ignoring the girls.

"I wouldn't let them keep their binkies so long," Evelyn said, "if I had it to do over again."

"Binkies?"

"You know, pacifiers."

"That's where they filmed *M*A*S*H*," Evelyn said later, lifting her aviator sunglasses. "That's supposed to be Korea."

They were inland from Malibu, on a two-lane road, climbing

through the dry hills that separate the ocean from the valley. George slowed down to look at the $M^*A^*S^*H$ buildings, set back off the road in a narrow canyon. Hawks circled above the ridge, riding a hot wind.

"Look at the hawks," he said.

"I see them," she said.

A few miles later, they came to the Lake Sherwood turnoff. A man sat on a folding chair at the end of a dirt road, cleaning his fingernails with a pocketknife. They paid him two dollars. He made them promise to leave the dog in the truck once they got to the lake. Dogs weren't allowed. He was willing to make an exception, as long as the dog stayed in the truck.

Barky jumped out as soon as the truck came to a stop under a eucalyptus tree, and the twins followed.

"Everybody carry something," Evelyn yelled to the twins. "You take the Playmate," she said to George, meaning the plastic cooler with the drinks inside. George was looking out over the lake. It was a fine spot. Steep green hills rose from the edge of the water. The sun glinted on the water's surface, breaking up into sharp points of dancing light and George thought it a wonderful sight. The lake seemed to be quite large, and L-shaped, although part of it wasn't visible from where he stood. Next to the truck, a field of orange poppies bloomed, and beyond that stood two small white buildings, the café and bait shop.

The children swirled around on the dusty path, trying to grab Barky by the collar.

"I know we shouldn't have the dog," Evelyn said. She walked lopsidedly, weighed down by the picnic basket.

The girls ran on ahead. A wind came up suddenly and lifted their dresses and George looked away, shy and embarrassed before their youthful shapes.

"I know we're going to get busted," Evelyn said.

"Wait by the dock," George told her. Inside the little store he rented a boat for three hours. He bought KitKat bars for the girls and stuck them into his pocket. He saw some fishing lures on a cardboard display that he thought he could make into a pair of earrings for Evelyn, and he bought two of them. They were beautiful metal ovals, speckled purple and yellow, and he could imagine them flashing from Evelyn's earlobes, catching light and casting pale hues of color onto her neck.

Once outside, he waved to his family from the porch and started walking toward the dock. It still surprised him that he had this family, that the identical girls in blue dresses, and the woman in a full yellow skirt and black sweater, who were all now waving back at him, their arms raised up into pale and fragile arcs, were actually his own.

"They're fishing, George," Lois said, pointing to some kids standing on the end of the dock. "Linda and I want to fish."

"Ah, fishing," George said. "We'll have to do that." He looked over the row of wooden boats bobbing on either side of the dock.

"Hurry up, honey," Evelyn said. "Pick a boat, any boat, and let's get going before somebody stops us."

The boats were white and in need of a fresh coat of paint. George frowned at them. Finally, he picked out one with an extra oar and helped his family climb in, then coaxed Barky aboard.

"George, is this a good idea?" Evelyn said, trying to steady the boat with one hand and pushing on Barky's haunches with the other, in an effort to get him to sit. She held onto the dock while George stepped over the edge, and the boat lowered deeper into the water. Someone appeared on the porch of the bait shop and yelled at them. George, with a firm push, sent the wavering boat gliding away from the dock.

"It's a very good idea," he said. "Just sit still. Pretend you don't hear him. Don't look at him."

Evelyn put her sweater over Barky's head and tied the sleeves around his neck like a scarf. She put her sunglasses on his nose.

"He looks very human," George said. "One of us."

George had met Evelyn on a Sierra Club bird-watching trip to Point Mugu Naval Station where, in marshes set among the test-firing ranges, they observed blue-crested mallards, willets, leggy egrets, and the rare clapper rail. Nearer the ocean, tide pools were also examined.

"We're here to observe what's above and what's below," Puff McGruder, the outing leader, said to the Sierra Clubbers as they disembarked from the bus. Since they all belonged to the West Side Singles Chapter, they were also there to observe what was next to them.

During a restroom stop at the golf course clubhouse, a long line formed in front of the facilities. George, who was standing near Evelyn, noticed the flower printed on the front of her T-shirt and asked the name of it.

"That's a giant *Coreopsis*," Evelyn said.

"How large are they?" George asked.

"Oh, about a thirty-six D," Evelyn said, and they both laughed.

George bought her coffee, served in cups with plastic missiles for stirrers, and they sat together on the bus during the rest of the trip. Soon, they were dating regularly.

In many ways, they made an unlikely couple. He was sixty-three, she just thirty-eight. He stood six feet four, she was just over five feet. The first time he hugged her, he felt the sharp point of her nose pressing against the bottom of his sternum.

He had never planned to marry, let alone marry a woman twenty-five years younger, and one with two energetic children. But Evelyn, in so many ways, was the perfect match for him. She was the only woman with whom he'd ever seen a future. It surprised him. It came late in life, when he'd adjusted to things going another way.

"If you'll have me," he said to her a few months after the Point Mugu trip, "I'm yours."

The lake was smooth and George found rowing easy. He faced his family and contemplated his luck. What would he have, twenty years with them? Fifteen? Life insurance should guarantee educations for the girls if he should go sooner. Recently, the heavyset black woman who was the dispatcher at work said to him, "I bought me an alarm clock, but you know, that thing runs backward. Now, I don't need that." But that's precisely what George wished he had, a clock that ran backward for a while.

He felt for the lures in his pocket and drew them out to show Evelyn, but she was looking through the binoculars, studying some birds feeding close to shore. He put them back and remembered the KitKat bars.

"Want some chocolate?" he said to Lois, who was holding her Barbie doll over the edge of the boat, dragging the permanently arched feet across the surface of the water.

"Yeah," Lois said.

"Say thank you."

"Thanks, George."

"Want a candy bar, Linda?"

"Thanks a lot, Georgio," Linda said.

George decided to row to the small island in the middle of the lake. It was farther than it looked. Progress was slow in the small boat, loaded down as it was, but he felt he could row like this all day. About halfway to the island, however, he began to feel a tiredness in his arms that progressed to an overall fatigue he was embarrassed to admit. He stopped for a moment, pretending to enjoy the scenery, and they drifted, borne by a wind that moved them toward another boat where people were quietly fishing.

"Hallooo," he called, and the fishermen gave a friendly wave.

By the time they reached the island, George felt he needed a rest and suggested they go ashore for their picnic.

"But it says no trespassing." Evelyn pointed to a sign, posted by the Department of Water and Power, that threatened trespassers with fines and prosecution.

"Who's the wiser?" George said, and put the boat ashore on a sandy strip between two rocks. He was the first out, stepping into shallow water in his chunky shoes and black socks, claiming the island as the sovereign territory of the Laytons.

The island was so small it took only a few minutes to climb to the summit where they had a view of the whole lake. Lois, Linda, and Barky ran down to a grove of oak trees while Evelyn spread the blanket and set out brightly colored containers of food. George felt out of breath and lay down close to her. He closed his eyes. Spirochete-shaped objects floated before him, rising and falling fluidly against the pinkness of his eyelids, illumined by the sun. He felt a little nauseated, his back ached, and his wet shoes were uncomfortable.

He looked up at his wife, who was spreading pimento cheese on crackers, her breasts full and free under her dress. Reaching out, he touched her, while Evelyn continued making sandwiches. He didn't fondle her breast, but held it still and firmly in his hand, enjoying its weight. It made him immensely happy that Evelyn allowed him to do this. From a distance, he heard the children's voices, singing in unison: "We are the thumb suckers of the thumb-sucking club," and the giggling that followed.

Evelyn frowned.

"Evelyn," he said, and when she looked at him, he smiled. "It's OK."

After they ate, the kids cracked rocks and examined their interiors.

"This one looks like an M&M, doesn't it?" Lois said, and held up a white rock with a black interior.

"This one is even prettier," Linda said, exhibiting a plain rock that wasn't very pretty at all.

Evelyn and George lay on the blanket and dozed, thinly aware of the world, the motorboat in the distance, the flies above their heads, the dog digging a hole, the girls hammering on their finds.

When he awoke, George called to the girls and together they climbed a large boulder at the very summit of the hill. He took two balloons from his pocket and blew them up and gave one to each girl, telling them to make a wish and let the balloons go. The balloons, a red one and a blue one, were carried by the wind out over the low trees, over the island's shore and beyond the boat, floating far out over the lake before they descended and skittered across the surface of the water.

"You will live long lives," George said, assuming an erect posture befitting his role as mock fortune-teller. "You, Lois, will marry a whale," he predicted, "and live happily in the sea. You, Linda, will marry a bear and be queen of the forest."

"George," Evelyn called. "We ought to get going. What are you guys doing up there? It's getting late."

The children ran down the hill, dodging clumps of cacti and the prickly bushes, racing toward the boat. Evelyn and George followed at a slower pace.

"George," she said, just before they reached the spot where the boat was tied, "would you like to have a baby?"

George laughed. "That's a new one." He felt his heart beat faster.

"I've been thinking we could have a child together if we do it soon. Lots of women have kids when they're my age."

"I don't know," George said, but he did know, and he would tell Evelyn later, when he had thought it through and knew exactly how he wanted to say it.

Rowing back across the lake, the sun was low and their skin glowed a golden apricot color in the light. George pulled at the oars, but his arms felt heavy and he was very tired. Frequently, he looked over his shoulder to check the distance to the docks, which never seemed to change. Lois hung over the side, dangling her doll, moving its legs so that sometimes Barbie swam, and sometimes she walked on the water. Linda slept, her head on her mother's lap. Each time he looked at Evelyn, she smiled at him so kindly that she appeared beatific to him. As they rounded the rocky point where the water eddied into a cave at the shoreline, something swooped out of the sky and darted past so quickly that for a moment George wasn't certain he'd actually seen anything. He thought some trick of the eye had fooled him. But then a second time the thing dove in front of him, and this time he saw it for what it was, a bat, moving out at dusk from some dank and darkened dwelling.

THE BOTANIC GARDENS

It was terrible to be alone in a foreign city. Every day you had to think of things to do, create everything from scratch, as though you were an artist confronted with an empty canvas or a writer peering at blank paper. It frightened her to look down the day at this stretch of empty time. But, by noon, as usual, she got up her courage and left the hotel and went down the street to the fish market and asked for the fish-and-chips, which they wrapped in newspaper for her. In the park, which was really a median of grass that separated two lanes of traffic, she ate her fish, feeling conspicuously alone. She imagined other people looked at her and once, as she brushed crumbs from her breast, she actually caught a man staring. (Why did she always drop crumbs on herself when other people seemed so neat?) She resolved to eat more carefully and nibbled at the chips as though they were delectable little morsels of caviar on toast, but then she was conscious only of the act of eating and didn't enjoy the food. There was nothing left except the grease stains on the paper when she'd finished.

She walked to the flower shop. The girls in the flower shop were a cold bunch. They watched her. Never a smile from these girls. Young and pretty, what did they have to worry about? With other customers they were familiar, even cloying. She bought a gardenia, only one, for forty cents and once outside, pinned it to her coat. That was nice, the smell of something sweet. Some people would say gardenias were too strong. Her fingers still had the feel of grease from the chips. She stopped at the corner where there was a public fountain and ran water over her hands. She took a hankie out of her purse and wiped them dry. The hankie needed washing; for two weeks she'd carried it in her purse, ever since leaving home.

There was still time, so much time left in one day. The post office was closed. She'd intended to buy stamps. Turning onto Edgerton Road, she walked toward the subway station. School was out, it was the weekend, and children swarmed in the streets. One bumped against her roughly. They had no manners, these children. She had to wait for a train. The sallowness of these people was astonishing. She had thought Australians were supposed to be a healthy, robust bunch.

The train took her to Martin Place, a plaza in the middle of the city. She'd hoped something was playing at the cinema but it advertised a movie she'd already seen. On the plaza, she stood in a group of people and watched a guitarist. His hands were delicate and white but the rest of him was dirty. When it came time to put money in his guitar case, she moved on, thinking he didn't deserve payment for his kind of music. Someone tried to give her a leaflet: "BAN SMOKING IN PUBLIC PLACES." She felt contempt for people who tried to ban things. The library was closed on Sundays or else she would have stopped in there. There was no place to go. Sundays were the most subversive days. That's when the culture threw you back on yourself, the day that families and lovers paraded their attachments. If you were single you felt it more. A laziness took over and she crossed the street and entered the high gates of the Royal Botanic Gardens. Sleep, that was the thing, a little nap on the grass beneath the broad-leaved trees. Pink and gray parrots pecked at the base of a tree before her. She lay down and the birds scattered, rising into the air rather laboriously, and settling on branches of a Morton Bay fig. An hour or so later she awoke because she was cold. Her soft flesh showed the imprint of grass. The gardenia on her breast had been crushed. She tried to tell herself it didn't matter about the gardenia, but it did, she felt the waste, the destruction of beauty, the loss of forty cents. She stopped in at the restroom in the subway station and, from a closed stall, overheard a conversation.

" 'So,' I said to Mother, 'it's me or him. I'm not living in the same house with that animal. He tried to touch me.' 'Where?' Mama says. 'What do you mean where? In the kitchen.' No, she wants to know what part of my body he tried to touch. It's just too disgusting."

"I like Harry, I really do. But you know what he told me? He says to me, 'There's only three things in the world I care about, my moustache, my mother, and Simon and Garfunkel.' I don't know if I can have a relationship with a man like that. I mean, where do I fit in?"

She came out of the stall and looked around but the women had left and she ended up staring at her own badly lit face in the mirror.

In the subway, she saw a flyer announcing free lunch-hour recitals on Mondays at St. Stephan's church, opposite the Botanic Gardens. Tomorrow's concert featured Schubert. On the train, her spirits felt lifted by the thought of the recital. It would give tomorrow a purpose. She hated religion and normally refused to enter a church, but for music, free music, and especially for Schubert, she'd make an exception. Poor Schubert, such a sad life, early death, poverty, the noble struggle for art. It was said he regretted never marrying. Wasn't this also her regret?

She returned to her hotel and ordered tea and listened to the ABC. Before going to bed, she wrote her mother a letter that began:

> You'll regret, I think, not coming with me on this trip
> when I tell you how beautiful Sydney is. I'm having quite
> a marvelous time. Today I took the subway to the center
> of the city, tomorrow I've scheduled a concert. Travel,

as we both know, is just what one needs to adjust one's perspective. I'm hardly thinking at all of Jorem.

The next day, she arrived early for the lunchtime concert. It didn't begin until noon and it was ten of twelve when she entered the darkened chapel. A kind of gloom emanated from the interior of the church, as it also did from Beatrice, who resented being so surrounded by religion. Religion struck her as a feeble attempt by mankind to bore itself to death in lieu of some long forgotten excitement. It was a baroque little way station on the road back to the beginning.

She had taken a seat near the front of the chapel where she could be certain to see the musicians. Two women came in and sat directly behind her.

"I'm more worried than excited," one woman said, "but once I go . . . " She left her sentence unfinished.

"It sounds bad," her companion said.

"Surgery wouldn't be the end of the world, would it? I'd give a pretty penny for a week's rest in hospital."

"In any case, it's in God's hands."

"Anything can happen through the power of prayer."

"When you pray, do you get on your knees? I can't get on my knees anymore. I wonder, does it make any difference?"

"Naw lovey, I don't suppose it does. But I like a proper supplicant's position. Try rolling a towel, like I do when I scrub floors."

"I don't suppose the position matters much, does it, as long as you get it right?"

"Like sex, love."

"Oh, you are bad!" Their laughter, inappropriate and coarse, echoed inside the domed chapel. Cheerily, one of them said, "I feel like getting me some seeds today and sticking them in the ground."

Just then, the Reverend Leonard J. Small took the podium. "This is the house of God," he said. "Worship with us through music. Remember God is present. Hand over to him all your burdens. Allow Him to take from your soul the strain and stress of daily life. Pray for others as you pray for yourself. Go forth in the strength which God supplies. Amen."

It's an awful lot to put up with, just for Schubert, she thought. But then the music began, and a sweet calm came over her as the frail soprano sang:

> Who is Sylvia? What is she,
> That all our swains commend her?

Beatrice looked around the church. She focused on a man near the windows who sat with his eyes closed, his face tilted slightly upward, as if sunbathing. His thick hair stuck up like a cock's comb and looked blue-black in the light filtering through the stained-glass windows. He had a thin moustache and wore a tie. Beatrice decided he looked like a poet. In his face, she discovered shades of James Joyce.

"Continuing with our emphasis this year on Bartók and Schubert," Reverend Small said at the end of the first song, "we shall next hear 'In der Fremde . . . . .' "

Beatrice closed her eyes, not completely, but so the light dimmed to a ghostly aura. In a foreign land . . .

When the concert was finished, she stopped on the steps outside to put her coat on. The man who had been sitting near the windows came out and stood next to her.

"Did you enjoy the concert?" he asked.

"Very much," she said. "Yes, it was nice."

"Wasn't it, though?" the man said amiably.

"Better than I expected," Beatrice added.

"An absolutely lovely performance," he said, and nodding to her, walked down the steps.

The sun shone on the doors of the library across the way where dozens of brass panels in bas-relief depicted the early Australians—the explorers, the distinguished settlers, convicts, artists, politicians, and the aboriginals of the old, red land. She watched as the man walked straight up the street at a brisk pace, past the library doors, until he finally disappeared into the Martin Place subway station.

During the afternoon, life had an unaccountable fullness and sweetness to Beatrice. She simply felt good. She enjoyed every activity without attributing her good feelings to their source, which was the concert, the Joycean man on the steps, and a general feeling that at last, on this journey, something had happened. When she returned to the hotel, she wrote about it in a letter to her mother.

It's odd how I felt in the church today. I resist going into churches but I always have this holy feeling when I'm there. All those ornaments, and the lovely colors in the window light, the arches with the sense of ascending space, and even the comfort of the padded little knee rests, which swing down so conveniently from the pew in front of you. It's all geared to comfort and grandeur so you'll give them more money, I suppose. But I was struck by the altar and the artifice and the edifice of it all. It got to me as it did in Notre-Dame and the time when Jorem and I were in St. Paul's in London at Christmas. The church today wasn't even that grand but I think if you had been with me you would have been struck by it too, and felt the pale slivers of faith working in you. Listen to me! I sound decidedly religious suddenly. I suppose the loss of a loved one can have queer effects but let's hope it doesn't turn me into one of those tiresome believers of one sort or another. At any rate, the discovery of the concert series is one of those fortuitous occasions that deliver unexpected rewards, and I will probably make these Monday concerts a regular event as long as my visit lasts.

Love, Beatrice

She went down to dinner. In the dining room, the pale waiter she was accustomed to served her with perfect obeisance. Beatrice's rule as a traveler was you had to spend a certain number of days in a place before you could judge it at all. First impressions were useful, but familiarity with shopkeepers, the budding friendship with a hotelier, or simply being recognized by a waiter who didn't despise his job in a restaurant that in turn didn't despise its helpers—these were the things that made a difference in how you *really* felt about a place. Sydney had been slow in serving up good impressions. Initially it seemed a very common place, rather like an ordinary American city such as Atlanta or Baltimore, quite uninspiring. But tonight everything felt comfortably elegant and suitably foreign. The waiter called her Mrs. Sharpels, exactly as she wished it, with no prompting whatsoever. The fish was perfectly delicious, fresh from the unpolluted water of the vast ocean surrounding the coastline. In the corner, a harpist offered Bach, not too loud, not too soft. The other diners, like Beatrice herself, had taken some care to dress for dinner, and the price of the place cut down on children, so that in general, most everything tonight was to her liking, right down to the Pavlova, the recommended dessert.

The waiter, who stood in the corner with his hands clasped, his legs stiff and buttocks pressed against the wall, raised his eyebrows and came at her call. He was a rather oily little man, really, once up close. Sometimes his cuffs weren't quite white. But he had the proper mixture of taciturnity and friendliness, adding up to that perfect obeisance. She called for and received the bill, added it, examined each item, left exactly the same tip she did every night, and went up to bed.

The week passed rather quickly, and pleasantly enough, until Monday arrived and Beatrice found herself once again in St. Stephan's at lunchtime, sitting in precisely the same pew as if some notion of order commanded it, looking up into the beady eyes of Reverend Small. She hoped the man with the poetic face would appear again. Perhaps because she was caught up in the feelings that the church seemed to automatically engender, this desire to see him again took the form of a rather devotional supplication. The exact words that crossed her mind were, *please God let him come again,* and no sooner had she thought them than she felt a kind of embarrassment that things had come to this, praying for strangers to appear.

Had Jorem lived, Beatrice would be Mrs. Herzog now, traveling in the company of her beloved and distinguished eye surgeon. So much had depended on his living, a future of companionship and gaiety and a mutual enlightenment, but he hadn't lived, which came as a surprise to everyone because he was healthy and vigorous, sharp and ready in wit, and so full of plans for his medical research you would have thought nothing could stop him from pursuing his years and years of ocular studies. But the brain tumor stopped him, felling him in the bathroom in the middle of the night as he reached for aspirin that scattered like petals around him on the pale green tiles. It happened three weeks before the wedding. "Didn't you suspect anything?" someone asked Beatrice. "Had you no idea he was suffering from a brain tumor?"

"He was a little surly the last few months," Beatrice said. "That's all, just a little surly."

Sitting in the church, Beatrice had a sudden thought: forty-eight is awfully old. She touched her hair. An embarrassment lingered. She had actually prayed for a man. What were things coming to? But with her mother no longer able to travel. With Jorem dead. She was required to go out into the world alone. And the world was so . . .

Just as the music began, the man with the Joycean looks appeared and sat just in front of her, next to a thick pillar against which he leaned during most of the concert, assuming a posture of relaxed and evident blissfulness.

And again, when the concert was over, he came out and stood next to her, as before, on the front steps. She was having difficulty finding the sleeve of her coat and he attempted to help, though in truth, she felt more awkward than if she'd been left to manage alone.

Once her coat was on he said, "There, I think we've got it."

She thanked him. A soft rain had begun to fall, although it had yet to make anything really wet.

"Goodness," she said, "I'd planned on taking a walk in the Gardens, but with this rain, I don't know. Do you think it's really going to come down, or is this a bluff?"

They both looked up at the sky, and then across at the gates of the Botanic Gardens.

"It could," he said. "It certainly could come down. Perhaps I could walk with you through the Gardens? I've an umbrella, you see."

"Fine," she said, "yes, that would be fine."

His name was Kevin McDonald, and when he pronounced it in his jaunty Australian accent, Beatrice found it very appealing. They walked along the narrow pathways, stopping occasionally to read the names of plants written on small plaques placed in the ground. The Gardens were immense, covering acres of ground. In the Gardens was evidence of man's will to explore, Beatrice said. When the world was still hardly circumnavigated, small as your village and otherwise terrifyingly abstract, botanists had gone forth in search of plants from other continents and had brought back evidence of the diversity of life on earth. In various sections of the Gardens, bits of growing things from Uruguay, Borneo, the Baltic coast, Ceylon—all the farthest reaches of the globe—had all taken root, lovingly placed in the new soil by the plant hunters. The world had been gathered together in the Gardens, and now, she herself was a witness not only to the multifarious forms of vegetation, but to the very spirit of conquest and acquisition that had sent the botanists forth. On such themes she expounded before Kevin McDonald, until they reached the restaurant in the gazebo at the center of the Gardens and he suggested they get something to eat.

Standing next to him in the cafeteria line, she was struck by the absolute blueness of his eyes. She had once heard a lecture on iridology. The woman who spoke said the irises in people's eyes become mottled out of evil and confusion, or sickness, and that for every organ in the body, there is a corresponding point in the eye. Corruption shows up as dark flecks, irregularity, discoloration. All babies are born with either blue or brown eyes. Hazel comes later, the lecturer said, as a result of confusion and evil. Could it be that Kevin McDonald was so free from evil and confusion that his eyes had retained the clear blue color of a baby's eyes?

He discovered she was American.

"I was in America once," he said, taking a small dish of prunes and a piece of banana cake from the display case and placing them on the cafeteria tray. "Loved Las Vegas."

"It is quite a spectacle, isn't it?" she said.

"I like a bit of gambling now and then. Made out good at the keno there." Thrusting a plate of greenish pie toward her, he said, "Try the Pavlova, it's the bloody national dessert, you know. Delicious, too."

They sat at a table outdoors where they could look down from the balcony onto a series of small, interconnecting ponds. The rain had eased up, there might have been some question as to whether it hadn't stopped altogether if the surface of the pond hadn't indicated that a few drops were still falling.

"What part of America do you live in?"

"I'm from California, actually," Beatrice said.

"Oh, that's a popular place, isn't it?"

"People have the most complex feelings about California," said Beatrice. "California is to America what America is to the rest of the world."

Kevin looked puzzled. "I'm not sure I understand you there."

"It's the land of milk and honey, don't you see?" Beatrice hastily swallowed a mouthful of food, anxious to go on and make herself clear. "In California, we're surrounded by prosperity and abundance and, of course, there's the physical glamour of a place so popularized by the movies. But many Americans think there's something vulgar about it, too, as if California were a modern-day Babylon, bereft of values, and harboring all sorts of decadence and extreme behavior."

"Is that right?"

"Oh, yes," Beatrice said. "So many people see California as an impoverished place in terms of its values, but at the same time, given a chance, they might live that way, too. It's so seductive, you see. There's a love-hate relationship. As an example of what can happen within a permissive framework, when resources are plentiful, California is a very interesting place to study. In terms of economic theory, it's the epitome of conspicuous consumption.

"It's my feeling that America looks this way to the rest of the world," Beatrice concluded. "That's how I come to say, California is to America what America is to the rest of the world."

She sat back in her chair, satisfied that she had elucidated the points of her thinking very precisely.

"Yes," Kevin said. "Well, I'm sure you're right about that. Above my head, though, I'm afraid."

Not an intellectual, Beatrice thought. Apparently he had no thoughts on the subject himself. That was all right. One couldn't always expect engagement.

"Where are you staying?" he asked.

She named a hotel in Double Bay.

"Double Bay? Got a bit of money, don't you, staying in Double Bay?"

"One comes to a new city quite blind. I booked in advance on the advice of my travel agent."

"Bit of all right, getting put up in Double Bay. I got an aunt in Double Bay whose flat cost seven hundred now. Didn't when she moved there. Used to be Hunkies and Poles and a few Wops. That's where those Eastern Europeans settled after the war. Now it's all fancy shops and big prices."

He tore off a bit of banana cake and threw it to the birds, who descended on it fighting.

"I'd like to get a place in Double Bay."

Beatrice asked him where he lived.

"Woolloomooloo," he said, "near the wharfs, right across the way." He pointed to a bluff visible beyond the treetops. The bluff descended sharply to the water where tin-roofed buildings lined a long wharf. Several large ships, magisterial in their height and layered tiers, were moored near the end of the wharf.

From where she sat, there wasn't a direction she looked where she didn't see the waters of the Sydney harbor. Little fingers of land extended out into the bay, creating a scalloped shoreline of many small coves, each with a pale crescent of sand for a beach.

"I certainly hadn't expected such a lovely city."

"It's a beaut, all right." He leaned toward her suddenly, his big hands gripping the corners of the table. "I lost my wife last year," he said. "Cancer. I couldn't stay in the house, so I moved to Woolloomooloo." He threw the birds another piece of cake, and settled back into his chair and sighed.

"I'm still adjusting," he said.

"Oh dear," Beatrice said. "Oh, that's such a coincidence. I lost my would-be husband last year. A stroke. No warning. Just like that, he was gone."

"So you know."

"Terrible to lose someone you love."

"Life can never be the same."

His face looked heavy with the sorrow of these losses. But abruptly, he brightened, although his eyes seemed veiled by something ineffable, so that they still appeared sad and did not match what was going on in the lower half of his face, where a smile widened as he stood up.

"Let's walk some more, Bernice," he said.

On the path, he took her arm. She felt it was a good time to correct him.

"My name is Beatrice," she said.

"Isn't that what I been calling you?"

"No. You've been saying Bernice."

"You look more like a Bernice than a Beatrice."

The remark upset her. Bernice was such an ugly name, whereas Beatrice had a touch of the poetic.

They walked slowly toward the gate. Frangipani blossoms lay on the ground like wayward, precious objects. Though it had stopped raining, the sky was still very wintry. "Tell you what," Kevin said. "I've got to go up to Whale Beach tomorrow to visit some friends in the afternoon. Maybe you'd like to come along. These friends have a place right on the water. Give you a chance to see a bit of the country. What do you say, Beatrice? Come along for the ride?"

Flattered, enlivened by the invitation, Beatrice accepted.

He shook her hand and said, "Good on ya, then, I'll see you at your hotel about noon tomorrow."

In the morning, she went out as soon as she was certain the shops were open, having decided a new outfit would give her mood the boost it needed. She knew she wasn't beautiful but her purchasing power gave her a style, an access to the easy lift, so that for a while, under the influence of something new, it was possible to believe she'd become more attractive.

At ten she left the hotel and walked past Rushcutter's Bay, through the park, just for the exercise, then turned and came back to the shops in Double Bay. She entered a store where, at once, and with absolute certainty, she determined the clothes were quite wrong for her. She entered other shops and left them as well. Then she stopped at a shoe store. Two homosexual attendants fell silent as she walked in. One of the men fit her in a sandal that she almost bought, but decided against. She left that store and entered others, and left again without buying.

In a way, during the walk back to the hotel, she had talked herself out of buying anything at all, foregoing the purchase of those items she originally imagined getting—shoes, a dress, or perhaps just a piece of inexpensive jewelry. But then she passed an Oriental import shop, and by the time she returned to the hotel, she was carrying a pair of beaded velvet slippers.

Kevin arrived in a utility truck that he called a "ute." On the side of the truck, it said McDONALD'S ROASTED NUTS, with a picture of a peanut with a human face. They drove out over the Sydney bridge and through streets lined with shops. He told her the names of the suburban towns, places with Aboriginal names like Kirribilli and Warrawee—wonderful names not at all like the towns themselves, which were ordinary and reminded her of the American Midwest. There was, however, something English about the places, too, as if the inclination to keep a small shop open, no matter how meager the income or mercenary the economics, overrode the paltry rewards. Also, the sense of scale, the smallness of the shops, was rather more English than American. Finally they left the suburbs and entered a wooded area called French's Forest. Kevin drove faster, until the ute shimmied with speed. A blue sky, fainter at the horizon where a line of pale hills was visible, was destined to turn cloudy by afternoon, Kevin predicted. More rain was on its way.

When they stopped, it was at the edge of a cliff that overlooked the ocean. By going down a steep driveway, they came to an apartment building at the edge of a beachfront road.

Jack Beal met them downstairs in the lobby of the stylishly new condominiums. His wife, Angela, waited in the upstairs hallway, standing outside the apartment door. She was a plump woman, sixtyish, with golden, stiff hair that curled like small ram's horns at her temples. Jack was tanned and handsome and had thick silver hair. A smile, more innocent than worldly, seemed perpetually in place.

"Who's this?" Angela said, turning toward Beatrice.

"Beatrice, meet Angela . . . Angela, Beatrice."

"You didn't tell us you were bringing anyone, Kevin. The house is a mess. Jack's just been for a swim and left his things in the bathroom. We had Mother here till four. I haven't even done our dishes today, but come on in. Just don't look at the mess."

Beatrice followed Jack Beal into a tidy living room. The mess his wife had spoken of was nowhere to be seen. Beatrice imagined that Angela Beal was the sort of woman who was always overstating her messiness. It was a peculiar thing the way some women did this. Perhaps it made the tasks of their lives seem neverending, cloaking what was really a lack of enough things to do.

"My, aren't those lovely things you have on your feet, dear?' Angela Beal said. "They look like the raja's slippers, don't they now?

"Jack, get them drinks," Angela added. "I've got some Pavlova in the kitchen."

Not more Pavlova, Beatrice thought.

"What'll you have to drink?" Jack Beal said. "Anything, anything you want, anything at all. The world is your oyster."

"I'll have a scotch," Beatrice said, thinking it was still early but hoping no one would notice, or if they did, they would not care.

Kevin sat down in front of the TV. Australian football was on.

"Midgame yet?" Kevin asked.

Jack said, "Manly, five to one."

"Has Dalgliesh done anything?"

"Oh, you should've seen him in the first quarter!"

Angela stuck her golden ram's horns through the doorway. "I've got five dollars in the pools. Manly better win! Just let me get the tea on and I'll join you."

Beatrice took her drink out onto a balcony that faced the ocean. There were tall pines growing in a row along the flat beach, two stories below. The water was the color of pewter, striated farther out by deep blue currents. Directly in front of her there was some sort of bathhouse or beach club, a building that, even though it was at the ocean's edge, housed an indoor saltwater swimming pool. Numbers of people were leaving the beach at once, as if having collectively agreed that, by virtue of the light or their watches, they'd fulfilled an obligation and, like quitting workers, were now making their way across the parking lot and splitting off in twos or threes to walk down the street. She turned and caught sight of Angela Beal through the kitchen window. Angela, oblivious to being observed, was arranging sweets on a tray—little buns and cookies and slices of the ever-popular Pavlova. The thought of all those sweets made her slightly sick. The barest tip of Angela's pink tongue curled over her upper lip as she worked. She plays the horses, Beatrice thought. Her mother spends most days here. Together they go over the racing forms. She loses more money than she should but she never tells her husband just how much. He's a dear. He's devoted to her. They're a good couple. Even though she's run to poundage as she's aged, he'd never think of cheating on her. They have all these little connections, the mundane rituals of coupling that pass for, and then eventually actually become, enduring serenity.

Angela looked up quickly and caught Beatrice staring at her through the windows. "Just a minute, lovey," she called. "I'm just finishing up here and then I'll join you."

All this was said in a sort of yoo-hoo voice, one neighbor holloing to another across the fence. Beatrice thought perhaps she was being antisocial by staying out on the balcony. But she couldn't bring herself to join the football melee or the preparation of tea. The outdoors held her fast, as if the stream of pinkened people slapping their rubber thongs against the heated pavement offered more opportunity for communion, even two stories below her, than the domestic configuration of football and tea.

She looked out at the sea, which had a farther-reaching feeling than the ocean in California did. She thought, It's always going to be like this. There would only be a series of wrong things, primary events turned sour.

"There," Angela said, appearing suddenly beside her.

"There," she repeated, "that's done." She made it seem as if some terribly difficult task, one which had been put off for days, had finally been addressed and overcome and she was free at last of the niggling burden of unmet responsibility.

"Tea's ready, I mean," she said. "Would you like to have a look around the apartment?" She started to move toward the glass doors, ready for Beatrice to follow her on a tour.

"No," Beatrice said, "not really." It was a moment of crushed hope. Angela looked disappointed, perhaps even wounded. She should have just allowed herself to be taken on a guided walk through the rooms, but it seemed so pointless, so terribly, utterly pointless to be so nice—to attempt nicety—when she didn't want to see the rooms at all, but only to stand out here in the lovely light.

She smiled kindly at Angela. "I would like another drink, though, please. It's just so nice out here. I was enjoying the view."

"Of course," Angela said, and went for her drink.

When Beatrice turned and looked at the ocean again, she saw something bizarre had happened. The sky was darkening with birds. Like swarms of bees, they appeared in dark clusters; wave after wave materialized from the horizon and circled the tall pines. From these birds came a screeching such as Beatrice had never heard. The birds settled in the trees, as if the trees were bottomless funnels that could absorb as many birds as could drop out of the sky. It was impossible to tell what kind of birds they were because the sun was behind them. They appeared only as black forms descending into black-branched pines, and soon they were all in the trees, and it was as if the trees themselves broadcast the terrible, beautiful screeching, which continued, rising to a constant, wondrous pitch.

"Parrots," Jack Beal said when he delivered another drink. "We get them every afternoon." He returned to the living room where he resumed watching the football game with Angela and Kevin.

Later, as Beatrice passed them on her way to the bathroom, Angela explained how you had to wiggle the handle on the toilet to get it to flush. When she came out, the Pavlova was being served in front of the TV. The screen showed a boy with a pink face taking a big drink of water on the sidelines and blowing it out on the ground. Half-moons of black had been painted under his eyes. He wiped his face on a towel and trotted back out onto the field.

"Come here and sit down," Kevin said to her.

"Kill him!" Jack Beal yelled at the football players.

Angela said, "Like as not they will kill each other."

"Don't they wear padding?" asked Beatrice, who stood near the doorway, still unable to make up her mind whether to sit next to Kevin on the couch.

"Naw, that's for Americans."

"Oh my God," Jack yelled, "he's going to do it . . . he's going, going, gone! All the way, Angie, all the bloody way!"

"Oooph," Angela said, when the runner was tackled, "that had to hurt."

Kevin patted the couch. "Come here and sit down, baby."

The word startled her. Baby? Strangely, it both repelled and excited her.

"They're never going to make it," Jack said. "Three more minutes left in the quarter. We can kiss our five bob good-bye, Angie."

"How about some tea, Beatrice?"

"I'll have another scotch, thank you." Already her head was swimming but Beatrice wanted to swim farther. Out beyond the breakers, heading out to sea, where the shapes of the currents ran a deeper blue today. She was feeling very much herself. Sweetly detached, bittersweet, and now slightly numb. Oh, it was nice. But it would always be this way. It was awful, really, but it would. A series of disappointments, when the poetic turned into the plebian, and the Joycean man was revealed as a nut-seller.

Another scotch was the one that sent her over the limit. Some time later, she felt queasy and knew, although there was plenty of time to get to the bathroom, that she was going to be sick. She knelt at the toilet. Oh God, she murmured, and emptied herself of scotch and kiwi and whipped cream. Afterward, she felt better, and used small squares of tissue, pressed into hard wads and moistened with water, to wipe her eyes, her cheeks, her lips, and filled her mouth with water that tasted of her own sickness.

She walked back toward the noise of the football game. With things moving about in a watery way, she managed to say, "I think I should go home," although it sounded strange, as if someone else, farther out in front of her, were speaking. No one heard her, however, and she sat down on the couch. She floated, and closed her eyes, resting her head, in a very still way, against the cushions. She imagined Jorem, standing on a beach in Hawaii. He was always saying, Take a picture of me here, and then in another spot, Take another picture of me here. Funny, but he'd never asked her to pose for the camera, or suggested asking someone to photograph them together. It was always, Take a picture of me here, and Take another one here. At luaus, in Oahu, on the rim of volcanoes, and beneath the porte cochère of the hotel.

"I'm not feeling well," she said to Kevin, and this time he heard her.

"I really don't feel well," she said again, this time to Angela.

"Ah, lovey, that's too bad," Angela said.

"Why don't you get her to bed, Angela?" Jack said.

"No," Beatrice said. "No, I must go."

At the door, Angela said, "You take care of her, Kevin." Beatrice lost one of her slippers walking toward the elevator and Kevin had to steady her while she bent over to put it back on. She turned and looked at the Beals. They stood outside their apartment door with their arms around each other. Just before the elevator came, Angela Beal leaned down and picked up a safety pin from the carpet. Then she waved at them, as if from a great distance.

The beautiful forest with the streaks of light falling like religious rays down through the gum trees was actually a very dangerous place, Kevin informed her, as they drove along. The deadly funnel web spider lurked there.

"A boy in Gosford was bitten by a funnel web last week," he said. "He was out in his backyard on his trike when his mum heard his screaming. He didn't make it, died in hospital. Funnel webs are the deadliest beggars. You wouldn't want to walk out there."

Kevin reached over and patted her knee, then slid his hand up along the inside of her thigh. Beatrice stared dully at the woods as if trying to make out the shapes of the deadly spiders, crawling with fatal precision, over twigs and fallen leaves.

"How old are you?" she said suddenly.

"I'm fifty-eight," Kevin said.

"How old do you think I am?" Her words, even to herself, sounded drunken, and she regretted this.

"Oh," Kevin said, good-natured, smiling at her, "I guess about forty."

"Wrong," she said. "Dead wrong."

"Am I above or below?"

"You are below," she said, "woefully below."

His hand, like those persistent spiders, continued to work its way along the tender flesh of her thigh.

"I think I suffer from loneliness for which there is no cure," she said.

"Ah, I think you're just a little drunk, love," he said. "Best not to think of big things when you're tight."

At last they came back to the part of the city she knew and she said, "I think I'll get out at the Mechanic Gardens."

She had meant to say Botanic Gardens, but she had somehow gotten her words mixed up. Still, he knew what she meant and after a moment he said he didn't think it was a good idea.

"If you went back to the hotel," he said, "they'd give you tea and you could lie down for a bit and then if you felt better you could go for a walk afterward."

"But I do feel better," she said.

And it was true, she did. She no longer felt like throwing

up, this was good. Her head didn't swim. The car ride had been a help, the air hitting her face. Even Kevin's strange, persistent hand at the height of her underwear, never going further than stroking the flesh where it met the elastic, was helpful in rousing her to steadier consciousness. It was as if he were petting some animal in order to calm it, a strangely pale sexual gesture.

He stopped the ute where she asked him to.

"Do you want me to come by the hotel again?" He reached across her and opened the door for her.

"I'm leaving."

"Oh, I didn't know," he said. "Where are you going?"

"India."

"India?"

"Yes."

"How wonderful," he said. "Have a good time."

"Thank you," she said. "But if I shouldn't go, I'll see you at the concert on Monday."

She walked into the Gardens, still quite removed, she realized, from scenes surrounding her, feeling lightly diffused, as if her mind were everywhere around her, rather than in her body. She had to work to keep her slippers on her feet. She had a feeling that she shouldn't have left him. She realized she would always be assaulted like this by feelings of being attracted, then frightened, starting conversations with them, the waiters, the museum guide, the tobacconist, or florist, only to beat her hasty retreat. She would continue to travel, impelled by the search, until death—when it finally did steal upon her as it had with Jorem and as it threatened to do with her mother—would quietly put her down. Disease might come first. It was dreadful.

In the beds of roses, Japanese tourists were taking pictures. They had large teeth for such tiny faces and they wore somber, funereal colors. She walked up a sunlit hill of grass. She climbed to the very top without stopping until, breathless, she came to the view she liked most where, near a monument called Mrs. Macquarie's Chair, she could look out over the entire harbor.

The harbor was full of sharks, trapped there by currents. The swimming beaches were netted and yet, she had been told, people were still attacked by sharks who tore holes in the nets. Just beneath the surface of the picturesque blue bay, she imagined thousands of saw-toothed monsters. She really would go to India tomorrow. Yes, I will, she thought. Below her in the rose beds, a different group was taking pictures. She looked down on them, these tiny, animated figures, and heard someone in the group say, "Beryl, move closer to Freddie." Then she went to see the grasses that she'd liked so much, the beds of infinite variety. Good-bye, she said to them in silent, drunken language. Good-bye, she said out loud.

Good-bye, she said to the small marigold bed and to the fir from Madagascar. Good-bye to the rose, and the sweet william rows, to the shrimp plant twigs, and the Morton Bay figs. A poem, an ode, to you all.

Good-bye, she said, on a more somber note, to traveling with Mother. Good-bye, again, to Jorem.

Take a picture of me here!

I don't like to eat alone, Jorem once said. I don't even like to have a cup of coffee alone.

In every case, with every single prospect since Jorem, there had come the moment when the fatal flaw was revealed. The lover of literature had turned out to be a distributor of Christian books who rattled his fork against his teeth when he ate. Herman was broke, Richard also. Werner used drugs. Peter had married someone he worked with. The Swede had already been married but by the time she discovered this it hadn't mattered much, since his smacking of lips during meals and his terrible taste in music had worn her attraction to a useless nib. You didn't try to reform each other, that's what everyone said, and yet there was none whom she could take without reformation.

She turned her back on the harbor and walked down the hill toward the main gates, but when she reached them, she discovered a small group of people had gathered. The gates themselves were locked. A sign posted on the fence said that the Gardens closed at 5:00 P.M. Beatrice looked at her watch and discovered it was twenty past five. The Japanese tourists she had seen in the rose garden were now standing in a group, slightly apart from the other people, their attitudes expectant and watchful, but quieter than the rest. *Something* will happen, they seemed to say.

"They can't just lock us in," a woman complained.

"Someone will be round I'm sure."

"Why don't they tell you when the place closes up? This is ridiculous."

"There is a sign."

"But where nobody can see it. Who looks at signs anyway? I never read signs."

"I'm sure someone will come around."

Meanwhile, they waited. A few more minutes passed. Just to make sure, Beatrice tried the gate herself. What if we are locked in for the night? she thought. Finally a man spoke up and said he thought perhaps the gate at the south end of the park was open. Everyone, including the Japanese group, followed him when he set off in that direction.

Soon they were standing before the other gate, which was also locked. The sun had set. Pink, fleecy clouds hung over the horizon of rooftops.

"Luck of the Irish," someone said.

"I don't understand this," the older woman said. "I mean, how are we supposed to get out of here? Where are the caretakers?"

"There must be a gate still open somewhere. They couldn't just lock you in for the night, could they? Still, it is odd, isn't it? You'd expect them to keep someone posted at the gates well past closing time, wouldn't you?"

Now a young man in blue jeans stepped forward and rattled the gate.

"I reckon we could climb the fence," he said. He spoke to no one in particular, but Beatrice stepped forward.

"There are those spires at the top," she said. "They might prove a little difficult."

The fence was made of wrought iron. Curlicues and scrolly

grillwork filled in the space between the tall uprights. The very forms in the Gardens were duplicated in metal, the leaves and buds and vines. Beatrice had never really looked at the fence before but now she saw how beautiful it was. Staring at it, she also saw a path for her hands and toes, a clear route before her, and without hesitation, she took her first step and began climbing. Her toes fit easily in the grillwork, her hands found their rightful holds. The velvet slippers gave her padding but didn't hinder her ascent. When she reached the top, she hesitated, wondering momentarily how she would make it over the spires. But then she felt the man's hand at her ankle and she looked down at him. He smiled in encouragement. She swung one leg over the top and felt him steady her, his hand sure and firm on her ankle. At the level of the fence top, a light breeze blew. She felt light herself, and suddenly she was on the other side, and then it was a simple matter to climb down. She stood on the ground on the other side. "Well done," the man said simply. She turned and walked away. She heard a woman say, "I'm not climbing that fence, I can tell you that right now. I'll wait here till hell freezes over before I climb that fence."

She crossed the street at the light in front of St. Stephan's Church. He stepped out of the shadows and surprised her.

"My God," she said, "you frightened me."

"I just wanted to make sure you got back to the hotel all right."

He took her hand. "Are you OK now? You feel all right?"

"You waited for me? But how did you know I'd come this way?"

"I figured you'd be taking the subway." He turned her hand over and looked at her palm. She'd scratched herself and there was a thin line of blood across her flesh.

"I didn't like leaving you when you were still a little tight, you see. I felt I might wait and see you back to the hotel. That way I could be sure nothing happened."

Beatrice looked back at the Gardens. The crowd had disappeared from the gate. It was as if they had never been there. Had they moved on in search of a caretaker? An unlocked gate?

Kevin studied her with his blue eyes.

"My God," she said, "you frighten me."

"I guess I shouldn't have surprised you like that."

She wanted to say, That's not what I meant. That's not what I meant at all, but she was so tired, suddenly, and he was there, guiding her down the street, his hand the lightest touch on her elbow.

THE RAKE
PEOPLE

••————————————————————••

Near my house there's an empty lot where, twice a year, according to city ordinance, the weeds are cut by a crew of Mexican men who work without interruption from the time the sun rises until it sets. The earth always looks damaged to me when they're finished. The green lot becomes brown and bare. It's too bad everything has to go like that, the wild poppies and morning glories and other plants whose names I don't know. They just come and chop things down and pass armfuls of vines and branches to each other. One man stands by a truck and throws the cuttings onto the bed. Another man stands in the truck and jumps up and down on the pile to pack it down and make room for more. These men don't work too fast, but they have a lazy, constant way of moving. They swing machetes, bend and lift, rake up cuttings into piles, moving slowly as if all their lives they've worked hard in the sun, pacing themselves throughout the day, in order to reserve energy for their other, better lives, which begin in the evening.

When I woke up this morning and looked outside and saw the men working, once again it reminded me of another time when we lived on a narrow street in a canyon on the outskirts of Beverly Hills, in a neighborhood where everyone had a gardener. On Tuesdays and Fridays, the days which, for whatever reasons, the gardeners preferred to work, the sound of their rakes carried from yard to yard. Worse, those portable machines that blow leaves and dirt from patios started up early in the morning and sounded like chain saws. There were so many gardeners working at the same time that their noises mingled all day, and it sometimes seemed like they were the only people you saw walking around outside. Everyone else stayed in their air-conditioned houses, or else got into their cars and immediately drove away.

We, too, had a gardener, since neither my wife nor I had time to take care of the place ourselves. His name was Lupe Batista, and he came with the house when we bought it. In other words, he had worked for the former owner and, out of convenience, we chose to keep him on. He arrived and left while I was at work, on Tuesdays and Fridays, so I never had much contact with him, or reason to think one way or another of him, until something happened one spring and we had to let him go. Or maybe he let us go, since the circumstances are somewhat complicated.

It began on a morning in April. My wife, Pat, stood at the sink looking out the window at Lupe working in the garden. Our dog, Elmo, had his nose pressed against the screen door. He was also watching Lupe, and barking with a grim persistence.

"Why do you think Elmo dislikes Lupe so much?" Pat said. "He doesn't dislike anybody and suddenly he's got this thing about Lupe. I don't understand it."

It did seem mysterious, the way the dog had turned against the gardener. I'd noticed it, too. Even the sound of a rake in another part of the neighborhood was enough to cause him to jump up and rush to the door barking.

"It's gotten so he goes crazy every time he hears a rake," Pat said. "Maybe Lupe hit him once, or poked him with his rake."

In truth, I found it sort of amusing. Elmo was a rather sedentary old Labrador retriever. His new quirk animated him.

"What is it, Elmo?" I said, looking into his large, knowing eyes. "Is it the rake people, huh? An attack of the rake people?" Elmo, his hair standing up along his back in a fluffy ridge, cocked his head and pressed his ears forward. Sometimes he gave me such intelligent looks I expected him to speak. I liked Elmo, though he wasn't my dog, he was Pat's. She had had him when I met her eight years earlier. People were always surprised to learn Elmo was twelve years old. He didn't look it, because he'd had a good life. We had a large fenced-in yard, and there was a hole in the fence that gave him access to the hills. At night, when coyotes howled, Elmo listened with an intense and distant look on his face. Deer came down regularly to eat the roses, and raccoons traversed a path that cut across the corner of our garden. All this was fine with Elmo. He sensed in this urban world a distinct trace of the natural order that preceded the more recent residents, who drove Mercedes and lived in houses on stilts, cantilevered over the chaparral. Each night, when the coyotes howled, he traveled a road back to the beginning, and sent up his own primordial cries.

But the barking, the hostility toward the gardener, was something recent and quite inexplicable. Armies of the rake people seemed to trouble him in some way that nothing else did.

I confess, I liked egging him on. "You're doing a splendid, absolutely splendid job, Elmo," I said. "Those rake people have been warned. They'd be fools to come closer."

Elmo barked even louder.

"Don't aggravate him, Russ," Pat said, trying to pull him away from the door. Elmo didn't wear a collar because Pat thought they were too restrictive, so it was difficult at times to get him to move.

"Alarm! Alarm! Elmo sounds the alarm!"

"I wish you'd cut it out, Russ," she said. We both looked out at Lupe to see if he'd noticed the racket, but he raked around the lemon tree, seemingly unconcerned, moving with that purposeful slowness that was characteristic of him.

"Honey," Pat said suddenly, "I didn't tell you this, but Lupe tried to kiss me last week."

"What do you mean he tried to kiss you?"

"Don't talk so loud, Russ, he'll hear us." She closed the door and sat down across the table from me. She told me that on Tuesday, while Lupe was working on the patio, she went out to ask him to cut the camellias back. His children were with him, the twin boys who sometimes came along when he worked. She asked him why the kids weren't in school. He said they were too young, but Pat knew they were beyond school age. She told him they really ought to be in school, but he just smiled at her and shrugged.

"In truth, I don't even know whether they let children like that go to school," she said. "I mean children of illegals."

"I don't know either," I said, wishing she'd get on with her story.

The day was warm, she said, and she felt like getting some sun, so she changed into a bathing suit and went outside. She offered Lupe a beer and gave the kids colas. They helped her clean out the fish pond, catching the goldfish with a kitchen strainer and transferring them to a pan while she hosed down the cement basin and refilled it with water. All the time they were cleaning the pond, the kids seemed happy, and Lupe worked nearby. She said she felt him watching her but she didn't think anything about it. Then she went inside to get him a check. When she came out, he was rolling up the hose. She handed him the check, and he reached out and took her hand. She regarded it as a gesture of gratitude, and squeezed it and said, "Yes, you're welcome." It happened at that moment. He reached up and put his hand on the back of her neck and pulled her face toward him. It was so sudden, and she didn't know how to react, but before he could put his lips on hers, she pulled back and said, "No."

"What happened then?"

"Nothing happened. I went inside."

"You didn't say anything to him?"

"No. I was so surprised. What could I say? I just went inside."

• •

Weeks went by. I didn't know what to think of Pat's story about Lupe trying to kiss her, but in time, we began to treat it as a joke. Actually, I was increasingly troubled by it. Could this have happened, I wondered, the way Pat said it did? Pat told the story to a few people. Everyone agreed it was pretty ridiculous, the gardener making a pass at her. At dinner one night, someone said, "It's just like Constance and the gamekeeper," and everyone laughed.

At least I thought I understood Elmo's animosity now. It seemed clear he was defending Pat. Through a system of signals and sympathies long established between them, they had an emotional connection. Obviously, Elmo had picked up on the situation.

Some mornings now, on Tuesdays and Fridays when Lupe was due for work, I delayed leaving the house in order to study him. I looked at him quite differently. I saw that he was about my age, maybe thirty-five—perhaps forty—but he was in much better shape. He always turned up in jeans and wore a clean, white T-shirt, tucked in. In fact, I realized he was quite handsome, though small in build. I was aware of his trim middle because that's where I'd recently put on weight and the first place I looked whenever I glanced into a mirror. Whenever I spoke to him, it wasn't clear how much English he really understood, but it seemed pretty limited. His manner was polite, but our few exchanges were vague and artificial. He seemed to prefer not to look at me when we spoke. He was mysterious to me. I didn't feel I could know him. As time went on, I wondered more and more what his life was like.

I began paying more attention to news reports that contained information on illegal aliens. In one month forty thousand Mexicans were arrested at the border and sent back. The border patrol wore helmets and masks with infrared lenses that made them look like creatures from space. A sweatshop was raided in East Los Angeles and the women, herded against a wall, were shown with their hands on top of their heads. In another report, it was disclosed that a motel in the Valley called The Snooty Fox was being used by the Immigration and Naturalization Service as a temporary detention center for illegals who were awaiting hearings. The detainees were shown on the nightly news sitting around the swimming pool, looking sullen and detached from their surroundings. The Snooty Fox had been enclosed by a chain-link fence.

Another evening, on the six o'clock news, I learned that more business licenses were issued to gardeners in Beverly Hills than to anyone else. There could be as many as ten thousand gardeners in the city, but the number was uncertain, since many gardeners were illegals who didn't bother applying for licenses. The average pay per household was sixty dollars a month, a rate that ensured that nearly everyone could afford a gardener, and thus could be said to have at least one servant. However, police had recently become suspicious that burglars were posing as gardeners, cruising the streets of Beverly Hills in trucks laden with rakes and lawn mowers, staking out houses to rob. As a result, spot checks were being initiated. Deportations were certain to result. During the following weeks, while driving home from work I several times saw police who had pulled a truck over and were questioning the driver, who was always Mexican or Central American.

Lupe's truck broke down one morning. He used the phone to call his cousin, but couldn't reach anyone. "Don't you have triple A?" Pat asked. I hooked jumper cables to the Mercedes and tried to get his truck started, but no luck. In the end, I gave him a ride to his apartment, and he came back later to get his truck. He lived in a pretty rough-looking neighborhood over near Sunset and Echo Park, in a building that was very run-down.

Pat's friend Marilyn took to calling and when I answered, would say to me, "Hi, darling, is Constance there?" It was going too far, but I really didn't know how to stop it. I felt maybe I ought to fire Lupe, but I couldn't bring myself to do it. I suppose

I had to admit that I still wasn't sure he was the one at fault, or what had really happened.

Then something interesting happened. Elmo had a change of heart. He suddenly took a liking to Lupe and began following him around while he worked, begging him to play with the ball he carried in his mouth. What's more, it was clear Lupe liked the dog. I felt it as an alienation of affection.

One day when I was home alone, down with the flu, I watched Lupe and Elmo from a place where I couldn't be seen. They had become absolutely buddy-buddy. Whenever Lupe stopped work for a moment, he scratched Elmo's head or threw his ball for him. In response, Elmo licked his hands enthusiastically. Since I was certain Elmo's feelings were a barometer of Pat's, I began to wonder, what did this mean?

I grew increasingly certain that Pat had been unfaithful to me, not necessarily with Lupe, but with someone, perhaps the house painter, a Greek with whom she had developed a friendship that lasted until he moved back to Ithaca. There was no evidence, only the fact that he'd called her frequently at night. Was my wife really true to me? In the past, we had talked about fidelity, but only in general terms. We had talked about it as if we were in a position to make policies for others, instead of holding the policies ourselves. A terrible jealousy began building in me. Sometimes I sat and thought, What's happening here?

"Do you want to pick up a lemon tree and plant it this week?" Pat asked Lupe. They stood just outside the door to my study, near the camellias. On that day, I suppose you could have said I was eavesdropping. Once again I had stayed home from work. This time it was an ear complaint.

"OK," said Lupe.

"All right then," she said. "Do you want the money now?"

"OK," he said again.

"Bring me a receipt," she said, "and I'll reimburse you."

Looking at his face, it was clear to me he didn't understand words like receipt and reimburse, but Pat didn't notice this.

"By the way," she said, touching his arm as he turned to go, "the roses look great. You've done a wonderful job with them. They've never bloomed like this before."

Later, Lupe's twin boys ran past the window while we were eating lunch and looked in at us. Pat waved at them.

"Do you know the boys' names?" I asked her.

"Hmmm," she said, thoughtful for a moment. "One of them is Manny, I think."

That night Elmo, who must have gotten out sometime during the afternoon, didn't come home. The next morning we noticed his absence and began looking for him. By night, he still hadn't returned, and Pat was in a terrible state.

"That damned dog," she said when we were in bed. Then she began to cry.

"He's never gone this long."

"Maybe after twelve years he deserves a night out."

"I can't joke, Russ. If anything happened to him, I don't know what I'd do."

The next morning, Sissy, who lived across from us, heard us calling around the neighborhood for Elmo and stopped us in the street. She said she thought she had seen Elmo in the back of our gardener's truck the day before yesterday. She couldn't be certain, she said, because he was driving pretty fast. But she thought it was Elmo she saw in Lupe's truck.

We didn't have a telephone number for Lupe, but of course I knew where he lived since I'd driven him home that time.

"What can we do but go over there?" Pat said.

I thought Sissy was mistaken. I didn't think Lupe had Elmo, and I told her that.

"But what can it hurt to just go over there and talk to him?" Pat asked.

The door to Lupe's apartment was covered with little paste-on stickers, goofy cartoon characters, Penzoil labels, trading stamps, even Chiquita banana logos. A girl of about twenty answered the door. "No here," she said when I asked for Lupe and she started to close the door, but Pat stopped her.

"Could you tell us where to find him, or when he'll be back?"

"No speak English."

"Does anybody speak English?"

The girl shook her head. Another woman, older, perhaps Lupe's mother (certainly not his wife?), came to the door and spoke rapidly to the girl. Then they just looked at us, silent and unsmiling.

"What about the twins?" Pat said to me. "Wait, don't let them close the door, let me get the twins." The twins, whom we had seen playing in a vacant lot next to the apartment when we first drove up, did speak some English, and Pat was certain they could help us.

"Just a minute," I said to the older woman, who regarded me impassively, but I felt her calm looks concealed an edgy traffic between fear and contempt. I tried to introduce myself and said that Lupe worked for us.

"No comprendo," she said.

Pat returned with the boys. "Is this your mother?" she asked.

"She my aunt."

"Tell her we need to find your daddy."

"He's in Mexico," one of the boys said.

"Where in Mexico?"

Before he could answer, the older woman spoke to the boys rapidly, as if scolding them, and they answered at length.

"Where in Mexico?" Pat said again. She took a few bills from her purse. "Where?" she said, showing them the money. "We owe him money," she said. "We're going down there on a vacation, we want to see him." Pat smiled. Pat laughed. Pat made it seem we wanted suggestions for tours of the old country. I couldn't believe it. I couldn't get over how effective, and determined, she was.

By the time we left, Pat, who had become persistent to the point of obnoxiousness, had bullied the woman into telling her the name of a café in Ensenada where we might find Lupe.

"Oh, God," she said, once we were in the car again, "I don't know what's going on. I don't know why Lupe would do this. We've got to go to Ensenada, Russ."

"We don't even know if he has Elmo. You didn't even ask them that."

"I couldn't ask them. They'd have never told us anything if they thought we suspected him."

"It's too convoluted," I said. "This is crazy."

"Revenge. Maybe he took him to get back at me for rejecting him. But it's so cruel. He wouldn't be that cruel, would he? What did we ever do to him except give him a job?"

"Yes, we're exemplary employers, cream of the crop."

"We've got to go to Ensenada, Russ."

"Look," I said wearily, "give it one more day. If Elmo isn't back by tomorrow night, we'll think about going to Mexico."

"We won't think about it, Russ. We'll just do it."

Elmo didn't show up, and two days later, Pat started packing. We were going to Mexico.

I didn't really want to go. When it came right down to it, I was a big chicken. I had no faith in the theory that Lupe had taken Elmo, but if he had, I didn't believe we would ever find him, and if we did find him with Lupe, I envisioned trouble, which is how it all came down to me being a chicken. I realized this. Little Russell Grover, the perpetual chicken, the fraidy-cat, no-dukes Grover, who, as he grew up, gave anybody anything he wanted as long as he agreed not to harm him. I didn't want to go to Mexico to get into a fight with somebody over a dog I didn't think he'd taken. But Pat had crawled right up to the brink of hysteria and was peering over the edge and the only way I could see getting her to back away was to make this last-ditch effort to locate what was ours. We would fling ourselves over the border, drop some cash in the corrupted economy created by tourist-gringos, and fetch back some cheap tequila or tin trinkets to remind ourselves that we had tried, by God we'd tried, to find what we loved.

• •

"Did you leave Sissy a key?" Pat asked while we were loading the car. I assured her I had. Sissy was to put Elmo in the house if he returned while we were gone.

"Keep the cooler out in case we want a beer," she said. Even in these tumultuous times, she thought of comfort, providing sandwiches and beer, magazines and tanning lotion, protective hats and sunglasses, and a dozen different tapes for the car stereo. We took off amid this panoply of middle-class props as if setting out on vacation, except our moods were subdued instead of festive.

The freeway from Los Angeles to San Diego is remarkable for its passage through industrial pallor, a gray, unspeakably fouled landscape at the edge of the City of Angels, which dissolves, the farther south you go, into the sublime green of golf courses and meticulously planned dream communities, homogeneous boxes creeping over hill and dale. I drove. Pat slept in the seat beside me. Just before Laguna, I took an exit, remembering a road that cut through the low green hills and dropped down toward the coastline.

With the green hills as a backdrop, the drive seemed suddenly much nicer. I began to feel better just looking at trees and rocks and the sky. We came out onto the highway that ran along the ocean, where it was possible to appreciate just how beautiful California really can be. Later, in trying to cut back to the freeway, I somehow took a wrong road, which came to a dead end in a college parking lot. Pat woke up.

"Where are we?"

"I got off the freeway for a while. Frankly, we're lost. I took a wrong turn."

"I need to get out and stretch my legs anyway," she said.

Just beyond the parking lot lay the college's experimental agricultural station. Above a ribbon of stream, a large barn sat atop a hill, surrounded by corrals filled with animals. As we walked toward the stream, Pat commented on how funny it felt to be taking a walk without Elmo there with us. We'd always taken walks because of him, it was true. Without either of us mentioning it, we realized at that moment how much of a triumvirate we were, a fact made clear by his absence. You can't understand loss until something's gone and then there's the mortifying realization that you might never see it again. You don't know the truth of this until you've lived with someone, even an animal, for so long that his daily sounds have infiltrated your thinking to the point that a precise presence, thick and rich, is created out of the absence of those sounds. So it was with Elmo, who could announce himself in so many ways: a door creaking, the clanging of a metal tag against a metal dish, lapping at the toilet, the muffled gathering of a throw rug into a nest, or a clack—distant yet growing—of toenails approaching across the wooden floor.

Pat picked up a stick and threw it into the stream cutting through the bottom of the ravine. The sheep, who were grazing in a pen opposite us, looked up, startled, and held their breathless pose.

As if reading my mind, she said, "When I go into a room, I expect to find him there. Even though he isn't, it's almost as if he is there."

Trees, their buds formed into perfect conical shapes, gave off a pleasantly pungent smell. We walked down into the ravine, stepped on stones to cross the stream, and climbed up the other side. Elmo, had he been there, would have been up the hill before us. I believed he was dead. I didn't know what had happened, but I thought, he is gone. Suddenly I felt this weariness and I just wanted to tell Pat about it. It wasn't Elmo I was thinking about then, but fidelity. Somehow I made that switch from one thing to another, so smoothly. I was sick of living in the clutter of our age. Just because we lived in the 1980s didn't mean we had to act like it. What I really wanted to talk to her about was love.

We walked up to the corrals and Pat put out her hand and flattened it, trying to get the attention of a big brown horse.

"I feel like we might just get lucky and find Elmo," she

said. When I didn't respond, she looked up at me. "You don't think we're going to find him with Lupe, do you?"

"I don't know."

"I don't think I did anything to make Lupe think I'd want him to kiss me."

"No?"

"Maybe I handled it wrong, though. Someone else might have reacted differently."

"It's no use imagining how Katharine Hepburn would have handled the situation," I said.

"But there's a point you're missing," I added, "and that is, Lupe may be our gardener but he's also just another guy."

"What do you mean, he's just another guy?"

"All this stuff is going back and forth between men and women all the time. Men make passes or women flirt, or the other way around. There's this big area of activity, you know, where people test things. The real question is, Are you settled, or are you looking? I thought we should try being monogamous but I don't think you're finding it too easy."

"You're so moral, Russ, you know where it all begins and ends. You know where chaos stops and order begins. You know at which point something that isn't possible becomes possible."

"What's not possible? What are you talking about? It's not so difficult, Pat. All I'm wondering about now is whether we're faithful to each other, whether we have been and if we can be from now on. Do you think it's important we're faithful to each other?"

There was a long pause, and then she said, "Do you believe me about Lupe?" I told her I thought I did. "Then why bring this up now?"

"Because it matters to me, the fidelity. I'm very corny about it. I want you, that's the point. Nobody else. Nobody gets you either. Isn't that crazy? You look at me like I'm crazy, but that's what I want."

A truck came down the road and the driver slowed down to look at us. When he'd gone, I continued.

"You just resist me on this," I said. "You won't give in."

Pat frowned. "What makes you think I haven't already given in?"

"Have you?"

"You want me to say it your way, spell it out for you, take away all your uncertainties. You don't have to ask for this kind of reassurance all the time."

"Just tell me."

"An old schoolteacher of mine," Pat said, "a woman who was in her eighties the last time I saw her, had one of the best marriages I'd ever seen. She loved her husband so much it wasn't funny, right up to the day he died. When she spoke about him, it was all still there, all that love and passion. And devotion. But she once said to me, 'I felt conquered by my husband. I told him once, "How does it feel to be the victor?" ' "

What was I supposed to think of this? There was a long silence while I tried to figure out what Pat meant by telling this story.

"We should go," she said, and turned and strode away.

Walking back to the car, I realized I hadn't said everything I wanted to, but the moment had passed. I wanted to tell her that in the whole terrifying length of a life—terrifying because of its shortness—I sensed that the only true available solace came through sincere devotion to another human being. Did this imply conquest? I thought not. Rather, within a transitory arrangement of elements, a fixed harmonious union was the means through which chaos became order. It was the point at which you found a location.

In Tijuana, we stopped briefly to buy *galletitas* at a bakery, then drove on through the dusk, as the light faltering over the ocean and land gave way broadly across the surface of things, until we found a motel on the coast, a few miles north of Ensenada. In the morning, after a breakfast on the terrace, we drove into town. It took us most of the morning to locate the restaurant where the twins had told us we might find Lupe. It was not in the main part of town that appealed to the tourists, but on one of the dirt roads that radiated out from the paved streets, where buildings were thrown together out of patchwork lumber, and a thick layer of dust covered everything. The restaurant had a piece of billboard for a door. Inside, a ceiling fan turned but barely stirred the air. In the corner, on an overturned wooden crate, stood a big jar filled with milky liquid. The place smelled of chili, roasted meat, and steaming beans. No one was in the restaurant except the cook, a boy who looked no older than twenty. Pat asked him if he knew Lupe Batista. He didn't readily understand her, but Pat repeated his name, then wrote it out for him, persistent, until the cook, now definite in his manner, shook his head and went back to work. He gave her an uninterested look when she tried to talk to him again, but Pat was unfazed. However, finally she turned away.

"It's still early," she said to me. "Let's try later."

We drove back into town and sat for a while on the steps of a wide, sun-filled plaza, then walked to the pier, where, at the edge of the water, in a shed that served as a fish market, men were cleaning their catch. The rough, fish-bloodied men looked Pat up and down as we walked the length of the shed. Coming out into the sunlight, I took her hand, and walking along, with our hands clasped and held high as though we were dancing, I felt something ceremonial in our attitude, and I finally remembered what it reminded me of—a scene in a Yugoslavian film I once saw, where the bride and groom, their hands clasped in just this way, came slowly toward a wedding altar.

"What are you doing?" she said.

"What?"

"You've got hold of my hand like you were presenting me at auction."

"Actually, I was thinking of a film where a couple are walking toward an altar."

"Well, there you have it," she said.

I looked down, saddened.

She touched my face. "Russ," she said. "Lighten up," and she jiggled my arm, and lifted our hands a little higher.

We returned to the restaurant, and the first thing we saw as we came around the corner was Elmo, lying on his back, all four feet up, warming his stomach just in front of the door.

"My God," Pat said, and jumped out of the car as soon as I'd stopped. Elmo greeted us in a faltering manner, as if he were having déjà vu and trying to recall where he'd seen us before. The door to the restaurant was open, and I saw Lupe, sitting at a table with three other men. Pat, who was bent over Elmo, patting his muzzle and kissing his head, didn't see Lupe. "Let's go," I said. But at that moment, she stood up and saw Lupe in the restaurant and walked right in before I could stop her.

She said, "Why did you take him? We trusted you." Lupe said nothing. He didn't look at either one of us. The fan overhead turned uselessly. I ought to be helpful, I thought, I should set something straight here. But I felt afraid to say anything.

Elmo had followed us into the restaurant and gone over to Lupe. Lupe picked up a scrap of meat, ignoring Pat who stood very close to him, and gave it to Elmo. The thing about Elmo was, he made friends very easily where there were prospects of a meal. One of the men at the table said, "Hey, Alamo," and dropped a tortilla on the floor for him.

Alamo? Did they really think his name was Alamo instead of Elmo, or was this their way of making a little joke? Lupe still didn't look at us, but tipped a full glass of the milky liquid up to his lips and swallowed it all down. It was a strangely obscene gesture to me. Then he put his plate on the floor for Elmo to lick.

The guy across from Lupe said, "*Qué quieren?*"

"*Quieren su perro viejo.*"

"*Se lo llevaron?*"

"*No, no me lo lleve.*"

The same guy turned to Pat and said, "Nice dog, lady."

I don't know why it happened then, but I felt I really had to say something. I said to Lupe, "You know, only a real jerk would steal a dog." He looked up at me.

"I mean, why did you do it? It's totally crazy to take somebody's dog like that."

He stared at me and shrugged his shoulders, his lips curling into a grin of dismissal, as if he couldn't care less that he'd caused us some little inconvenience.

"Take your damned dog," he said to me, and then looked at his companions and jerked his head toward the door. He looked at me again. I stared at him. I can't say what passed between us at that moment, but I knew it was only between us, that he had cut Pat out of everything, that he'd managed to avoid even acknowledging her presence and that he would continue to do so, dealing only with me. In truth, I felt calm for the first time in a while. I'd spoken up and nothing terrible had happened.

"Don't come around again," Pat told Lupe. "Not ever. I'll land your ass in jail if I ever see you in our neighborhood." Her voice was hard and firm. He still did not look at her. I didn't know whether she got this or not, how completely she was being ignored.

We tried to leave then, but Elmo, who seemed caught up in divided loyalties, wouldn't follow us when we called to him, and he even resisted, as he had always done, any attempt to force him to move. Lupe stood up. He gave Elmo a pat on his haunches on the way out. Each of the men, as he filed past us, said, "Adios, Alamo," and once outside, we heard them laughing as they walked down the street.

At the border, we were stopped because we didn't have the proper papers for Elmo. We needed something certifying that he'd had a rabies vaccination. Over and over again, to one official after another, Pat tried to explain the situation. Our dog was stolen by an illegal alien. We'd come down to get it back. We hadn't thought about papers. Couldn't they understand this? The officials peered into the car. They looked at Elmo, who placidly gazed back at them. They looked me over. They studied Pat. They seemed to think there was something we were hiding, some truth we hadn't told. At one point, we had to open the trunk so they could search inside. They turned their flashlights onto the backseat and they looked in the glove compartment. Pat, who became more and more outraged by their behavior, scolded them for not showing us more sympathy. Finally, perhaps convinced of our innocence, or perhaps because they'd exhausted their authority or just grown tired of us, they let us cross over the border, and, under a moonless sky, with music filling the car and Elmo nestled on the seat between us, we drove toward home, a triumvirate, somehow miraculously restored.

IT SURE IS COLD HERE AT NIGHT

Right now I'm living with this guy who fought in the war. I can't believe it, he's so much older than me, but suddenly, in the last three or four months, I don't feel so young myself.

It happens so damned gradually you almost don't know what's going on. At first, I thought I might just have tension and that was causing the corner of my eye to feel funny. But it isn't tension. It's a wrinkle that's shown up and feels like a little pinch. All those years of smiling in the sun are years I suddenly regret.

Angus says, buy some cream, which I do, twelve dollars a jar at Drugtown. It says, use sparingly, and believe me, I was. Lately, however, I've begun using it generously, with absolutely no regard for cost.

On Saturdays, Angus goes out to a shooting area near the American Falls reservoir. I go along and sit in the car and knit while he shoots bottles and cans. Sometimes he puts holes in refrigerators and water heaters that have been abandoned in the nearby dump, or blasts old TVs, couches, paint cans, you name it. He shoots into the straw-stuffed targets that are really meant for the archers and blows small branches off of trees. But I'm not interested in shooting, and I'll never go hunting with him again. Not after he shot the wet doe. The minute he starts cleaning it and that knife cuts into her milk, I know there's an orphan out there. What difference it makes, I don't know, dead is dead, whether you're a baby or an adult.

In fact, Angus said during the war he saw babies die and he saw adults die and for him, it was worse seeing an adult die than a baby. This goes against what you'd normally think, doesn't it?

Only once during the war did Angus shoot somebody, and that was by accident. It was a mess for him. There was some kind of inspection and Angus went to his locker to get his weapon—that's what they call it, never a gun or a pistol, but his weapon—and some guy sitting on a bunk nearby asked him a question. Angus turned to answer and somehow that thing went off. Without him having aimed it, purely by chance, the bullet went through this guy's neck. Angus, you can imagine, was freaked. The guy lived but Angus was subjected to an inquiry where he had to convince everybody it was just an accident. The guy didn't trust Angus again, he never spoke to him, though he healed up OK.

War isn't a thing a woman can understand too well. Oh, I guess if you were a woman in Europe in World War II you'd understand some things about war, not what it was like fighting, but what it's like living with the effects of war, relatives sacrificed, a fear for your own life, the destruction all around you. We in America are pretty blasé about war, like real young babies who don't worry too much about who's holding them because they can't yet focus their eyes to see the difference. Maybe it's not quite like that, but I'm only thinking how we, too, are blind to what we can't yet see. We can't see war because it isn't anyplace except on the television set.

Angus comes from Pocatello. His family are the Dooleys of Dooley Tires. His grandfather started the business that now has branches all over the state. Sometimes we'll be driving (we drive a lot—you can't stop that Angus when he gets behind a wheel) up by Coeur d'Alene, or over by Weiser, or Burley, and suddenly we'll see a big billboard that says DOOLEY TIRE COMPANY, and there'll be a moment of surprise and recognition, a little thrill.

Angus wants to stop drinking and pay off our credit cards so that's what we're working on.

We're watching a movie on TV when Angus says, "This is totally unbelievable. I can tell you, these guys would have skis or something."

The movie is called *Where Eagles Dare*, or maybe it's *Where Eagles Soar*—something like that. Clint Eastwood and Richard Burton have parachuted behind enemy lines. They've landed on a snow-covered mountain. They're wearing all-white outfits and are hardly distinguishable from the wintery background. Big white tubes with supplies have been parachuted in with them. Both Angus and I think that when they open these tubes, there's going to be skis inside, or at least snowshoes, but there isn't anything like that. They struggle to walk around in the deep snow. We can't figure out how they're going to get very far. In fact, it makes us nervous to watch them trying to walk. It's such a basic thing, knowing you can't walk in deep snow. We know that, how come the movie-makers don't? Who planned this expedition and left out snowshoes? Who planned this movie and forgot something so basic? It's very annoying to both of us, just watching them struggle through the snow.

"It's very unbelievable, isn't it?" I say.

"Unbelievable? Yeah, I'd say. It's ridiculous."

"It *is* ridiculous. How could they not think of that?"

"Not just ridiculous," Angus says. "It's plain crazy."

"How are they going to get anywhere?" I add.

This week is "War Is Hell" week on KCOP, Channel 13. Every night a different war movie. Angus is in heaven. He's a big fan of war movies. Anything with guns and generals and action gets his vote for our program viewing. Christ, Angus, I say, can't we watch something romantic? But for Angus, I think war is romance. When again is he going to get to go to a foreign place as exotic as that, with everything paid for, including the trips to Hong Kong and Bangkok where there are lots of beautiful Asian girls? On one level, he feels like he's seen the world. He was scared, I'm sure, but even the scariness had its romance.

When he talks about that place, you'd think it was a paradise in some respects. One time he started talking about the extreme heat and humidity in those jungles and he described it as sensuous. With those light, loose-fitting clothes, the way the native people moved, so loose-limbed and graceful, so small and light. It was very nice, he said, just the feel of that kind of heat on your skin.

You should have seen the beaches, he said. Beautiful. You should have seen them from a helicopter.

This is what some of the guys did. They took a picture of a naked woman, like a pinup girl. Each guy had his own pinup. He divided her body into 365 sections with a pen. Each day he filled in a section. That's how everybody marked time. By the time somebody finished a tour of duty, he had obliterated a woman, so she was a blackened form, like the charred remains of a corpse or an anonymous silhouette. Angus said, I never did that.

Some guy in Angus's platoon asked his wife to dress up in sexy clothes and take pictures for him and send them. As soon as he got the pictures, he passed them around for everybody to look at. The thing was, Angus said, you wouldn't have expected this guy to have had such a beautiful wife. She looked great. It wasn't like some of those pictures you see in girlie magazines that men take of their girlfriends and send in, where the women usually look so awful it's sad to think their boyfriends would do that to them. This woman was so beautiful, Angus said, she could have been a model, and here she was, married to an ordinary grunt.

• •

If Angus wants to be sociable, he can be, but more often than not he keeps pretty quiet. One exception is when we go out with Billy and Marion. Billy didn't fight in a war, but he's been in a mental institution. Angus feels comfortable with him. Billy creates an edge around everything, too. This edge is hard to explain but it's as though you have to prove yourself to Angus, and to Billy, too, before they'll let you cross over and get anywhere near them. They're not frivolous in any way, and they make it hard for you to be.

An example: Angus and Marion, Billy and I are sitting in the Melody Inn, a bar in Chubbock, just outside of Pocatello. A kid in a cowboy hat walks in. "I can arm wrestle anybody in this place and beat them." He looks at Angus, then at Billy.

Angus says, "We believe you."

"You want to try me?"

"No," Angus says.

The boy looks perplexed. "Come on," he says. He's young and everything registers on his face. He's only trying to have fun. He comes over to the table and sits down. "Either one of you guys want to play pool?"

"Get lost," Angus says. He says it with enough of an edge, the boy just gets up and walks out. Marion and I look at each other. Things like this happen all the time. Angus and Billy. They're sort of rough on people.

Another time during the war, a guy Angus knew was going on R&R in Hawaii. This guy's wife was coming from the States to meet him in Honolulu for a week. He came back with his wife's underpants. He told Angus he could use them for you-can-guess-what, but Angus, who thought it was a weird offer, didn't take him up on it.

Sometimes I get off work and come home and find Angus just sitting in a chair, doing absolutely nothing, just looking and listening. The first couple of times I caught him doing this, I thought, is he OK? He says he's listening to the music of the spheres. This is an old idea, he says, one that comes from

Pythagoras. Silence, says Pythagoras via Angus, is the music of the spheres. If you just sit and listen, you can hear it. What does it sound like? I ask Angus. Don't be a dumb shit, he says.

Whenever I ask Angus a question like this, I can tell he's going to get mad because he thinks I've got to live it out for myself. This is a problem with living with an older man. The rates of discovery are different.

One time, before I gave up hunting with Angus, we went out with some of his buddies to shoot doves. Doves are about the smallest thing you can try to shoot with a gun. All morning we tramped around in cornfields outside American Falls and nobody shot one dove. Finally I sat down near a fence and told Angus I didn't want to hunt anymore because it was boring me. He and the others took off. After a while I heard gun shots. A flock of doves came and landed on the telephone wires in front of me. I picked up my gun and shot two of them off the wires. A little while later, there were more shots off in the cornfields and another flock of doves flew over and landed on the wires. Angus and his buddies were just flushing birds for me, like good hunting dogs. I had so much time to aim, and they were sitting so still for me, that I didn't have any trouble hitting them. Over the next hour, the doves kept flying out of the cornfields and I kept shooting them off the wires. The funny thing was, when Angus and the other guys returned, they hadn't shot one single dove. We had to divide my birds among us for the walk back to the truck so that if we got stopped by a game warden, I wouldn't get a fine for being over limit.

"How did you get all those damned doves?" he asked me later.

"I just picked them out of the blue," I replied. I never did tell him how I shot them off the wires.

But after the wet doe, I stopped hunting.

"It's a fantastic little side business," Angus's father says. "High profit margin. Almost no overhead. Minimal investment."

"Right," Angus says.

"I wish I'd ordered more. I sold out in three weeks. But I

got another order placed, and I should get some more in about ten days."

"Right."

To everything his father says, Angus replies "Right." His father, as usual, is talking about something that doesn't interest Angus much. This time it's pistachio nuts. He's importing them from Turkey and selling them in the tire store. Customers get free samples. He's put a sign up in the store on the counter: NUTS TO YOU. We saw it when we went in last week.

Angus's father is always selling something, besides the tires. Before the nuts, it was bootlegged eight-track tapes, mostly country-western music. Before the tapes, it was hula-dolls for the dashboard. He wants Angus to work for him, like his brother does, but Angus has no interest in it.

"We could put these nuts in bars and do very well, I think," Mr. Dooley says. "Package them in different sizes. People love pistachio nuts, more than almonds or peanuts."

"What about cashews?" Angus says dryly.

"Well, cashews are popular, too," his father says, "but I believe we could get the pistachios into bars and convenience stores and make quite a profit. I'd be willing to go partners."

Angus declines. Later, over a beer in the Melody Inn, Angus says, "I just don't have that merchant mentality. He's got it, but I don't."

"What kind of mentality do you have?" I ask.

"Warped," he says. Then he takes me seriously and thinks about it.

"Mechanical, I guess," he says. It's true that when he does work, it's fixing other people's cars or motorcycles, even fiddling with TVs and toasters for friends. But it's hardly an absorbing occupation. Yet, it's with real feeling that he says, "I've always liked putting things back together after I've taken them apart. It's the only thing that seems real to me."

My Uncle Arlo was some kind of officer in World War II. He was a difficult man. His wife, Aunt Mattie, nearly went crazy with him before he died last year. She probably wouldn't have become an alcoholic except he was one. Now she's worried about me because she sees that Angus drinks too much. Angus, however, doesn't change much when he drinks, whereas Uncle Arlo became the most obnoxious person on earth when he drank. Lots of times, at family parties, everyone would just go home early rather than have to put up with Arlo's drunken war stories.

Ray is different. He's my mother's cousin, or maybe something more distant than that. He was also in a war, Korea or what he calls "The Korean Conflict," which makes it sound like a miniature war, but he doesn't talk about it much. Ray's a serious person, but also very kind. I think he's quite religious, though he doesn't talk about that, either. He's married to Hella, and they live on a farm near Blackfoot.

Hella's of German extraction, her family were Nazis. When she was a teenager, the war was on, and she got conscripted for service. She said she was given three choices: She could work in an underground munitions factory; she could get posted at the border and man searchlights at night; or, she could become a tramcar driver in the city of Hamburg. She chose the tramcar driver, a job that turned out to be pretty rough. During air raids, the tramcar drivers were the last ones to go into the shelters, and the first to come out. So Hella saw all this destruction and death and that was pretty horrible for a teenager. After the war, Hella didn't want to stay in Germany, she wanted to forget and, not knowing a soul here, she came to this country.

Can you imagine, I said to Angus, being a teenager, so young, and having only three choices, each of which put you in danger by making you part of the machinery of war? Angus didn't say anything. And then I realized that he'd only been given one choice, the army infantry.

"Can you believe it?" Angus's father says. He's mixing himself another bourbon. It's his fourth. He keeps mixing them for Angus, too, and I wish he would stop. He's upset because he's just learned he can't get any more nuts.

"More potato chips?" Angus's mother says to me, and passes a bowl.

"There's something wrong when you can't have free trade in the world."

"What's free trade got to do with it?" Angus asks.

"Apparently they're trying to keep some balance of trade with Turkey. They're not taking something of ours so the government here won't let these nuts come in anymore."

"Sounds complicated," I say.

"Well, it's over our heads, all these international agreements," Angus's mom says.

"You can say that again," says Angus. "There's a group of people running this world that we don't know anything about. Truth is, we're ignoramuses. There's a bunch of people who are outside governments, outside laws, outside everything. They decide what happens. These guys are tied to networks of anticommunist, right-wing organizations, and international cartels. Everybody else is just their puppets."

"Oh, horseshit," Mr. Dooley says so angrily that he spits. "I hope you're not going to start with that conspiracy crap again. I don't think you know, son, just how full of shit you are about that. This is a free country. It's a good country. The people we have to be afraid of aren't people in this country, and they're not some guys in corporate offices. They're the damned terrorists and the communists and all the rest!"

Mrs. Dooley says, "Let's not spoil a good time."

Mr. Dooley stands up. He teeters slightly, the effects of his several drinks. He kicks the lawn chair as he heads toward the barbecue. He picks up his barbecue fork and jabs at the meat lying on the grill.

"How can you have fought if you don't ever remember?" he sputters. This sounds suddenly profound to me. But I don't know what it means. I'm thinking about it when Mr. Dooley backs up and steps on my toe. It hurts like hell, but I smile instead of yelling.

"Ooops, Ollie," Mrs. Dooley says. "You just stepped on Brenda. Did it hurt, dear?"

I shake my head.

"I listened to this conspiracy crap about Kennedy and about

King. Now it's the whole goddamned world." He turns around and points the barbecue fork at Angus and shakes it.

"Just find a better goddamned country," he says. "Go ahead."

Later on, when we are driving north on the interstate, I sit as close as I can to Angus. He was awfully mad when we left his parents, and he hasn't been able to get over it. He's sullen and driving too fast. Between us, we don't have much money or else I would suggest stopping to get something to eat. We hadn't stayed long enough to get any steak at his parents'. I begin to feel hungry. Our credit cards are maxed out. We can't even charge anything.

Suddenly I think of Hella and Ray, who live not far from where we are. I say to Angus, Why not go there and spend the night? and he agrees.

It's nice when people make you feel welcome, and Ray and Hella surely do. They give us the pull-out couch in the TV room to sleep on. Hella, who is tall, with gray hair and steady blue eyes, fixes us something to eat. We watch TV with them until it's late and then fall asleep. Hella is up early and leaves for her job at a nursery. Ray is busy with farm chores all day. When Angus and I get up, we take a walk, sit on the porch, stroll around the pens looking at the different colors of cows, and decide to spend another night. Instead of staying a night, we stay four.

There isn't a morning we don't wake up and smell something good cooking in Hella's kitchen. Cinnamon rolls. Doughnuts. Blueberry muffins. Angus takes a liking to a flop-eared dog and the two of them disappear for long stretches during the day. The good life takes us up while we're there, and we hardly drink at all. They live very simply. The house is old, and there isn't much room. Hella, for instance, keeps her sweaters in boot boxes, stacked on shelves near the dining room table. Food comes fresh from her garden. Nothing is wasted. Hella, who is robust from her work at the nursery, actually looks stronger than Ray, who is thin and coughs into a hankie a lot.

One night, when we're looking for something to read, Angus finds Ray's diary that he kept when he was in the war, and though we know we probably shouldn't, we read some of it. There are just short entries:

October 16, 1952: I am on the front lines now. We do most of our work at night. The enemy is about two or three hundred yards in front of us. We are on one hill and they on another across from us. If we move around in the daytime they start shooting at us. After dark, patrols are sent out from our lines to try to find out about them. They have a lot of land mines in the area so you have to watch out where you step, and that is hard to do in the dark. We had four boys get wounded about two nights ago from one that blew up.

October 18: It sure is cold here at night. I was on patrol last night. We left the front lines about eleven o'clock and stayed out until four in the morning.

October 23: I'm so glad when morning comes and I can get into my warm sleeping bag. We have a place dug into the ground and covered over with sand bags— it is about six feet deep and has room for four people to sleep in. At night we stay out in the trenches, which are about six feet deep. A patrol was out the other night and made contact with the enemy. Three boys were injured and one killed. They couldn't bring in the one who was killed, and when they went back the next night to get him, the enemy was waiting with guns set up all around.

October 30: We have to go each day about half a mile to get our chow and carry it back across a field and up over a ridge. They can see us when we cross the ridge and fire at us with machine guns. They sure make us run. They've hit two boys.

November 1: I go out on patrol every fourth night. There is one officer and one platoon sergeant to each platoon, and there are three rifle platoons in a company. We take fifteen men on a patrol with a radio and a telephone, and a roll of wire. We roll the telephone wire as we go out and have the phone hook on the wire so we can talk with the company commander about what goes on around us. If the enemy gets in behind and cuts the wire, we always have the radio to fall back on. We never start a fight with them. We have good medical care. We have a hospital corpsman along with us. If a person is wounded real bad they call a hospital plane and they can have him back in the Division Hospital within an hour.

November 4: We have been on the front lines one month and will stay about another six weeks, then go back for a month. We had another boy killed last night and one the night before.

November 6: It is getting dark again so I must get ready for a night of work. I go up and down the trench lines at night and talk to the boys. They are all young kids—eighteen to twenty-one years old; fine boys. They talk a lot about their families. I guess everyone feels near their families when they are away from home like this. I think we all feel we need God's help, and feel near Him when we are in trouble or in battle.

We read like this for a while, Angus propped up on pillows with the diary leaning against his knees. My head is on his shoulder. Every once in a while Angus reaches down and smooths my hair. I like it and think he's doing it because he feels close to me. But then I realize my hair is tickling his nose and he's brushing it out of the way. Still, I think, this is the most peaceful we'll ever be. I move my head away from his cheek. Through a window that is open, the cool air comes into the room. Noises come too. A calf moos. We hear the crickets. We can smell the turkey pens and, from time to time, hear their silly gobbles.

Suddenly Angus snaps the diary shut, as if he's angry or has just had a brainstorm.

"Are there any of those Fritos left?"

"I don't know."

"Get up and see, would you? Bring a Coke, too."

When I come back from the kitchen, he has the black-and-white cat on his chest and he's kissing it or something. Then he sees me and shoves the cat away and puts his hands behind his head. He looks up at me, blank-like. I try to hand him the bag of Fritos. But he just stares at me.

"Take these, Angus," I say.

He doesn't move.

"What'd I bring them for, then?" He can make me feel very frustrated. But just then he comes out of his trance and takes the Fritos and I sit down with him and together we finish off the whole bag so that I have a kind of sickly full feeling from eating too much of one thing.

Angus pulls me over close to him and holds me.

"I don't really think there's a world conspiracy," he says.

"I didn't think so, but it probably doesn't matter."

"It matters," he says, "but you can't go getting paranoid, can you?"

"No," I say, "it's not a good idea."

We are quiet for a while.

"We used to see the dawn in Vietnam every day," he says.

The turkeys gobble wildly all of a sudden. Something must be out there scaring them, I think.

"I really appreciate Ray not talking to me about the war."

Sometimes I'm convinced he just wants to forget. He doesn't want to remember. But then I think, Why are we watching all these damned war movies?

Whatever was bothering those turkeys, it doesn't go away. They gobble off and on until dawn, which breaks, curiously, at a time when both Angus and I have opened our eyes and are laying there together, looking out the sliding glass doors at the expansive brown fields, and the brilliant red glow at the horizon, which is spreading upward and widening, bringing in the light of day.

THE DEATH OF A MORMON ELDER

Between Springville and Mapleton, on land that lay for at least part of the day in the shadow of Mount Nebo, the church owned a large farm, which was run by a Mexican convert named Emilio Carranza. While always profitable, the farm had done even better under Emilio, who had arrived from Mexico three years earlier. So much profit, in fact, was being realized each year that the welfare program was booming, and still there was money left over. The church had been able to buy more land, and then more, until it owned most of this eastern slope of the valley.

Emilio lived with his wife Gloria in the farmhouse at the uppermost edge of the property. The area was called "the bench" after a narrow flatland left behind as a shore mark when the prehistoric Lake Bonneville had receded. In fairness, the church could be said to own ninety percent of the slope below the bench, and the Waterfalls—a family who had been in the area for generations—the remaining ten percent.

In Mexico the Carranzas had been poor and Catholic until Vernon Waterfall, then barely eighteen years old, arrived at their door, wearing a blue suit and riding a fine bicycle, and gave them the first of the gospel lessons. From that moment on their fortunes had changed. Now, thanks to the Waterfalls, who had been their sponsors, the Carranzas were church members, living in the United States in a handsome house, eating better than they ever had before, and getting paid a salary by the church that was twenty times what Emilio had earned in Mexico. To be sure, theirs was an unusual story. Most converts didn't come to Utah; they stayed in their native lands. The Carranzas had simply been lucky to have the Waterfalls as their benefactors.

Although the lands were not actually his, there were times when Emilio, standing above the fields, looked out over the tender green crops, the rows of sugar beets pushing through the ground, the tassled corn and herds of cattle, and thought himself a rich man rather than just the overseer of the church farm.

The Waterfall family, in spite of their land holdings, were decidedly not rich and never imagined themselves so. They lived in a basement house, a concrete block that rose only a few feet above the ground, just to the level of a normal house's foundation, and ended there, forming a square concrete pad about half the size of a tennis court. The children, by merely stepping up onto the concrete pad, could walk on the roof of their house. They could play war there, or roller skate, or dribble a ball. Because it was always the intention of Clayton Waterfall, the father, to build a proper house on top of his basement foundation, the iron rods that formed spines inside the concrete walls had been allowed to rise in antenna-like extensions, which in time were bent into loops in deference to the children's safety.

At the time of the events in this story, the Waterfall children had all grown up and left home, although the grandchildren and the children and their spouses all continued to spend a lot of time there. The second story, the aboveground addition that Clayton had planned for years, had never been built, and it was accepted now that it never would be.

It seemed to Emilio Carranza that the Waterfalls' house was like a relic of the past. Every time he visited, descending the stairs into the basement rooms, it stirred an ancient memory in him of living underground, in dwellings where people awoke in earthen or cavernous chambers, still warmed by the previous night's fire. Of course, the Waterfall house was clean and proper, but Emilio, who had never seen such basement houses in Mexico, found it a curio.

In contrast to what had happened to most of the families in the community, the Waterfall children had stayed in the area. It was a big, close family. The women used each other to sound out their family problems, had pregnancies simultaneously, and got everyone together for holidays. The men were always ready to labor on each other's behalf. Within the community, the Waterfalls were known as good church members, hard workers, kind people. By some process of natural selection, which acknowledged age and wisdom, Clayton Waterfall each year took charge of the Fourth of July celebration, flipping the hotcakes himself, organizing the cleanup crews, taking control with the combination of firm direction, humbleness, and good humor that made everyone love him.

Clayton owned his own excavating company, Waterfall and Sons. Both Vernon and Leon, his youngest and oldest sons, worked for him. So, too, did Emilio Carranza until the opportunity to manage the church farm came up. With a small fleet of equipment—the prize piece being an expensive frontloader capable of digging great holes and moving quantities of earth, of even lifting large boulders in its bucket—the Waterfalls earned fair livings from jobs as small as digging fence posts for farmers to subcontracting portions of the Great Salt Lake Causeway. The prized frontloader was a recent acquisition. Sometimes, when it took a boulder in its bucket, it seemed as if the back tread rose so far off the ground there was nothing left in contact with the earth to enable it to move. It was like a rearing animal, a bucking and groaning thing. There was always danger to this work, the fear of a tractor rolling, a chance that at these precarious angles, a machine might tip over. But experience had prevailed, as it often does, combining with luck to protect them from harm.

Early in the morning on the fourth of June, Clayton Waterfall left home to drive to the site where he had contracted to dig a foundation for a house, a job that he hoped to finish in three days. The first day, he and Vernon, his youngest son, known for his slow speech and slow ways, arrived at the site just as the sun was rising. They said a prayer before they began to work, as they did at the start of every job.

Vernon bowed his head.

His father said, "Our Father in Heaven, we ask thy blessings and protection for this day. Amen."

His head rose and he said to his son, "I'm going to walk these lines, you go ahead and start up at the point where the road comes in." The son climbed up in the driver's seat. Father and son had done this hundreds of times before, so no words were wasted trying to tell each other what to do. They couldn't have been heard above the machinery anyway. They had, instead, a language of symbolic hand movements, much like those used by football referees, by which they could say stop, dump, more to the left, more to the right, and so on. Clayton turned and walked away from his son. Vernon started up the machinery.

A little while later, Clayton Waterfall, who had lately felt a hitch in his hip as if something hesitated and faltered there, like a gear that's slow to mesh, slipped and fell to the ground. When he tried to get up, his leg failed him again, and once more he went down. It happened at a moment when Vernon, looking out over the valley, was thinking of Earl Gibson, whom he could see below him, walking from his turkey pens toward his house. Vernon backed up, his eyes still on Earl Gibson. He took several more bites out of the earth with his bucket. He backed up farther and farther, swinging the machine around deftly as if he were doing a brody in his own car. As he scooped up the next load of earth, he noticed a bit of colored cloth in the load. When he dumped the contents of the bucket, the body of his father was included in the mounds of dirt that came tumbling out.

He ran to his father. He saw he was dead. Instantly, Vernon felt the impossibility of this. For seconds he imagined there was something he could do, something he *must* do. It was inconceivable that he couldn't change things. He panicked. He touched his father's face and threw himself across the body. He began sobbing. With fierce insistence he denied this thing could happen. Then he jumped up and ran around wildly. He began wailing, running first in one direction, then the other. His eyes were wild and he looked everywhere, all around him, seeking some immediate, urgent help. He went to the lip of the hill, the bench created those thousands of years before by the prehistoric lakeshore, and he began yelling in a voice that would have startled any living thing that heard it. Earl Gibson, who was standing in his driveway, heard the strange noise and stopped and listened carefully. He looked up at the hillside. He saw a man waving his arms and realized the cries were coming from him. Instantly he started running up the hill. As he would later tell people, he was the first person to arrive at the scene of the accident.

Emilio Carranza sat in the clinic, which occupied a wing of the hospital. The doctor, with tweezers poised, was about to remove a tick from Emilio's torso when a nurse rushed in and summoned him. "Excuse me a moment," the doctor said. Not until the doctor was in the hallway did the nurse tell him that the body of Clayton Waterfall had just been brought to the hospital.

Emilio was left sitting, shirt off, with his feet resting on a shelf that pulled out from the end of the examination table. After a while, he grew uncomfortable and lay back on the table and stared at the doctor's ceiling.

The doctor didn't return. The tick, still fully alive, continued to fatten itself on Emilio's blood, tickling his stomach as it wiggled its legs. It was just this sensation in the night, the barest tickling like the light, playful touch of a lover, that had awakened him and had led to the discovery of the tick, already embedded and engorged and looking like a tiny bruised appendage. He was for pulling it off, but his wife advised against it, in case the head remained and gave him fever. Instead, she lit a match, blew it out, and touched the smoking, charred tip to the end of the tick, a trick that should have made him back out. But it didn't work. She tried again with another match. Still, the tick didn't retreat from Emilio's soft flesh. "He's going to die if we keep sticking matches against him," his wife said, and kept him from lighting another. "You don't want him to die still in you." Finally, against his will, Emilio was persuaded by his wife to wait and see the doctor in the morning.

The doctor still hadn't returned. He was gone so long that Emilio, who wasn't a patient man, began to have thoughts of getting dressed and leaving. He stood down on the cold floor and walked to his clothes. He put his socks on and walked back to the table. Suddenly the doctor opened the door, giving Emilio a fright, as if he'd been caught doing something wrong. The doctor wore a grave look. He told Emilio Carranza that Brother Waterfall was dead.

"It happened above Earl Gibson's place. They were digging a foundation. One of the boys apparently didn't see him and ran over him with the tractor."

Emilio made a soft whistling sound. He wondered which son had been driving. This was his first thought. Was it Leon or Sweego or perhaps Vernon, the one who stuttered? Vernon, of course, he felt closest to, since he'd converted Emilio and his wife to the church, but as a result of the friendship with the whole family, the other boys had become close, too.

"Which boy was driving the tractor?"

"Vernon," the doctor said.

"Can you imagine his feelings?" Emilio mumbled, shaking his head. "This is a terrible thing for that family."

"Clayton Waterfall wasn't an old man, either."

"No, he wasn't."

"And one of the kindest men on the face of the earth."

"True," said Emilio.

As the doctor removed the tick, Emilio felt a wave of sorrow. Brother Waterfall was gone; death was abrupt and cruel. He felt fear for the family. He also felt foolish that something as inconsequential as a tick should have brought him to the hospital on the day Brother Waterfall was killed. (That such a silly problem should compete for the doctor's time!) Mostly, he felt awe that death should be so swift.

The tick was removed. The doctor stepped gingerly on the pedal of the trash can and disposed of it. He washed his hands.

As if to give his situation more weight, Emilio asked the doctor whether there had been any recent cases of fever from ticks in the area.

"Near Fish Lake," the doctor said, "but that was maybe two, or perhaps three, years ago. There's been nothing more recent."

"Well, doctor, if I live to be ninety, I'll have you to thank for saving my life."

The doctor, failing to grasp the joke, nodded and left the room.

Before the morning was over, Emilio had broken the news of Brother Waterfall's death to a number of people. He told Barry Wadman. Clark Hatch, the druggist, learned of the accident when Emilio stopped to buy pads for his bunions. So, too, did Grant Markle, who was delivering milk for the dairy when Emilio saw him. Each time he told the story, the tragedy struck him anew. Almost everyone commented on the fact that death was swift, and their awe lay in the knowledge that one moment a man was alive, another he was dead. Because these were religious people, their reactions contained a reverent wonder, tinged with a fear inspired by the sublime. The deity that unaccountably allowed for the death of good men in violent accidents was also supposed to be their protector. Whom, and when, would He call home next? Yet these things only deepened their faith. It confirmed their belief in the magisterial and unfathomable workings of God, who could take anyone, at any time, from this earth. His demands could be ruthless. He could even make the sons the instruments of their fathers' deaths.

Around noon, Emilio headed home, remembering that a class of Mia Maid girls was coming to pick string beans. The girls were already waiting with their teacher, Sister Plowgian, when Emilio pulled the truck up alongside the house. No sooner had he gotten out of the truck than the Bishop arrived. The Bishop had spent the morning in Nephi and hadn't yet heard about the accident. When Emilio broke the news to him, he left immediately for the Waterfalls'.

Emilio supervised the girls in the fields. He checked on the cow with the infected foot. He mended a gate. He thought about Brother Waterfall, a good, fair man. He thought about his gentleness and his good, kind disposition. He had been like a father to Emilio, even though there had been little difference in their ages. He had seen to it that Emilio had everything he needed to begin his new life in America. He cared for him and watched over him. Perhaps his memory would be kept alive by people, like himself, who loved the man. Whenever they thought of him, it would be with warmth, and then it would be as if he were there among them again. Perhaps the dead needed only to be remembered in order to have their realm.

All these things he thought throughout the afternoon. Brother Waterfall was with him, as he was with others who were discussing his death. When Emilio took a load of beans to the wardhouse where the women were waiting in the kitchen, ready to begin the canning, he found them discussing the accident.

"Poor Vernon. He's had such bad luck. First his daughter, then this," said Sister Wadman. She was referring to the retarded child born to Vernon and his wife earlier in the year.

"You wonder why the Lord would put such difficulties on a good boy."

"You can't wonder such things."

"It's the good ones who get tested."

"Like the Ross family. You wonder how much a family can stand, and then they do, they just stand it."

"The back broadens to the burden."

"You know, that Vernon's a sweet man. I remember when he was just a boy and he came around selling Watkins vanilla. He had an imaginary friend named Larry, and he'd say, 'Larry wants to know if you need any vanilla.'"

"He was an unusual boy," said Mrs. Cain, the retired schoolteacher. "I had him in first grade. I remember once I asked the children to compose poems about something that had happened to them that day. I'll never forget Vernon's poem. He wrote,

"When I am walking down the
Stairs at school, I don't think
About anything else. I just
Walk down the stairs.

"He's always had a sweetness about him."

Mrs. Cain enjoyed recalling a student for whom she felt a curiously strong fondness. "And then another time," she said, "he told me, 'There is something in my stomach that knows everything, and that's magic.'"

"I believe he's going to need more help than his mother to get over this."

"Lord, I hope he has the faith to pull him through."

"I'm sure he does."

"Oh, I'm sure he does too."

Emilio spoke up suddenly and said good-bye. He had decided to go and see the family now, to pay a visit of condolence to the Waterfalls.

Emilio found his wife tweezing her eyebrows in front of the tin mirror decorated with angels that had come with them from Mexico. If Gloria Carranza didn't regularly pull out the hairs from between her eyes she would have had one long eyebrow extending from temple to temple. She had been to Nephi shopping. Emilio noticed the Mode-O-Day bags on the bed.

"Spending money," he said.

"Just a little."

"A little is already too much."

"You've got to pick up those steers tonight," she said, not looking away from the mirror. "Brother Cranston called and said to come get them."

"I'm not picking up any steers," Emilio said. "Not tonight anyway. I'm going to see the Waterfalls." He pulled his boots off and looked for his white shirt in the closet. "There was an accident today. Brother Waterfall was killed. Vernon ran over him with a tractor while they were working up on the hillside."

"Oh, no," Gloria Carranza said, and she crossed herself out of the habits of the old religion. But she did not ask any questions. The difference between her and the other people to whom he'd broken the news during the day was she didn't want to know any details of the accident. Being superstitious, she had a fear that the details of a death could linger and cause trouble in the form of nightmares or bad luck. It was bad enough that someone had died tragically—much worse, in fact, in terms of *mala suerte* or bad luck than if they'd died a natural death.

"That's terrible news, terrible for that family." She made a clucking noise. "Such a tragedy. But do you think you should go visit them so soon?"

Emilio stared at his wife. She talked to him and yet she continued to stare at herself in the mirror. "Does it help to screw up your mouth like that when you pull hairs from your eyebrows?" he asked. Since he'd walked in, she had not stopped plucking her eyebrows for one second. It seemed everything, including the news of a death, was secondary to the removal of these wayward hairs.

"It hurts," she said. "I can't help it."

"Where are my black shoes?"

"Where they always are. What will you say to the family?"

Emilio Carranza shook his head and sat down on the bed, staring at the back of his wife's head.

"I don't know." He hadn't really considered this. What if he couldn't find the right words? When such a terrible thing happens, what can you say? He saw himself intruding on fresh grief, wordless, dark, private grief, which the family might wish to suffer, at least initially, alone. His words might cut into that like a bad noise.

"Maybe I should wait until tomorrow," he said. He felt inexplicably tired all of a sudden, and was sweating in his underwear. He longed to lie down and close his eyes.

"I think that would be better," Gloria said. "Wait and go in the morning." She went into the kitchen to check on her soup.

They ate dinner in the small room with windows looking out onto the rows of Lombardy poplars that protected the beet fields from the winds that came out of the canyon every afternoon. Emilio told his wife how the body of Brother Waterfall had fallen out of the tractor bucket right before Vernon's eyes.

"Stop!" she yelled, and dropped her spoon. "Do you want to bring tragedy on this house, too? Now I will see that dead man falling in my dreams. When you know a thing like that, you don't forget it, Emilio. You give the dead too much power. Don't you know they want to be free to go over to the other side? They don't want to be pulled back here every time someone imagines the horrible details of their deaths."

"Don't be foolish."

"It's you who are foolish to provoke bad luck."

"I'm sick of your superstitions. You put your faith in the wrong place, like a pagan, instead of trusting God."

"I never said I didn't trust God. Don't twist my meaning."

"You are as superstitious as your mother and almost as crazy. A *bruja!*"

"God forgive you, Emilio, for talking about my dead mother in such a way."

"Don't give me this holier-than-thou memory of your mother. You know what happened to her as well as I do, how she saw omens everywhere. Even you didn't want anyone to hear her when she came running in to tell us how she'd just hoed up a devil in the garden. How she thought cats could see ancestral spirits in the corners of rooms. I remember if you don't." He added, "Tell her to come haunt me, I don't care."

"You are bad to speak this way."

"Tell her to send one of her cats to come around and scare me. What kind of woman puts doll clothes on cats, Gloria? A crazy one, that's who."

Gloria began whimpering. "So she put clothes on her cats.

Did that hurt anyone? No. Oh, you're so cruel, Emilio, to say bad things. It can't be good for a husband to talk so bad about his wife's mother, I tell you that now."

"Your mother was crazy and not because I say so now. I'm telling you that your superstitions are the seeds of your mother's craziness and if you continue to believe in them you could make yourself as crazy as she was." He was weary of the way his wife straddled beliefs. She wasn't a Mormon and she wasn't a Catholic, even though she'd been baptized the former and given up the latter. She was some crazy hybrid, like that tree next to Albert Skanky's house. Half of it was bing cherries and the other half pie cherries. He hadn't seen another tree like that. Part of the tree had deep ruby fruit, the other yellowish red. His wife was like a tree with two different kinds of cherries growing on it.

"You might as well ask me to give up my liver as to give up my intuition. And what is it to you? All I asked was that you not tell me anything more about Brother Waterfall's death. I don't like the details, thank you anyway. Is that so much to ask? You have no respect for me."

Emilio said nothing, for he could see that she was now truly worked up.

"I have a husband who treats his cows better than his wife." She pulled her apron to her face and sobbed into it. "If I could only see my sisters. Sometimes I wonder why we came here. You leave everything, then what? There's no one to console me, no one to confide in. Who really cares for you like your own family? Nobody, that's who." She sobbed harder.

This whole act was false to Emilio, as false as her eyelashes and her nails. Her obsession with cosmetics had been all right when she was twenty, but it had grown worse as she aged and became less suited to so much makeup. He looked at her. She was nearly fifty. These days, she sometimes looked like a bad woman to him. He was sorry to think this, but it was true. Even worse, more and more she looked like her mother.

"I'm tired," he said, pushing away from the table. "I'm going to bed."

"The sun's still up," Gloria said loudly, "and you're going to bed."

"Does something terrible happen to a man if he goes to bed while it's still light?" he said gruffly.

"Something terrible happens when people argue about the dead. That's what's terrible, Emilio, if you must know. That's very bad."

Emilio walked out of the room, and she was left alone, sitting before the panes of glass that faced the purple mountains to the east. Mount Nebo was still capped with snow. The deepening sky drew a clear black line against the ridges.

Many hours later, Emilio pretended to sleep when he felt his wife crawling into bed beside him. He lay still until her snoring told him she was asleep. Then he opened his eyes and looked out the window at his favorite constellation, the Pleiades, or Sisters. The moonlight on the covers of the bed comforted him. He thought about their life in America. He had adjusted to the new country better than his wife had. For him, America was the place to be. Her talk of relatives in Mexico left him empty. He had no desire to go back. The inflation, the lack of enough money, the squalid shanties that passed for houses in the area of Rio Canario where they had lived. What was there to go back to? The river ran yellow, not with minerals, but with the filth from a factory. When cows drank that water, they dropped their calves stillborn. There was no progress, only penury. Yet, while he had taken root in the new country, he felt his wife had stayed aboveground, floating, like a saint in a religious picture, above the real world. He made friends with the men in the ward. She kept her distance from the women. She passed her time alone or shopping or in the beauty parlors. She had grown heavy and lazy. She read books with titles like *Dangerous Moonlight*. He suspected her of continuing to say the rosary, although she claimed she kept the beads only for their sentimental value, since they had belonged to her mother. Never once had she stood up in Fast and Testimony meeting on the first Sunday of every month. When other people arose and testified, she sat mute and still. She was not a good Mormon, she was not a Catholic any longer: she was nothing he could understand, but something female, too witchy for a man to know. She was always bothering him with this or that idea about bad luck. When you grow old with a woman, you can't tell whether she will become more or less familiar as the years go by. Emilio felt his wife was becoming less familiar. Or was it this new country? Or even the religion that had split them?

He got up to close a shutter that banged in the wind. As he latched it, he looked down and saw the rosary lying curled in a dish on a table among his wife's beauty potions. It was for him the symbol of her incomplete conversion. He picked the rosary up and looked at it. The linked metal chain and amber beads draped his fingers with a coolness, like water. He went quietly to the closet and slipped it into the pocket of his work pants.

Gloria Carranza awakened first and, feeling the dampness in the bed, knew that her husband was sick.

"It's the fever," she said to him when he opened his eyes, and she went into the bathroom for a cold washrag.

"It's not the fever," he said. "It was hot last night. That's why I sweat."

"Not that hot," she said. "I'm calling the doctor. If it's the fever from the tick, he'll know what to give you."

"Anybody would sweat in this heat." He nudged his wife's rump with his foot. "Let me up."

"Where are you going?"

"To get the steers."

"No," she said and pushed him back against the pillows. While he had grown thinner with age, she had gotten heavier, and she could easily hold him down, especially this morning when he felt a buzzing in his bones, like something alive and malicious was working there.

"At least let me up to go to the bathroom," he growled.

"All right, but then you're going back to bed until the doctor can see you."

While he was in the bathroom she called the doctor, who said for Emilio to come in at four.

"What are you doing?" she cried when she found him dressing. "Emilio, stay in bed," she pleaded.

"Stop annoying me, I feel fine this morning."

He put on his work jeans, then hesitated and began taking them off again.

"That's more like it. Come back to bed and I'll make you some breakfast."

"I changed my mind. I'm going to see the Waterfalls." He reached for his good pants, and feeling suddenly dizzy, sat down quickly on the edge of the bed.

"I think you're delirious!"

"What did you do with my shoes?"

She shook her head and then angrily picked up the shoes lying concealed by the edge of the bedspread and, holding them at the level of her breasts, she dropped them, so that they landed a few inches from his feet.

"There," she said.

"If those had landed on my corns!"

"It would have served you right. Maybe then you would stay in bed where you belong." But she had already given up on getting him to stay home. She sat down at her dressing table and opened a jar of cream, made from the hormones of turtles and reputed to be effective in removing age spots.

After her husband left, Gloria Carranza prepared to do the laundry. She made a pile of dirty towels in the hallway, another pile of tablecloths and dishtowels in the kitchen, and she was in the process of making a third pile in the bedroom when she discovered her rosary in the pocket of her husband's work pants.

He meant no good by this, she knew. Why he'd taken it from her dressing table, she didn't know, nor what he'd intended to do with it. But this rosary belonged to her mother, and thinking of last night's conversation, it seemed a bad sign that he'd removed it from her dressing table and put it in his pocket. He certainly didn't take it because he intended to use it in the way it was meant to be used, for supplication, prayer, communion, or meditation. Oh no, not Emilio. When he had given it up, he gave it up completely. No icons, no images, no crosses were permitted by the Mormons, and Emilio, who was truly a good Mormon, had no difficulty surrendering to this. For her, it was a little different. The saints, for instance, had been with her all her life, and it was difficult to erase their influence on her thinking. She saw no reason why you couldn't take a little of this, a little of that, to make something for yourself. The rosary, after all, was not only pretty and a gift from her mother, but also a mystical tool which, when held with devotion, brought you closer to God. Nothing could be wrong with this, especially since no one knew her thoughts on the matter.

For a long time she sat on the bed staring out at the fields and thought about the situation. If she confronted him with his theft (for that was what it amounted to), he could deny any malicious intent. If she said nothing and simply put the rosary back among her own things, she would never know what had been in his heart, what he was capable of doing. If she returned it to his pocket, she stood a chance of losing her mother's rosary, an object so cherished it hurt her to think of being parted from it. That he would even think of taking it from her upset her deeply! No matter how long you live with a man, you never know him completely. Or was it the change that had occurred when they moved to America that made them seem stranger to each other than ever before?

It was important that she somehow outwit him, in order to learn his intent and, thereby, his capabilities and his true nature. As she sat on the bed thinking, the cows outside gathered at the barbed-wire gate. She saw them crowd together until the single wire holding the gate to the fence post snapped and a narrow opening gave them access to the alfalfa field. One by one they leapt over the bottom wires, like sheep clearing a fence in a nursery rhyme, and began grazing in the thick green alfalfa. She ought to shoo them back into the pen and fix the gate. But she could only think of her rosary at the moment, how to save it, and know her husband's workings. She watched the cows trample down the alfalfa, unable to rouse herself to stop the damage.

Finally it came to her what she should do. At the end of a canyon, beyond the road that led to Fish Lake, there was a Trappist monastery, a silent order of monks who raised bees and sold honey in their bookstore. There, among the religious books and the honey that came flavored with walnut, orange, blackberry, and lemon, she remembered seeing a display of rosaries. The chances were good that she could find a rosary that would be an acceptable match for her own. Her husband was not the kind of man to notice detail. If she were to buy the new rosary and put it in his pants pocket, keeping her own safely hidden from him, she would perhaps be able to find out what he intended to do.

The idea grew within her until she saw it as the perfect device for discovering the truth. Perhaps, if nothing was said, she would one day complain that her rosary was missing and see his reaction. If he lied, she would catch him.

Or, if he didn't return it, possibly she would let him think she hadn't missed it. And then one day, lo and behold, she would bring it out, very casually, and say, "This is the most cherished object I own because it was Mama's," and let him wonder where it came from. Let him think it was *milagra!* The *bruja* at work!

She hurried to the car. For her plan to work, she needed to get to the monastery and back before Emilio returned from the Waterfalls'.

Emilio parked at the end of the driveway that led to the basement house. He descended the steps that so often before had taken him into the underground chambers where the Waterfalls lived. Before he reached the screen door, someone opened it. It was Leon, the oldest Waterfall boy.

"Hey, Emilio," Leon said. He shook his hand. He had a big, handsome, ruddy face.

Inside, children played on the floor. There were kids of varying ages and sizes, but one thing they all had in common was the black Waterfall hair.

"Ah, it's Emilio," Edith Waterfall, the widow, said. Her eyes were a river of tears. Emilio could see that. There had been no end to the crying. In such a soft woman, the emotions are always there. Now they gave her a look of someone who would never stop crying. No, that wasn't true. One day she would stop. But she would always be sad, though such sadness can actually make someone more beautiful.

"Aren't you dear to come," Edith said. She smiled and such a beauty shone out of her that Emilio found it almost unbearable. There, in the dark basement, she was light. With death all around her, she was life.

"Bring him a chair. Get him a chair to sit on," she said. "David, get Brother Carranza a chair," she told one of the children.

"Tell Vernon to come, too. Tell him Brother Carranza is here," she added.

A folding chair was brought. Vernon was roused, apparently from sleep or a sleepless nap, since he had the marks of a bedspread on his cheek. Slowly—always the boy had done everything slowly—he crossed the room and shook Emilio's hand with a stiff arm, and he mumbled something in his usual slurred way, something Emilio couldn't understand, but which he took to be a kind of greeting that didn't require anything but a nod to answer it. The boy, even in the middle of tragedy, had the shy kind of half-smile that seemed forever in place, but now it gave him a look of terrible bewilderment, like a man who has just been told that he's missed a plane, and half-hopeful, half-embarrassed by his incompetence, he stands there, rather disbelieving. This was Vernon's state.

Emilio sat on the chair. "This is a terrible thing that has happened," he said, rather too loudly. "I am so sorry for the loss to your family."

Leon said, "He was a good old man."

"I'll miss him, Lord will I miss him," Edith said, and Emilio had no difficulty understanding what she meant. He could already see the terrible emptiness of the days before her. She put her arm around her big son Vernon. She looked into his face and he looked into hers. This seemed to be a ritual they had performed many times in the past few hours. Emilio felt the tears pushing against the back of his eyes. He could hardly stand to see them this way, the dazed son, the saintly mother.

"He sure loved you," she said, and smiled at Emilio. "He surely did. He thought you were about the best convert Vernon ever made down there in Mexico. He said you knew more about farming than any ten men from around here. Long as you were running the church farm, he said we'd always have plenty of food to keep the welfare program going. Isn't that right, Vernon?"

"Right," Vernon mumbled.

Again, she looked into her wounded son's eyes. She seemed to be trying to keep him afloat, to keep him with her, her forgiveness and love a palpable raft she was forming right in front of him. And from the dark eyes, from behind the glittering reflections that crossed the lenses of Vernon's glasses when his head turned toward her, you could see him trying to be with her, struggling to hold his life more dear than his father's death, but the death was all but extinguishing him, and he was hardly aware of, or in, the world.

"Have some food, Emilio," the widow said suddenly, and with an abrupt and vigorous rubbing of Vernon's back, released him temporarily from her ministrations. Turning toward Emilio, she pointed to a table where various dishes had been set out.

"There's a pie there that Arda Stringfellow made. A lemon pie. It's absolutely delicious."

Emilio accepted the pie. The Bishop, an avuncular figure with a long groundhog's face, arrived along with his two counselors, Brother Wadman and Brother Skanky. Vernon's wife came into the kitchen and began rubbing a chicken with salt, preparing it for the oven. A child on the floor ran a toy truck back and forth near Emilio's feet, all the while making a noise that was intended to emulate an engine. The basement rooms seemed to fill up suddenly with activity and noise. Once again, Emilio felt the dizziness. Sweating and flushed, he rose abruptly—too abruptly, for his head became light and the room assumed a reddish, then yellow glow, and he stumbled forward.

Leon grabbed him by the arm. "You OK?"

"I just stood up too fast. The blood goes slower than I do these days and I have to wait for it to catch up." With politeness, he said good-bye to everyone in the room. To the widow, whose eyes were darkened with her beautiful sadness, he said nothing, but he took her hand and kissed it, something he had not done with another woman since arriving in this country, where such a thing was clearly never done, and the gesture made him feel old and foreign and foolish, and gallant and noble as well, and—for a moment—almost equal to her grandeur.

Leon walked him out to the car. "How's Gloria?" he asked.

"Gloria," Emilio said softly, as if intoning the conclusion of the rosary. "Sometimes I think Vernon didn't convert her good enough."

Leon laughed. "It's hard to make a woman into anything she don't want to be. I learned that from my wife." Leon's laughter sounded like it was coming out of a long tunnel.

The truck was parked beneath some cottonwood trees. The sun was very intense on his head. Emilio thought, If I can just make it to the cottonwood trees. Then he reached the trees and their leaves gave gracious shade. He turned toward Leon. A yellow worm had lowered itself on a silvery thread from the branch above his head, and it twisted and spun before his eyes like a hypnotist's charm.

Looking at the sweat on Emilio's face, and his dull, fixed eyes, Leon Waterfall realized the man was sick and offered to drive him home, but Emilio, though he confessed to feeling like he was coming down with the flu, insisted on driving himself.

Twice during the drive home Emilio had to stop when the feeling came over him that his hands were growing lighter and lighter on the steering wheel, as if he were being drawn by an imperceptible force, upward and through the roof of the cab.

"I've been studying the twelfth Psalm," said the monk. "Jehovah's rule in the midst of ungodliness." He smoothed the page in front of him. "It begins, 'Help, Jehovah, for the godly man ceaseth.' "

He looked up to see how the woman was doing. She was Mexican. He'd never seen her before, but being Mexican, of course she was Catholic. He'd been reading when she came in. Speech was such a privilege, the prerogative of those whose turn it was to work in the bookstore. He'd been delighted to see a customer and hoped to engage her in conversation, just to indulge, and receive, the peculiarities of sound and the pleasures of the human voice.

"Yes, the godly man ceaseth. The Psalms are perhaps the most lyrical of all the books in the Bible."

Gloria laid a rosary, encased in a plastic container, on the counter. "How much?" she asked.

"Seven ninety-five," he said.

"I'll take it."

The monk consulted a tax chart. "Must pay Uncle Sam," he said merrily.

"Uncle Sam?"

The monk smiled at her. "The government."

This was the part that was annoying to a foreigner. She didn't get the nuances.

"Ha-ha, of course."

"It's curious," the monk said, "that in the Psalms we find the Lord addressed by three different names. There is Jehovah—or 'the becoming one'—and Elohim, as well as Adonai—"

"I don't need the receipt," Gloria said. "Thank you."

"But you've given me too much money," the monk protested.

"Give it to the poor," Gloria called from the doorway.

◆ ◆

"Where have you been?" Emilio Carranza asked. He stood on the porch and watched his wife get out of the car.

"To the grocery store."

"Since when do you go to the store and come back with no food?"

"I only needed lard for the beans but they were out."

"What beans? There's nothing cooking."

"Of course not! I told you I needed the lard."

Her husband still wore his good clothes. That meant he hadn't been inside to change yet. This was lucky, fortune smiling on her plan, perhaps Mama's hand guiding things from the other side. She only needed to distract him for a moment in order to switch the rosaries.

"How was Vernon?"

Emilio waved his hand, a gesture of dismissal. "Very sad."

"Do you want something to eat before you go to the doctor's?"

"I'm not hungry. Besides, I need to let the water in at two."

"Before you do that," Gloria said quickly, "can you bring me a few onions from the garden?"

Emilio protested. "I have whole fields to take care of, can't you get onions from your own garden?"

"I've had to go to the bathroom all the way home from the market," she said, dancing jokingly up the porch steps and rushing past him. "Just bring me the onions, OK?"

While he was out gathering onions, she removed her mother's rosary from his work pants and left the new one in its place. She hid the old rosary in a box containing her finest nylons and placed it at the back of a drawer where he'd certainly never discover it.

The water rose and darkened the old boards of the sluice gate. Emilio stood over the irrigation water and looked down. Weeds clogged a culvert leading to the fields and he reached down and pulled them free. He flung the clump of wet weeds, limp and pliable as a small deceased animal, over a nearby fence. Water began running into the hard earthen ditches, pushing forward in clear, thick beads which, when they broke, turned quickly from liquid into nothing, descending instantly into the dry and insatiable earth.

He took the rosary from his pocket and held it over the water, which was backed up behind the irrigation gate to a depth of two or three feet. He dropped it quickly, before he could change his mind, lest the fear, or guilt—whatever it was that made him feel trembly—should stop him. It fell like a handful of pebbles and hit the water with a light hiss before disappearing. In a matter of days, the rosary would be buried in the silt, which was rich and dark, the best topsoil, carried by the water from melting snows, borne by streams and rivers through the system of narrow channels that finally dispersed everything back to the land. Rains fell and lake water evaporated, but it was the same old water. There was no new water and there never had been. The water that was here now was the same water that had rained and evaporated, going on in its endless cycle, as when the dinosaurs had lived on the shores of Lake Bonneville. He stared into the eddying water, once again mesmerized by nature, as he had been by the worm turning on the thread below the cottonwood tree. There was power in what God had put on earth.

Somewhere between the culvert and the barns, he collapsed. The doctor said it was the flu and not the fever caused by ticks. By noon the next day he had grown seriously ill. He was hospitalized, surrounded by a plastic tent infused with oxygen. His lungs succumbed to bronchitis, and then pneumonia. He slept much of the time, resting in a state that resembled a coma, seriously weakened by his battle for breath. For two days and nights, he lay this way. Gloria stayed by his side until the nurses sent her home each evening at nine o'clock.

On the third day of his illness, Gloria said the rosary, using the amber and silver beads that had belonged to her mother. She invoked the names of favorite saints, and promised further votive offerings, as well as personal sacrifices and constant devotion, should her husband be made well. She felt he was close to death. She smelled it in the breath coming from his nose. The doctors, however, assured her that this was not the case. He was certain to recover.

While Gloria prayed over her husband, the sick man opened his eyes and saw his wife holding her rosary, making small clicking noises as her red nails moved along the beads. She had drawn back the plastic oxygen tent. Her head was bowed a few inches from his own. The beads loomed large before his eyes. With his own eyes he had seen these beads sink. He thought of them falling, and the slight hiss they made when they hit the water, as though they had been made of fire, and he knew it was impossible that she was now holding them. But there they were, in her hands, and he felt as if all the mysterious and incomprehensible forces in the world were threatening him, and the worst of these, death, was coming for him. He felt so weak he couldn't imagine resisting its call. He closed his eyes. In his mind he repeated the beginning of the mass he had learned as a child. Then he hallucinated and saw faces that he believed were the visages of those on the other side who waited to give way, parting to make a path, in order for his soul to join them. Among the faces was Gloria's mother, and she frightened him, for above all others she seem to beckon him with the most forcefulness. He prayed, but he got his religions confused. He would begin the sacrament prayer that the Mormons said over the bread and water, only to have it turn into Latin words of the Mass. He thought, I am dying and my wife has her rosary back. She had drawn it back from beneath the water. Anything was now possible. Oh, living grace, momento mori, gloria, gloria.

He took a turn for the worse. Even the doctors were worried. They could no longer be so optimistic. Every cough brought up a small issue of blood.

Gloria called Leon Waterfall, who came to lay hands on Emilio, and he brought with him his brother Vernon, and the long-faced Bishop with the rodent-like teeth. Surrounding Emilio's bed, they poured a small amount of olive oil, taken from a bottle consecrated for this purpose, in the middle of Emilio's forehead, just at the point where his cap had protected the upper part of his face and left it a lighter brown than the rest. Then the elders placed their fingers on his head over the oil, very lightly, so that just the tips of their fingers rested on his flesh, and Leon, in the sonorous voice of one who is called and temporarily infused with the power to heal, pronounced a powerful prayer over the ailing man. They left after the prayer, seemingly exhausted and quieted by their task. Gloria, who was deeply moved, was left alone by the side of her gravely ill husband.

The next day, Emilio started to improve. The elders came again and administered to him once more, and by evening, the improvement was even more pronounced.

Gloria threw away her rosary.

The rising of a testimony in Gloria Carranza was sudden and—as the people of the ward observed—coincided, not surprisingly, with her husband's illness and miraculous recovery. She stood publicly in the next Fast and Testimony meeting, which fell on the first Sunday of the month, and bore her testimony to the truthfulness of the gospel. In time, she became unusually devout. By fall, her name was put forth at Ward Conference, and she was appointed to the Relief Society presidency, along with Alma Lewis and Meada Fuller. Even higher callings were to follow. As a person, she grew softer and warmer. People remarked how her entire countenance had changed.

Emilio recovered from his illness completely, although as he grew older, he developed a decidedly fragile bearing. From a distance, he could easily be mistaken for a woman. In the time that followed his illness, the rosary was never mentioned. More and more he came to trust in the guidance of nature. He felt a womanly, feminine thing had come into him, something that seemed the province of the other sex but through some exchange, like waters mixing between sluice gates, had begun working in him. There was magic in the world he didn't understand, but he felt he'd been called into a circle to witness it.

Although he never told his wife, he began planting by the phases of the moon. He noted omens, auspicious signs, coincidences. To others he appeared quite unchanged, but privately he spoke to certain stars, particularly the Sisters, and some trees he felt held his ancestors in their branches. He also threw away a photograph of Brother Waterfall, whose image he preferred to remember rather than see. From his mind he removed all memory of the details of his death, believing finally that his wife had been right; such things can linger in the form of bad luck. *Mala suerte* did exist in the world, surely, but fortunately, so did *buena suerte*.

PRETEND
WE'RE FRENCH

In 1954 my father and his brother Ed got into a fight and stopped speaking to each other for five years. This happened when I was twelve years old. It's easy to remember when the fight started and ended because my Uncle Ed owned a Buick dealership in Salt Lake City and he'd always gotten us good deals on Buicks. During the years my dad and Ed were mad at each other, we stopped driving Buicks. My father bought a Pontiac instead, which he drove until they made up. The argument was bracketed by a '54 Pontiac and a '59 Buick, purchased the year of their reconciliation.

During those five years, my father didn't once speak to Ed, although they didn't live far from each other. No one knew exactly what started the fight, except my father and Ed, and possibly their wives. The kids were left in the dark. We only knew that something had happened and we didn't see our cousins anymore, and that was too bad because I had a girl cousin my age and I liked her a lot. Her name was Marcelline.

Living in Salt Lake City had given Marcelline a cosmopolitan air that I didn't have, coming, as I did, from a small town thirty miles away. She had a way of moving and acting that made me feel I was awkward and boyish. She was capable of making boys stop and stare, of winning everyone's attention without appearing to be trying to do so. Even as a child she had that indefinable something that I later heard people call "presence."

One time our parents took us to Patio Hot Springs up the canyon for a picnic. This was before the fight and I remember Ed and his wife, Meada, and my mom and dad joked all during the drive. Meada had brought a potty seat for her youngest and it was sitting in the trunk next to a chafing dish full of baked beans. Everyone thought this was funny. It seemed to me an example of adult humor, which was based on talking about things you shouldn't talk about, alluding to parts of the body you weren't supposed to mention. This seemed even dumber than childish humor, which was based on perfect silliness. I didn't feel I was part of either world. I was in between. I was at that age when I was discovering such things.

When we finally got to Patio Hot Springs, Marcelline and I were the only ones interested in swimming. Everyone else headed for the baseball diamond or began setting up the picnic.

It had been a while since I'd been on an outing with Marcelline. In the dressing room, I saw how pretty and bright her bathing suit looked next to mine, which was faded from last summer's use. She had painted her fingernails and her toenails a pearly white. In the time since I'd last seen her, she'd acquired shapes to her body that I thought came when you got much older. Even the way she walked was different. I had no notion how to get that walk. She had braces on her teeth, and yet she managed to make them look beautiful, like jewelry for the mouth.

I followed Marcelline out to the pool, where several boys about our age were gathered at the deep end, doing cannonballs off the diving board. Two of the boys were older than we were. The younger boys were growing up but not out. They were rangy, bony, and white. The older ones had muscles and suntans, as if the two went together.

Marcelline, without even looking their way, got the boys' attention. It was as if she had a mental vacuum cleaner and she could draw boys' thoughts to her the moment she appeared on the scene. It wasn't until much later that I realized that most girls flirted to make this happen. But Marcelline wasn't flirtatious. She didn't have to work hard at being what she was. She had that natural grace that others lacked. Why is it she was born with this and I wasn't? And how, I wondered, would I ever get it?

Marcelline and I got into the pool. When we were in the water up to our necks, she pulled me close to her so she could whisper in my ear.

"Pretend we're French," she said.

I didn't know how to do this. I waited for cues from her. I wondered how you acted if you were French.

"Ooo la la," she said, and dipped her hand into the water. She let the water drip through her fingers as if the drops were diamonds, falling one by one.

"Iss tray chood est eet no?"

I nodded. She nudged me and frowned. I was supposed to say something French-like, but I could think of nothing that would sound like that.

The boys looked our way. One by one they got out of the pool and jumped off the diving board, grabbing their knees in midair so that they made a big splash as they landed. One of the older boys did a back dive and went over too far, slapping the water with his stomach.

Marcelline said some more French words and looked at me. I knew the game rested on me, but I felt that if I opened my mouth, my non-Frenchness would show and give us away.

The boys moved closer to us and did handstands on the bottom of the pool. Their feet waved above the water. One boy's lips had turned purple from the cold. His chest was concave and white. He had knobby sticks for legs.

"Can you do a handstand?" he said to me. I stared at him and shrugged. These were the kind of boys who always talked to me.

Marcelline suddenly broke into a long string of French words, which sounded perfectly right, very foreign, and utterly smooth. She was so convincing that I felt she must really be studying French in school. She ended her speech by flopping on her back and floating face up. She had very nice brown hair, which she'd streaked with blonde by poking holes in a rubber cap and pulling strands through the holes and dying them with peroxide. Her hair floated in long wavy tendrils around her head, and the peroxided parts turned deeper gold while the brown got darker and richer. She kicked her feet and paddled her hands. I would have liked to have gotten my hair wet, too, but that wasn't a possiblility. My eyesight was so bad I'd left my glasses on, which meant I couldn't put my head in the water. I moved over to the edge of the pool and kicked my legs while I held on to the side.

Marcelline came up out of the water and said something quickly in French. I realized that she had powers of spontaneity that I totally lacked. She had the ability to make things up on the spot. Only later did I realize that this was the basis of social intercourse, and that I didn't have those fundamentals then, that day at Patio Hot Springs, and that I wouldn't acquire them over the years. I would always be awkward when I met people. Initially, I would find it difficult to think of things to say. I would always end up waiting for someone else to lead the way, to show me the shape of a conversation.

After Marcelline's last spontaneous outburst, the boys looked quite bewildered. They whispered to each other. I was quite sure we had managed to convince them we were French. It was all Marcelline, of course. I say "we," but it was she who assumed, with such utter composure, the guise of a French girl and didn't break the surface of her make-believe character.

Later, I realized that Marcelline had revealed to me the nature of feminine guise. She showed me that day that a woman can make herself over and become something totally different and get away with it. As an adult, I saw it happen again and again. I watched women transform themselves for social purposes, and I saw the multitude of guises available to choose from. Providing you understood the possibilities, there were endless ways to present yourself.

In my heart, I was trying to feel French, and looked for the words to express it. But I couldn't find them. I was sort of a mute participant in the overall enactment of something I wasn't equipped to effect. This feeling I also remembered later, when I developed the longing, but not the appropriate words or gestures, to attract someone.

Marcelline was becoming slightly annoyed with me for not carrying my half of the conversation in French. I'm sure she felt I was dangerously close to ruining the groundwork that she had laid. As we floated and bobbed in the pool, I was trying to think up some French words that I might say when Marcelline spoke up first, and I had a sudden brainstorm.

I repeated what she said, but I made it sound like a question. It was the only thing I could think of doing, and I saw that it worked. I said, "Como say vah?"

"Tray bone," she said. "Wee!"

"Wee. Tray bone."

She looked enormously pleased. I realized something, and it was also to prove of value in understanding events that occurred later in life. I learned you could survive through sheer duplication. Imitation offered instruction and relief. If I couldn't think of French-like words myself, I could take Marcelline's and repeat them, or recombine them, and it would be possible for me to be a part of things.

I listened to Marcelline's phrasing, and culling a few words from her, I moved them about and formed my own little sentences. Now we were actually having conversations! There could be no mistaking that we were French girls who'd simply landed in Utah for some strange reason. I made up a story for myself about our backgrounds: We were sisters. Our American father had fought in the war. He met our French mother in a little café, fell in love, and later married her. After the war, they stayed in France because they liked the French life. Marcelline and I were born. Two girls, just what they wanted! We lived in Paris. This was the first time we had ever visited our American grandparents, who owned a mink ranch in Porterville, just up the road.

·· ··

The blue-lipped boy stopped trying to get me to stand on my hands or turn somersaults under the water, and I felt that we'd proved our foreignness at last, and the uselessness of trying to talk to us. One of the older boys, however, suddenly swam up to Marcelline and said, "Where are you guys from?"

This was Marcelline's finest moment. She looked him in the face and shrugged. Her face was a sweet blank. "Je nuh pawl American," she said. There could be no doubting her. It was the most perfect enactment of a lie I'd ever seen.

However, instantly everything was thrown into danger. Marcelline's father, my Uncle Ed, came out of the men's dressing room and strolled over to the edge of the pool. Uncle Ed didn't look at all French. He had on the kind of big boxer swim trunks that they sell in department stores for men his age. He wore black socks and a pair of rubber flip-flops that he had trouble keeping in place because the socks didn't allow for the rubber piece between his toes. He had on a pair of those sunglasses that you clip at the nosepiece over your regular glasses, but they were flipped up, creating a little awning that stood out from his forehead and gave him an odd appearance. Worst of all, he was cleaning his ears with a toothpick. He stood at the edge of the pool, a rather grim and distracted look on his face, and poked a toothpick cautiously into his ear, withdrew it to check the level of wax, and then reinserted it.

I was certain French people didn't clean their ears with toothpicks, that it was a habit peculiar to Utah, and perhaps to my family, since I'd never seen anybody outside my family do it. But none of this seemed to matter too much because I was sure Uncle Ed would speak to us momentarily in English and our whole game would be over.

However, Marcelline—the ever-inventive, spontaneous Marcelline, who in her youthful wisdom understood the workings of the world so well—made a bold move. She turned instantly toward her father and began speaking French to him. She gestured and laughed and spoke more French. To my surprise, Uncle Ed hesitated only for a moment, and then he spoke

French back to her. I mean the mock-French, because he could no more speak real French than I could.

He cleaned his ears and spoke French. He took off his socks and flip-flops and got into the pool and spoke French while he paddled around on his back. He spoke French and banged the side of his head with his hand to get the water out of his ears. The boys moved to the deep end of the pool, as if our foreignness were such a tangible thing that it pushed them into a tight little corner. Our alien credentials, by virtue of being sanctioned by an adult, were now unquestionable.

I felt a fondness for Uncle Ed that hadn't been there before. He was very game, our coconspirator. It was nice of him to have fun with us like that. I saw that within the world there were men who would be perfectly happy to help women assume any kind of identity they wanted to, although I'm sure I'm making too much of this point in restrospect, since Uncle Ed would certainly have done the same thing for one of his sons. I guess I mean I understood that there were players in the world. If you knew how to enlist their help, they would always assist you, rather than detract, at a crucial moment. But it required a boldness and a swiftness that I have come to associate with sensuality. That's what Marcelline had. She was terrifically, naturally bold and swift. I wasn't then, and still am not, that way. After a while, we left the pool, all three of us together, and joined the picnic. We were still babbling happily in our made-up French.

This happened in 1953, when Uncle Ed and my father were still speaking. Then they had their argument, or whatever it was. The years went by and I didn't see Marcelline until, as abruptly as they'd stopped speaking, my father and Uncle Ed suddenly resumed contact. They acted as if nothing had happened. No explanation was ever given. My father bought a new Buick from Ed, a two-tone Roadster—green on top, yellow on the bottom—and this solidified the reconciliation. We were invited to Marcelline's wedding, which took place in the same month, just a day after her graduation from high school.

• •

In the years since I'd last seen Marcelline, I had done a lot of thinking about what I would do with myself as I got older. Sister Stringfellow, our teacher in Mutual, asked each of us girls to write down what we hoped to become in life. I put down that I wanted to become either a stewardess or a secretary. I also added that what I really wanted to do was to become a wife and mother, since that was the highest calling in life. But I didn't have much faith in this last part, not because I didn't believe what I'd said was true, that it was the highest calling in life, but because I hadn't had any dates yet. I was becoming a pragmatist. I could see that it might be difficult to become a wife and mother if boys didn't even look at me, if I hadn't had even one date. So I put down that I'd like to be a stewardess or a secretary because that seemed to offer some possibility for having a life of my own and a future to think about.

Marcelline, as I expected, had only become more of what she already was in the five years since I'd seen her. She had become more beautiful and more confident and moved even more fluidly and effortlessly among people. She had chosen someone for a husband who was as attractive and sure of himself as she was. On that evening, she was in complete command of the events surrounding her wedding. I heard someone say, as we stood in the basement of the wardhouse before the reception began, waiting for Marcelline to freshen her makeup, "I have never seen a more beautiful bride."

I remember a boy came to the reception that night. His name was Arnie and he'd been a former boyfriend of Marcelline's during high school. She took me aside and told me about him. She said he'd been All-State Basketball. He was also an exceptionally good golfer who was considering a life as a pro. They had talked of marriage. But she had broken with him when she met the man who was now her husband. Arnie had the palest blond hair I'd ever seen.

He stood outside the door for a long time before coming inside the recreation hall. When he finally did move down the reception line, his congratulations were perfunctory. Then he got out of there in a hurry. He didn't stay for refreshments. When he left, I followed him as far as the doorway. I watched him get into his car. He didn't drive off immediately, but sat for a long while, staring blankly out the windshield at the dark fields beyond the church parking lot. A streetlight illuminated him, slumped down behind the steering wheel. He had the saddest look on his face. I felt very sorry for him. Here was a man in complete defeat. He'd lost.

I didn't become either a stewardess or a secretary. I became a writer, and no one was more surprised than I. I moved away from home, traveled, actually learned to speak true French in a somewhat limited way. Many times I had reason to think of Marcelline, in many different places. We're in our forties now. I often wonder, where is she?

In fact, I hadn't seen Marcelline in many years, although I'd heard that she was on her fourth marriage, had several children, and had left the church. But recently I saw Uncle Ed at a family reunion. The reunion was held in St. George, and attended by so many relatives that I really didn't have a chance to talk to him. However, I learned that he'd been divorced and was now remarried. His new wife was named Lola. His old wife, Meada, was said to be very bitter. He was no longer in the car business, but sold hot tubs in a ski resort. I wanted to talk to him, to ask him about Marcelline, but I kept missing him, then the day came that I'd planned to leave, and I packed up the car and said good-bye to everyone early in the morning.

Before leaving town, however, I stopped at a place called Dick's Café to get a cup of coffee, and there, at the counter, was Uncle Ed, sitting with his new wife, Lola.

I sat down with them and talked for a while. Uncle Ed had gotten thinner, and of course he looked much older to me. He wore a hairpiece. It looked terrible. I know lots of people wear wigs, but I looked at Uncle Ed and felt as if some travesty had been perpetrated by allowing a man to walk around wearing something as awful as the toupee he had on his head. It was criminal activity, selling a hairpiece like that. It looked as if his hair had met with some terrible mishap involving egg whites and a steamroller. Lola, his wife, seemed very nice, but I thought both of them were trying to be a lot younger than they really were.

Finally I asked about Marcelline.

"Oh, she's OK," Ed said. "She just got married again. She's got three kids, you know, and she's pregnant again. Can you believe that? I'm so upset about it. She's crazy. I told her I thought it was crazy but she went ahead anyway and got pregnant. She's forty-two years old! It's time to knock that stuff off. Lola and I love her kids. We live close to her so we baby-sit all the time. But I think it's terrible she's pregnant again. Can you imagine it?"

I did imagine it. I thought of Marcelline's boldness and swiftness, and I thought I understood perfectly how it could happen. It bespoke the sensuality before which all men, particularly fathers, tremble. I thought it was wonderful the way Uncle Ed was talking about Marcelline. On the one hand, he seemed thoroughly disgusted that his daughter, at forty-two, was going to have another baby, more disgusted by this than by the fact she had had four husbands. On the other hand, when he spoke of Marcelline, he gave every indication that he loved her so much it didn't matter what she did anymore. Marcelline was Marcelline. He may not have liked it that she was pregnant again, but he would tend this baby, just like he had the others. I imagined Marcelline was just as sensuous, as indomitable in her choices, as she had ever been. She had accepted the highest calling in life, not once, but four times.

I finished my coffee, which I noticed Uncle Ed was also drinking, ignoring the Mormon Word of Wisdom, just as I was. I guess we were all falling away from the church, changing bit by bit. It made me very happy to see him, even with the toupee, which gave him an air of defeatedness, a clownish imbalance, an appearance of inappropriately suspended age. Before leaving, I managed to deflect all questions about myself by saying that I was engaged in research and lived alone.

I kissed them both good-bye.

Just as I reached the door, I turned around. I had a great urge to say something to Uncle Ed, although I hesitated, because I still haven't acquired that ability to be spontaneous. He and Lola were talking, however, and not looking in my direction. If they had been, I would have spoken up. I would have said, *"Au revoir, Oncle Ed! Avez un vie jolie!"*

WHAT IS
THIS MOVIE?

Phyllis called her mother long-distance but her mother could hardly hear her for the noise on the line.

"What's that terrible noise?"

"What do you think it is?" Phyllis said. "Take a guess."

"I don't know."

"Just guess."

"A generator. Some kind of machinery. I don't know, Phyllis. Just tell me."

"It's my espresso machine. I'm steaming milk while I'm talking to you."

"It's pretty annoying."

"It'll end soon. See. Just a second. Now it's over, and I have delicious cappuccino."

"I'm in the middle of a movie. What'd you call for? It's a bad time."

"Pardon me for living, Mother. I'm your only daughter, you can spare me a few minutes. How's Susan?"

"She wasn't having such a good time I don't think. Then she met a boy. He clips the lawn here. Now she's in heaven. I'm witnessing the effects of love."

"Fleeting, no doubt."

"It doesn't matter at that age. You're willing for things not to last, as long as they're intense while they do."

"Mother, you sound depressed. Are things OK with Arnold?"

"Arnold who?"

"Funny, Mother. You think I don't know anything. I've talked to Susan."

"I'm missing so much of my movie I won't know what anything's about."

"She says he's a very nice man. So why is it I have to learn everything from Susan? Why don't you tell me when you're seeing someone?"

"I'm seeing a lot of people. They're all over the place down here, in the supermarkets, on the streets, at the laundromat."

"Is this your way of saying you don't want to talk about it?"

"Open your eyes and you see people. You can't help but see them."

"Let up, Mother. I get the point. Well, anyway, you can't hide him from me when I get there. Sooner or later, all will be revealed."

"Is there anything else, Phyllis? Otherwise, I'm getting anxious to get back to my movie."

"One thing. I think it'd be a good idea if when I come to pick up Susan you come back here with us for a while."

"When are you coming?"

"Thursday. I thought I'd drive down in one shot. It's only about six hours. You could drive back with us, stay a week, then I'll pay for your plane ticket home."

"I'll think about it."

"That's what you always say."

"The boy in this movie is getting beat up by some ruffians. Ooooph! They're really working him over. He'd better learn karate pretty quick or there's going to be nothing left of him."

"What is this movie you're watching?"

"*The Karate Kid.*"

"You think about coming back with us."

"I'll think about it, Phyllis. Good-bye. I'll give Susan your love."

• •

The hardest thing about having her granddaughter visit for a month was giving up sleeping with Arnold. Alice didn't think it was right for Susan to know that her grandmother had a boyfriend who slept over. Now every movie where there were love scenes, she began to think about Arnold's kisses and hugs in the middle of the night, and how much she missed them.

There were, however, no love scenes in *The Karate Kid*, except a few moments between teenage kids, when they sort of rubbed their noses together in friendly yearning, like rabbits who are checking each other out. What the movie was really about was friendship and courage. There was a lot of Oriental philosophy in the movie, too, and Alice liked that. A boy from the East Coast moves to California with his mother, who is divorced, and they take an apartment in a building where an older Oriental man works as a handyman. The kids at school give the new boy a rough time. The boy and the handyman become friends. The story was pretty good. But everything took place in California, and Alice was a little sick of seeing so much California in movies. The light looked impaired out there, either too bright or washed out. But there were some nice scenes on the beach showing how when the waves curl, you can see right through them.

What made the movie so good was its presentation of good versus evil. The boy has to learn to defend himself against the bullies at school, and the old Oriental handyman gives him lessons in karate, but not until the boy has learned to approach mundane tasks like trimming bonsai trees and sanding floors and painting fences with an attitude of focus, purposefulness, and devotion. The moral was that hard work and good attitude gave you power. By the end of the movie, Alice was choked up with emotion and cheering for the boy to win the match against the evil kid in the local karate contest, and when he did, she smiled. Now that the movie was over, ending on the victory, she felt a peculiar calm, as if she'd just had a good long talk with someone she felt close to.

• •

The day that Phyllis was to arrive, Alice rented two more movies, *Pharlap* and *The Secret of NIMH*. *Pharlap* was a big disappointment. It was all about horses and though Alice liked horses well enough, she didn't care to see a whole movie about one. The film was predictable. You knew the horse that nobody believed in was going to become a big winner. At moments when the music suggested these were the big emotional scenes, Alice didn't feel anything. *The Secret of NIMH* was an animated film about rats that were trying to escape from scientists who wanted to experiment on them. (NIMH stood for the National Institute of Mental Health.) It was a very sympathetic portrayal of rat life. You saw how they had families and feelings just like everybody else. The movie hadn't quite finished when Phyllis arrived, and Alice felt a little embarrassed that her daughter had found her watching a cartoon, although Phyllis didn't say anything.

"Mother, this is very nice." Phyllis embraced Alice in the room where she stored her gardening equipment, a porch-like enclosure attached to the entrance of the trailer. It was the first time Phyllis had visited her mother in her new mobile home.

"Well, come see it all," Alice said.

"Where's Susan?"

"With Ricky, the lawn boy."

Phyllis followed her through the rooms in the trailer and out into the small garden.

"It seems the perfect place, Mother."

"Well, perfect is a little strong but it's very nice." Out of the corner of her eye, she saw Arnold come out of his garage across the way, turn on the hose, and begin watering his lawn. Suddenly he looked up and saw her and waved. Alice raised her hand in return.

"Who's that?" Phyllis asked.

Alice said, "That's Arnold."

"Oh, Arnold. So that's Arnold. When can I meet him?"

"Anytime," Alice said. "Right now if you'd like."

"Oh, Mother, not till I clean up. What I could really use is a bath and a drink, after that long drive."

"As you wish. Beauty first," Alice said.

When Phyllis came out of the bathroom, Alice noticed something was different. Her glasses were gone. She tilted her head back in a funny way and blinked often. She had a bemused, distant look that gave her an air of preoccupation. All her attention seemed devoted to making her eyes work. Alice asked about it and Phyllis said she'd recently made a trip to New York and she'd gotten contact lenses at a cut rate from an optometrist in SoHo.

"I've got an artist friend there," Phyllis said. "I've been going in regularly to see him."

Phyllis picked up the lid to the cookie jar and seeing nothing inside, replaced it.

"What do you do all day, Mother? Do you get out and see things?"

Alice felt like saying, What do you think I am, an invalid?

"I go out," she said. It sounded so feeble. She meant, I go out with Arnold. We go out all the time. We go to paper collectors' conventions. We go out and dance to Cole Joy and The Joy Boys at Zito's Supper Club. The truth was, of course, that she didn't go out much at all. She liked to say home and watch rented movies.

"Of course I go out."

"It seems like you're always watching movies when I call."

"What would you like me to do, Phyllis? Run for the city council? Volunteer for some social cause? I worked all my life. I'm resting now. I like movies. They make me feel I know what's going on out there."

"I just don't like to think of you vegetating."

"Vegetables do all right," Alice said. "They have their seasons and cycles. Think of me as a carrot, or lettuce, turning to seed."

"Oh, Mother," Phyllis said. She was trying to hold the fridge door open with one foot while she set a container of milk on the counter. It made her stretch out and balance on one leg. Strangely enough, it looked like one of those karate positions on *The Karate Kid*.

"What do you do all day?" Alice asked her daughter. "As long as we're on the subject."

"I'm in charge of all the student galleries at school now. It's a sixty-hour week for me. I'm also teaching a class in gallery and museum management. Fortunately, I get along with the chairman of the department. Otherwise, it could be hell." She lifted up tinfoil covering the ham in the fridge. "Can I have some of this?"

"*Mi casa es su casa,*" Alice said.

"It's a grueling schedule, though. When I get home from school, I'm exhausted. Susan is all I've had time for.

"But while Susan's been gone I've met someone," Phyllis continued. "His name is Jerry. He's the one who lives in SoHo. The artist. Very large paintings. I'm wondering how Susan is going to take to him. He's a little nervous about meeting her, too."

"I imagine Susan will like him if you like him."

"That's not necessarily the case, Mother. Susan hasn't always liked my boyfriends. It's a jealous thing, I suppose, Oedipal or something. But I understand you're just trying to make me feel optimistic."

Alice thought of a line from yesterday's movie. *I need the power or else those guys will know and I won't be able to win.* That was the boy asking the old Oriental man to help him go back and face his enemy. Somehow it seemed to Alice that all Phyllis needed was the power to feel good enough about her choice of Jerry, and Susan would feel comfortable around him. That, of course, was assuming he was a good man.

"Is he a good man?" Alice asked.

Phyllis, blinking to keep her contacts moist, said, "What do you think I'm going to do, Mother, pick a dork?"

Alice invited Arnold for dinner and they barbecued on the patio.

"Scott is so cute. Don't you think he's cute?" Susan held up the picture of her boyfriend back home. It was one of those school pictures that make kids look extraordinarily bland and alien, even to themselves.

Phyllis said, "Jerry is staying at the house while I'm gone. He's taking care of the cats. Mickey's got a sore on her neck. She fights with the neighbor's cat."

"Does anybody not like their burgers rare? Let me put it another way. Nobody likes them well done, right?" Arnold looked up from the grill and raised his eyebrows in question.

"Rare-ish is OK," Phyllis said. "My neighbor's got a Siamese, too. She's got another cat that's part Siamese and has both stripes and spots. It's some kind of experiment to create a new breed. She wants to show it but there's no category for it yet."

"Ricky's pretty cute, too, though," Susan said.

It seemed to Alice that there were as many conversations going as there were people. No one was paying any attention to what was said. It was the kind of thing that annoyed her, but she was trying to be calm. The sunset was beautiful but there was no need to point it out to everybody. She looked up at the colors in the clouds, following the striations of pink and purple.

"Scott has these really, really blue eyes."

"Okeydokey, baby doll," Arnold said. "These have about two more minutes to go."

Phyllis looked from Arnold to her mother, as if it were cute he called her baby doll.

"I had to give up on some foods," Arnold said, rubbing his stomach. "I miss Italian most. But you can't take all that fat and salt after a while."

"He's so nice, too," Susan said. "You'll meet him when you come home with us, Grandma."

"What was your profession before you retired, Arnold?" Phyllis asked.

"Fourteen years with UPS," Arnold said. "Dry-cleaning business before that."

"Hmmm," Phyllis said.

"And your mother tells me you teach at an art school?"

"Yeah," Phyllis said. "I never have enough time for my own work. But I suppose if I had time for my own work, I'd never have enough money."

"Who do you think is cuter, Arnold? Ricky or Scott?"

"Would somebody stop changing the subject here?" Alice said, feeling quite annoyed with things.

"Better idea," Arnold said. "Let's put food in our mouths."

After dinner, Arnold asked Susan if she'd like to play cards with him. Alice and Phyllis cleaned up the dishes and then sat outside on the two folding chairs Alice had placed at the end of her driveway. They had a view of the trailer next door and the garden and a few trailers up the street. In front of each trailer was a small, but very neat, square of bright green lawn.

"Camelot Mobile Home Park," Phyllis said out of the blue. "What a place to live."

Alice didn't know what she meant. Was this good or bad?

"Why don't you and Arnold get married?" Phyllis asked. "He seems so right for you. You could sell one trailer and move in together."

"Don't," Alice said. She felt herself blushing and was annoyed.

"What?" Phyllis said innocently.

"Why don't you and Jerry get married?" she snapped.

"We don't know each other well enough. We're taking things in increments."

"Why don't Susan and Scott get married! Why doesn't everybody get married! We could have a wedding together. I can see it in the papers. 'Three Generations of Linders Marry in Triple Ceremony: Grandmother Looks Haggard.' "

Phyllis suddenly stood up and stared at the street. "The light out here is very beautiful. I'm just going to get my camera."

She came out with her video camera and began taking pictures of everything. She pointed the camera at Alice, at the carport, the trailer, even the flowers in the garden. She walked out to the street and panned along the rows of trailers. She pointed it up at the street sign that said "King Arthur Way." She moved up close to Alice and said, "Mother, how do you like living in a trailer park?"

"Is that thing on?"

"Yes. You're being filmed," Phyllis said. "Actually, you're being videotaped."

"It doesn't make any noise. I didn't know whether it was on or not." In trying to act nonchalant, she felt herself becoming stiff and self-conscious. She had never liked having her picture taken, but at least with a regular camera, somebody pointed it at you, pressed the button, and it was over. With this thing, it was always aimed at you, silently, and there was something sneaky in not knowing when it was going and when it wasn't.

"Have you gotten to know your neighbors?"

"Somewhat," Alice said. "I think I'll go in now and see what Arnold and Susan are up to."

"Yes, let's go inside," Phyllis said, as she trained her camera on her mother's back and followed her up the steps.

Arnold and Susan had given up the card game and were sitting side by side on the couch watching baseball on TV.

"I'm trying to talk Arnold into going swimming with me," Susan said.

Phyllis said, "Is there a pool here?"

"Oh, we've got a beautiful swimming pool down by the clubhouse," Arnold said.

"Do you go swimming much, Arnold?" Phyllis asked. She pointed her camera at him as she spoke, and Alice wondered if she could be taking pictures inside the house. It seemed too dark for that.

"No," Arnold said, "I'm not much of a swimmer."

"What do you do for fun?"

"Squire your mother around."

Phyllis laughed. "You two were lucky you met, weren't you?"

"You bet," Arnold said. "Luckiest day of my life."

"I sure wish we had some ice cream," Susan said.

"This can be arranged, Sweetie," Arnold said. He stood up and jingled the change in his pockets. "I'll just go down to the 7-Eleven. Come on, Alice."

Arnold's car was an old van. He had to move some papers from the seat so Alice could climb in.

"She's a nice woman," Arnold said as they were driving down the highway. Alice knew he was talking about Phyllis.

"She's got a new boyfriend," Alice said. "An artist named Jerry."

They drove along a wide boulevard lit by blue lights.

"Are they talking marriage?" Arnold asked.

"They're talking increments," Alice said. "They can't think too far into the future."

"Well, that's OK," Arnold said. "As long as she's got some-body there for her." He paused and then said, " 'Last night I dreamed the secret of the Universe: Man was not meant to live alone.' That's Clifford Odets," he added.

Once Arnold had suggested marriage to Alice. She had said marriage wasn't for people their age. Companionship was more suitable. Marriage was based on the idea of growing together into a future. Alice had already grown up to the edge of future. There wasn't that much left of it.

"Oh, I don't think that's right," Arnold had said when she explained these thoughts to him.

"We could have parallel lives just as easily," Alice had said, but she didn't really see them as parallel. She saw them more in tandem. She envisioned her and Arnold living in their sepa-rate trailers, and imagined two railroad cars, joined by some grinding apparatus, with passages leading back and forth, al-though she couldn't really complete the metaphor because when she imagined that apparatus, she saw it as a hazardous, sway-ing platform, accompanied by signs that said, "Do not stand here too long! Move on!" It seemed a dangerous spot, this transitory connection, capable of uncoupling and sending one car into an uncontrollable backslide.

The light changed, but Arnold had to wait for traffic before turning into the parking lot of the 7-Eleven. Alice watched him enter the store. He had a round, firm belly and a trim face. His health was good. He was cautious about butter and salt. He planned on living to be ninety. If he took his clothes off, you could see a scar from an appendix operation, but that was his only experience with illness in sixty-eight years. Arnold and his wife had owned a dry-cleaning and laundry business for many years, and his skin, as a result of continual exposure to moisture and steam, was uncommonly smooth and youthful. In short, he was handsome and healthy, and it seemed to Alice that he might live as long as he wanted to.

He came out with a quart of fudge-ripple ice cream and a box of Fig Newtons. Before starting up the van, he leaned over and kissed her.

"I love your lips," he said. "Beautiful, beautiful lips."

Phyllis was on the phone when they returned. From the way she sat hunched up at one end of the couch, as if trying to make an individual private space for herself, Alice assumed she was talking to Jerry.

"Did you water the backyard, too?" Phyllis said into the phone. "How about the cats. Are they OK? Is the sore on Mickey's neck any better?"

"You are so nice, Arnold, to get me ice cream," Susan said. "Isn't he nice, Grandma? I think you should come and visit us in New Jersey."

"New Joisey," Arnold said, exaggerating Susan's pronunciation. "I'm afraid I'd start talking like you if I came to New *Joisey*."

"Did I have any messages on the machine?" Phyllis said. "Did Marcie ever return my call?" In a burst of laughter, she revealed a pink tongue and her broad, white teeth. "Oh, baby," she said, "I'll be home soon."

• •

Sometime during the night, Alice woke and saw the pale moon framed by the window. It was beautiful enough to make her feel teary. Throughout her life, she had tried to be a sensible woman, tried not to feel more emotion for a subject than it deserved. Lately, the tables had turned. Emotions rose easily. The movies seemed to have made it worse. She often sat watching a rented movie on her VCR and cried at a scene, giving herself over to the drama, even though at such moments, or perhaps later, when she had put some distance between herself and the film, she saw how everything—the music, the script, the dewy eyes of the actors and actresses, and the highly improbable situations—had all conspired to manipulate her feelings. But during the moments when she was actually caught up with the drama, her own life seemed tangled with those of the actors. In her own past there seemed to be loves lost, people missed, such tender moments, surfacing into an overall sense of pain. But these were just feelings. When she tried to attach a face to the loves she mourned, nobody came forth.

Now, looking at the moon, she was mourning something again, but she couldn't figure out what it was. So it seemed that she was affected just by the beauty of something like the moon, and that was awful, for it was certainly giving a subject more emotion than it deserved. A slight imbalance had come upon her. Before she fell asleep again, she decided it might be a good idea to go home with Phyllis for a while.

When, in the morning, Arnold heard she was leaving and going up to Phyllis's for a week, he said, "You'll have a wonderful time." He helped them pack the car. Phyllis, who had been wandering around all morning with her video camera pointed at things, went into town to get some postcards with scenes of Virginia Beach. When she returned, they were ready to leave. Smiling and waving, Arnold stood in the driveway as they backed out. "Call and let me know what time to pick you up at the airport," he yelled, and pursed his lips in a kiss. He was still waving when they turned the corner, and Alice felt unaccountably sad as she looked back at him.

.. ..

She hadn't meant to become lovers with Arnold. Sex, she thought, was a dead issue. She was living up to all the expectations people have for anybody over sixty-five. She relinquished sex as completely as she had given up teaching, as if it were also regulated by compulsory retirement laws. In fact, she had missed teaching when it ended much more than she had ever missed sex. Sex had fallen into a long, slow, shabby decline, even when her husband was still quite young. Not once had she considered sex with anyone after his death. Not until Arnold. "I just don't think I can do it," she said when he asked her to come into his bedroom with him. "Nonsense," he said.

They could do it, they did do it, although Alice had not liked undressing in front of him and felt as if she were a terrible actress in a terrible play. But over time he convinced her she was desirable. He was robust and slow at the same time. Arnold said, "The important thing is to please yourself. You can't be thinking of the other person all the time. It's just the opposite of what they tell you. It's a backward Golden Rule." It took a long time for her to figure out what she liked, even longer to articulate it, but Arnold coaxed and talked, putting matters forth in his straightforward way. Slowly, it was better. "It always gets better," Arnold said. "Better and better."

Susan, leggy and suntanned in her shorts, sat in the back of the car until they passed the Virginia border, and then she traded places with Alice. The corn was high and Alice enjoyed the sight of the fields flashing by in geometric rows that converged, like some exquisitely planned design, at the horizon. At Charlottesville, they stopped for hamburgers at Wendy's. A tall, sunburned boy behind the counter flirted with Susan. She looked very tantalizing in her shorts. When she walked, she tilted her hips back and pushed her high, full breasts forward. Susan's entire life revolved around boys, and she dressed and behaved as if each action were a movement, an encoded part of an age-old mating ritual.

They sat at a molded plastic table with indentations for their trays. Plastic seats were attached to the table, and, although they swiveled, they didn't allow for much independent movement and weren't very comfortable.

"Jerry won't expect us tonight," Phyllis said. "He thinks I'm coming back tomorrow. I think I'll just surprise him. Or maybe we'll call."

Susan said, "Who is this guy?"

"He's an artist," Phyllis said rather importantly, as if that should explain why he was a terrific choice for a boyfriend.

"Old or young?" Susan asked.

"He's my age," Phyllis said. "Forty-one. Does that make him old or young in your opinion?"

"Young," she said, "or at least younger than the last one. He was a dinosaur."

"Sometimes you're disrespectful, honey," Phyllis said dryly.

Seeing a storm brewing, Alice changed the subject, and began talking about her meal, a baked potato with bits of bacon and broccoli and cheese on it. The potato sat in a little carton in the shape of a boat, which said "SS SPUD" on the side. The potato was pretty good, she said.

"Wait right here," Phyllis said. She went out to the car and returned with her camera, turned it on, and pointed it at Alice.

"What is this movie you're making?" Alice asked.

"I thought I would just look at everything in my life," Phyllis said. "It's an art piece, I guess. Like scenes from my life. My real life." She trained the camera on the remains of Alice's meal.

What did she mean, real life? Did she have a life that wasn't real?

"A baked potato is a scene from your life?"

"It's an American phenomenon," Phyllis said. "The hundred-and-one different things they throw on baked potatoes these days. A fad. I exist within a culture. I'm filming that culture."

"Yawn," Susan said, and opened her mouth into a big fake yawn.

Alice lit a cigarette.

"People are dying from smoking," Susan said, waving the smoke away from her face.

"People are dying from all sorts of things, Susan. Don't bother me, I've already told you that."

"I just want you to live, Grandma."

"I call this living," Alice said.

She looked at Phyllis. "Is that thing on again?" Phyllis had been pointing the camera at her for the last few minutes. She felt annoyed.

"Yes," Phyllis said. "You can tell it's on when this little red light is lit up. Do you want to try it? It's really very simple." Phyllis handed her the camera.

"Hold it like a gun, Mother." She showed her how to push the trigger-like lever to make it go on and off, and where the viewfinder was.

"What do I do with this?" Alice said, looking through the viewfinder.

"Just shoot whatever you want. But try and move the camera smoothly. Also, as a rule of thumb, if it's worth shooting at all, it's worth ten seconds. In other words, don't hop from one thing to another too fast."

She tried pointing the camera at her daughter but she felt embarrassed, as if she were being rude by sticking something in her face, and she turned away from Phyllis. She looked around, wondering what to take a picture of. Outside the window, tall trees bordered the highway. Alice looked through the viewfinder at the trees and pressed the button that brought them closer to her. It was as if she had suddenly moved outside, or the outdoors had come to her. Looking through the camera, she framed the leaves and zoomed in closer on them. The leaves were moving so slightly. What fascinated her about that movement was the light on the leaves. Everything was flattened out, a wall of color and light right up against her eye. She'd never seen things this way before. It was wonderful. Alice pressed the trigger. She held it there for a long while and then she handed the camera back to Phyllis.

After lunch, Alice drove for a while and Susan sat in the front while Phyllis napped in the backseat. Alice and Susan talked about Susan's cats, her horse, her past job at a Kentucky Fried Chicken franchise, and her present one at a Hallmark card shop in the mall.

"They've got some really neat stores in the mall where I work," she said. "You can get Perry Ellis shoes for twelve dollars at this place I know."

Phyllis, who was supposed to be sleeping, spoke up. "Those can't be real Perry Ellis shoes," she said. "They're knockoffs."

"What about college, Susan? Do you think of that?" Alice said.

"I don't want to go to school beyond high school. When I get out next year, that's it. I'm tired of going to school."

"But learning," Alice said, "you must keep learning, Susan. Learning from work or some kind of meaningful pursuit, if not from school. What are you going to do? You can't learn things from frying chicken or selling greeting cards."

"I told you I want to get married and have a baby," Susan said, pushing her jaw out slightly like she did when she became stubborn. Something happened to her eyes at these times: they glazed and retreated, as if when you challenged her, by settling deeper into themselves, they created a forceful front to protect the ideas emanating from her brain.

"It's not what you might want me to do but it's what I want to do," Susan added.

"I don't get it," Alice said. "Are we moving backward here? I struggled to get my master's degree so I could be useful and independent and make a good living as a schoolteacher. Your mother managed to get her bachelor's, even though she wanted to be an artist, so that she could ensure some financial security for herself. Now you don't even want to go to college. You want to get married and have babies. That's what my mother wanted to do! Four generations and we haven't gone anywhere!"

"When I think about it," Phyllis said from the backseat, still not opening her eyes, "I feel like I might have been a better artist if I hadn't gone to college. Maybe it was a mistake. Sure, I can make a living. But I don't have the time to make art. So I'm not one thing or another. That doesn't mean I want Susan to get married at eighteen and start having babies. I definitely don't want her to do that."

"Why not?" Susan said.

"I want you to want to do something."

"What makes you think being a teacher is better than being a mother?" Susan asked, acting very defensive.

Phyllis said, "You answer that, Mother. I don't know how to."

Susan said, "At least I might not get divorced. I might give my children a happy home."

"Ouch," Phyllis said.

"Oh, dear," Alice mumbled. "Don't go on. I don't know why we talk about ourselves so much anyway. There are much more important things going on in the world to think about than us."

"Like what, Mother?"

"Like South Africa," Alice replied.

"That's an awfully big subject," Phyllis said.

Later, as they slowed down for a construction site, Alice had another idea, and she asked Susan, "What about music, Susan? You've always loved your music. Maybe this is a direction for you."

"I'll always play the piano, Grandma," Susan said. "I love playing the piano. That's how I met Scott, you know. I was the accompanist for the choir at school and he sang in the choir. Scott was so cute. I couldn't believe it when he asked me out. I really wanted to go out with him but I didn't think he was going to ask me. Finally he said something to me. I wanted to go out with him so bad. He just came up to me and said did I want to go out on Friday. I was so happy. Then we went out and we've been going out ever since. If it hadn't been for my music, I never would have met Scott."

"Oh God," Alice said.

One of the front tires was losing air and they stopped at a station on the outskirts of Baltimore. Phyllis pulled up to a self-serve pump, and while Susan filled the car with gas, she went to phone Jerry. Alice sat in the car watching a bright blue candy wrapper blowing across the pavement. After a while, when the attendant didn't come, she got out and began fiddling with the air hose. Phyllis returned and stood over her.

"Do you know how to do that, Mother?"

"No," Alice said, "I'm learning."

"Jerry wasn't there. He didn't leave the machine on either. That's not like him."

Alice, who'd managed to attach the hose to the tire, was trying to figure out how to make the air come out.

"Maybe he went out for dinner," Phyllis said.

"Ah," Alice said, "you push this little gizmo." Air began hissing into the tire.

"Don't you need one of those gauges?"

Alice said, "I think that's enough." She stood up and kicked the tire with the toe of her shoe. Then she walked back and kicked the rear tire the same way. She returned to the front tire and kicked it again.

"Yes," she said, "they're just fine. Let's get going."

Phyllis's house was dark when they pulled into the driveway, but Jerry's car was parked at the curb out front.

"He's home," Phyllis said happily. It was after midnight. The air was cool and fresh when they opened the car doors.

"Mickey," Susan said to the black-and-white cat who appeared from out of the darkness, and she scooped him up in her arms. "Mickey, Mickey, Mickey," she sang, "la, la, la. Oh, Mickey, did you miss me?"

The front door was unlocked. Inside the house, a smell like fried onions hung in the air. It was warm and close and dark.

"Jerry?" Phyllis called.

Susan turned on lights in the living room and the kitchen, and then went upstairs and turned on more lights in her bedroom and the bath. "Nobody up here," she called.

"Hmmm," Phyllis said after inspecting the downstairs rooms. "Maybe he's not here."

Suddenly a door opened at the top of the stairs and Jerry appeared in a T-shirt and jeans. He didn't have any shoes on and he blinked, as if adjusting his eyes to the light. The room he'd just come out of was the spare room. Phyllis hadn't thought to look in there.

"You are here," Phyllis said. "We decided to drive back a day early. Come down and meet my mother."

"Oh," Jerry said. He made no move. He looked down at Alice, then at Phyllis. "Hi," he said. He lifted a hand at the same time, and waved, as if she were too far away to hear him. In fact, standing up there on the landing above them, Jerry appeared to be a traveler, who, looking down from the deck of a ship, was about to sail away and was bidding farewell to well-wishers on the dock.

"Marcie is here," he said. "She just came over to watch TV."

A small woman with brown hair came out of the room behind him. "Hi," she said. "You're home. How was your trip?"

With a sudden, terrible feeling, Alice understood. And she saw, though it was slower in coming, that it was dawning on Phyllis, too. She looked stricken and couldn't do anything to hide it.

"Fine," Phyllis said quietly. Susan had come out of her room and was looking at Jerry and Marcie.

"Susan, this is Jerry and Marcie," Phyllis said. The way she said Jerry and Marcie, they became even more of a couple.

Susan said, "I've met Marcie before." She frowned at them.

The next moments were, for Alice, like watching a terrible part in a film. Marcie stayed long enough to talk about the American Playhouse production of a Clifford Odets play that she'd come over to watch, and to explain that once she got her own TV fixed, she wouldn't mooch off other people. Phyllis, content to subscribe to this fiction, or rather forced to, actually let Marcie kiss her on the cheek when she left. After a little while, Jerry left, too, saying he needed to get back to his loft because a dealer was coming early in the morning and he still had things to do. Susan went to bed. Alice and Phyllis were left alone in the living room.

Phyllis said, "You're not going to think much of Jerry after this."

"I'm not going to think much," Alice said indignantly. "What about you?"

"I don't think I'll ever get it right with men."

"Well," Alice said, and then found she had nothing to say.

Alice considered cutting her visit short. It wasn't much fun being at Phyllis's. Phyllis, who was tied up with school matters much of the time, had a forced cheerfulness about her when she was home, and it made Alice weary. Jerry didn't call, and Phyllis said she hadn't had any luck in reaching him. She kept trying, however, saying there were obviously things they had to discuss. Finally, one afternoon, he called and asked her to meet him at a café. After Phyllis left, Alice turned on the TV. The Million Dollar Movie was just starting, and her spirits lifted, as if this were a piece of unwarranted luck.

When Susan came home from work at the card shop, she found her grandmother watching Kim Novak and William Holden in *Picnic*. She got some Cheez-Its and a Coke and sat down with Alice to watch the movie.

"The best thing about this movie is William Holden," Alice said.

"Which one is he?"

"He's got the torn shirt on."

"Do you like dark men or light men, Grandma?"

"Dark," Alice said.

"William Holden looks light."

"I'm making an exception."

"I like both. Scott is light, but Ricky was dark."

This conversation made Alice feel unaccountably buoyant, like she and Susan had suddenly dissolved the years, as well as the other differences, that separated them.

The movie, in spite of being rather corny, got their full attention, and they were sitting in the warm room, in very dim light, watching the part where Kim Novak is trying to decide whether to stay with Cliff Robertson or to run off with William Holden, when Phyllis came home. She sat down and looked at them as if she wanted to talk, but she had a hard time speaking. She waited for a few seconds, during which she appeared rather catatonic. Alice thought she looked awful.

"Jerry says he can't make any commitments at this point in his life." Phyllis shook her head. Alice thought, Must they always use this boring, overworked terminology, like commitment and relationship? Phyllis looked very pale and spent and Alice felt sorry for her. But at the same time, a sense of annoyance was working in her.

"He didn't mean to start anything with Marcie. It just happened. Now he's confused. He doesn't know whether he wants to see me until he sorts things out."

Susan said, "He's a creep, Mom."

"Thanks, Susan."

"He doesn't even look nice. He's got a mean mouth."

Phyllis pretended she was watching the movie.

"If Scott were seeing my best friend, I'd never speak to him again."

"Marcie isn't my best friend," Phyllis said. "She's just a friend."

"It's complex, anyway," Alice said. "I'm sure you'll think things through and decide what you want to do."

"When you talk like that, you sound so cool and disinterested," Phyllis said. "It always drove me crazy, that voice."

"Dump him," Susan said. "That's my advice."

Phyllis turned toward her mother. "Mother, it's like you've already decided it's not worth it. The truth is, I didn't have any arrangement with Jerry that would stop him from seeing somebody else."

"What did I say?" Alice asked. "Did I say anything?" In her mind, she was thinking, In your own house, in your very own place?

"We didn't have any claims on each other. Sure, I want a

significant other in my life and I thought maybe Jerry was that person."

"Significant other?" Alice said. *Significant other?*

"You don't like him."

"I don't even know him."

"What if Arnold were having an affair with somebody else. Would you think it was worth it to wait for him to figure things out?"

Alice felt her face go hot with anger. "I have no reason to distrust Arnold. He's a good man."

"And you think Jerry's a flake?"

"No," Alice said, "I think you're the flake."

Alice packed that afternoon. She found a flight that left Kennedy at 8:00 P.M. She called Arnold from the phone in the upstairs den to ask if he'd meet her at the airport. Enough was enough, she said. She was ready to come home. When she told him what had happened, beginning with their discovery of Jerry and Marcie in the spare bedroom, Arnold said, "Somebody ought to let the air out of that guy's tires."

The thought gave Alice a lift. Things had been so tense around there for days, but now, talking with Arnold, everything felt lighter. She laughed and said, "It's been an awful visit, really."

Arnold said, "When you get home, would you like for us to just shut ourselves off for a few days and watch movies? I could rent a few on my way to the airport."

They made a list of films for Arnold to pick up. Alice went downstairs and found Phyllis sitting at the kitchen table reading the newspaper. There were still hours before her flight, but Alice wanted to leave then. Without looking up, Phyllis said, "Sure, we can go whenever you'd like."

"I bore myself, sometimes," Alice said. "It must be dreadful for other people." Susan, who stood at the sink, turned and smiled at her grandmother.

"We could all be better at talking to each other."

Phyllis raised her head and looked out the window.

"Oh," she said.

"I don't know why we all can't just be what we want to be," Susan said. "We keep trying to make each other over."

Phyllis picked up her mother's suitcase. "Let's just go."

Once in the car, Alice said, "I was wondering if we could make a little detour on the way to the airport."

"Where to?"

"Jerry's place."

"Mother, I don't want to see him," Phyllis said.

"Oh, we won't. And hopefully, he won't see us."

"But why?"

"Just drive me by," Alice said. "I want to see how these artists live. Call it sightseeing."

The smoke stacks of factories rose above the city's skyline and a few burned bright with flames, putting out clouds of pale colors, yellow and pink and mauve, shades very like those found in candy Easter eggs. The oncoming night was deepening the color of the sky behind the buildings. Driving across the bridge over the Hudson, Alice looked down and saw a wake left by a boat, although the boat was nowhere to be seen. Once in SoHo, they navigated their way through thick traffic until they came to Broadway and Broome. Phyllis made a left and pulled up in front of a building with bolts of cloth in the windows. She pointed to blank windows on the seventh floor. "Up there," she said, "that's where Jerry lives."

"And where would his car be?" Alice asked.

They found it parked around the corner, across from a shop with a big cat sitting among cans in a window.

"I'm surprised he left it on the street," Phyllis said. "He usually pays to leave it in a garage on Spring. What do you want his car for?"

"I want to leave him a message," Alice said.

She got out of the car and motioned for Susan and Phyllis to follow. "Susan, you go down to the corner and keep an eye out for him. If you see anything, get back here quickly."

Alice knelt down by the front tire. She took a pen out of her purse, while Susan and Phyllis stood nearby, watching her. The air began hissing out of the tire as soon as Alice depressed the valve.

"Oh, Grandma," Susan said, "nice move, nice move," and ran down to the corner to take up her post.

Phyllis looked down at her mother, bent over and squatting by the curb. She had her jaw set in a determined way, but otherwise, looked very placid and calm. "Oh, God," Phyllis said, "why didn't I think of this?"

The surprising thing was how much time it took to let the air out of two tires. Alice was exhausted when she'd finished, though Phyllis had relieved her and done half the work. The car had a dispirited appearance when they stepped back to look at it. Susan, responding to Alice's wave, ran back from the corner, out of breath. The three of them stood for a moment and admired their vandalism.

"It's terrible," Phyllis said, but she was smiling.

"I know," Alice replied. "Awful."

"He'd kill us if he ever found out," Susan said.

"He won't, though," Alice promised. She sighed. Suddenly she thought of Arnold, and the strangest image came up. It was of his delicate, beautiful hands, moving so gracefully, and with such deliberate precision, as he turned a page in his stamp book.

"We'd better get going," she said. She looked at Phyllis and realized that she was now shorter than her daughter. For years, she'd been considerably taller.

"Yup," Phyllis said, "before somebody stops us."

"Onward and upward," Susan cried, raising an arm in the air, "forward into the future." She turned and ran on ahead of them, and then stopped, breathless and happy, to wait for them to catch up with her.

CAMP ROSE

◆◆ ———————————————————————————— ◆◆

Looking up, she sees her father and brother above her, digging a hole near the road. Her brother stops and puts his arms out in a stretch. She thinks her brother has the most beautiful body of any man she's ever seen. She thought this after seeing him naked the first time, when, as adults, they shared a sauna at a place called Miracle Baths, and it occurred to her again this morning when he stepped from the shower and walked into the kitchen, naked, and said, "I hope my nudity doesn't offend you."

"No, no," she said quickly, thinking of their parents, Ray and Ada, who were upstairs playing pinochle. He is so long and thin and white, he has a spectral beauty. She wished her body were more like his. She would like his legs.

"I am into nudity," he said, with his very precise style of pronunciation, and looking a little mischievous, walked back toward the bathroom. "Up here we just forget our clothes," he added. He turned and smiled sweetly.

Up here is what her brother calls his place in the country, which he recently bought for very little money. It needs a lot of fixing up but it has great possibilities. It has a nice view of a purplish-brown river that runs so slowly Ann gets mesmerized watching it. The house itself sits below the road, on a steep hillside rising above the river, and like other places around it, was originally built as a summer cottage. The garden is large. Oak trees covered with moss rise up and form beautiful, shady canopies, and slender Madrones border the property. There's a hammock. Meals are eaten outside on a wooden deck. It feels to Ann like a summer camp and in fact her brother, Peter, gave her a T-shirt when she arrived with "Camp Rose" printed on it. Underneath this is written "Naughty Pines."

When he finishes stretching, Peter goes right back to his digging. Ann nudges a large rock with her shoe and wonders if she's strong enough to lift it without hurting her back. For some reason, a phrase from her mother's repertoire of homilies comes to mind: *It takes a heap o' livin' to make a house a home*. She finds it so sentimental it makes her laugh.

"What are you laughing at?" her father calls down to her from his place near the road. He is wearing a Stetson and a denim shirt and dark glasses and he looks like an old-time cowboy.

"Nothing," Ann says.

"I thought maybe you were laughing at the Old Poot." The Old Poot is Ann's father's name for himself.

"I'm getting a little old to be doing this kind of work," he says. "I could fall and break my neck climbing around up here."

"Take it easy, Pop," Peter says. He reaches out and touches the old man's shoulder, but just for a second, and then he bends his beautiful white back to the sun and begins mixing another bucket of cement.

She watches her father for a moment longer, then she picks up more rocks and carries them down to the lower garden where she is building a wall, rock by rock, around a planting area.

Ann, who arrived by plane and bus according to instructions mailed by Peter, found the trip not at all tiring. The plane from Los Angeles to San Francisco was only an hour, and at the airport, a bus marked Santa Rosa was just pulling up as she came out of baggage claim. She took the seat behind the driver. When she saw how empty the bus was, she spread her things out on the adjoining seat, ate a tuna sandwich she'd made for the trip, and drank coffee from a thermos. They drove along a freeway for a while. Then the freeway ended and they were caught up in the thick traffic of the city. When they were about to cross the Golden Gate Bridge, the driver, an older man with a friendly face, turned around and said, "Quite a view, huh?"

Ann glanced back at the city's skyline from the bridge. It looked too pretty to be real. It must always look this way, she thought. Charming San Francisco. She wondered what it would be like to live in a beautiful city instead of Los Angeles. Ann, who had been very depressed by her recent breakup with Stanley, felt happier just looking at the city and the picturesque blue bay.

When the bus finally stopped an hour later, it was in front of the Holiday Inn in Santa Rosa. Ann spotted her mother sitting in a car in the parking lot. Peter stood on the curb and greeted her.

"Hello, Sis." Peter put his arms around her.

"Is she your sister?" the bus driver asked Peter.

"Yes."

"You've got a nice sister."

Ann had hardly said anything at all during the drive. How could he know whether she was nice or not? Nevertheless, when Peter agreed with the driver and said, "I know," Ann couldn't help feeling good. This might be a nice visit, she thought. Maybe her family would help take her mind off Stanley.

She leaned into the window of the car and kissed her mother. Her father was nowhere to be seen.

"Don't you look nice," Ada said. "I like your short hair."

"I've got to get a drink of water," Ann said, feeling terribly thirsty. "I'll be right back." She walked inside the Holiday Inn with Peter and got directions to a fountain down the hallway. Before they reached the fountain, she saw her father. He looked lost. Then he saw her and laughed and put out his arms as she came toward him. "Hi, doll," he said.

"I need a drink of water," Ann said, hugging him.

"Say," her father said, "I think you look better than I've seen you look in years. That's a pretty sharp haircut. You look about ten years younger."

Ann drank deeply from the fountain. Her father drank after her, bending over and taking long, repeated gulps of water. They shared the belief that drinking lots of water is good for you. When he stood up, he said, "I'm mighty glad to see you, honey." He looked dapper and trim, his gray mustache very neat, his hair slicked down with some kind of oil or pomade, and a turquoise stone decorating his string tie. He caught her staring at him.

"You can tell this eye is a little skeewhumpus, huh?" he said.

"Not really," she said.

"It's shrinking, I think," he said. "Getting smaller than the other one."

The original idea had been to go to Hawaii, but neither Ann nor Peter wanted to spend that much money on a trip just to please their mother, Ada. Since recuperating from pernicious anemia and her brush with death, Ada wanted nothing more than to take a trip to some far-off, exotic land. She thought Hawaii would be perfect. She even checked with her friend Sybil Wadman to see if Sybil's condo on Oahu would be vacant. But because Ada had just recovered from her illness and still had some trouble getting around, Ann and Peter thought Hawaii was a bad idea. Also Ada had always liked to play cards and eat meals she didn't have to cook and take drives through the countryside, and they saw no point in going all the way to Hawaii to do these things. When they proposed going to Camp Rose for a week instead, Ada agreed happily, and, at the last minute, Ray decided to come, too. All Ada really wanted was to take a trip. Above all, she wanted to feel that life wasn't passing her by. It would be so easy at her age to feel that most everything that was going to happen had already happened, but Ada, cheerful and adventurous, was quite determined to go out and make more happen.

Ann, who has just dropped a large pink rock near some smaller, undistinguished ones, looks up to see her mother's face in the second-story window. Ada lifts her hand and waves at Ann, opening and closing her fingers as if she were counting by fives . . . five, ten, fifteen, twenty. The face in the window is that of a plump and graying grandmother, pink and sweet. Tiny spider veins blossoming on her cheeks have given her the complexion of a ruddy, happy peasant.

Two months earlier Ann received a letter from her father in which he complained that Ada read trashy novels all day long. He couldn't understand putting such junk into your head. He wondered why Ada didn't read something more worthwhile. He called them "sex books," though they were really romance novels, thin little paperbacks with couples on their covers. "Sometimes she reads two or three in one day," Ann's father wrote. "They stack up on the back of the toilet, she's got four or five by her bed. Pretty soon they'll take over the whole house."

Ann, who had determined to treat her father in a more direct and honest way, wrote back: "About Mother and the romance novels . . . I think the reason she reads them is because she wants the feelings they give her. I think she's a romantic. From what she's told me, she always enjoyed sex with you. As the years have made the possibility of intimacy more and more remote, she probably reads these books in order to satisfy the longings she has for romance. It doesn't seem such a bad thing to me."

She mailed the letter and then began to worry. Would he think she had gone too far by talking about his sexual relations with her mother? Would her frankness embarrass him? Since he never responded to the letter, she couldn't be sure, but she felt he hadn't really meant for her to comment on the subject. He had meant for her to regard it as he did, as a light, humorous topic for a letter. So far this trip, neither he nor Ann had mentioned the subject of Ada's romance novels.

But as she looks up at her mother, she sees one of the novels in her hand. With one hand she is waving; with the other, she is clasping a small, colorful book.

The next morning, the second of their vacation, they are up early and working in the garden again. So far all they've done is work—move rocks, dig fence-post holes, transplant gladiolus bulbs, tear out some old berry bushes. It seems like working on houses is part of what has always kept their family together, and anytime they all find themselves in one spot, they immediately get busy. Peter and Ray are digging more post holes, filling them with cement, and then setting thick, green posts upright in the ground. Ann is hauling more rocks. Her jeans have dirt ground into them from where she's rested rocks on her thighs. Thick little pads of skin have begun to build up where her fingers meet her palms. She can smell her perspiration on her shirt. As she climbs the stairs to the upper garden for another load of rocks, she meets Peter coming down from the workshop.

"Some vacation," he says, "making you work like this."

Ann smiles at her brother and thinks of the way they played together when they were kids. There's only eighteen months between them. At one point in their lives they were mistaken for twins. On her wall at home there's a photograph of the two of them when they were six and seven. They're each holding two ripe peaches in exactly the same way, one in each hand, just at the height of their chests. Thinking of this picture, she feels even fonder of Peter and is happy to be here with him, working on his place.

"We can fix some lunch soon," Peter says, "and then we'll go down to the river and take a swim. Come on up to the workshop for a minute." Ann smiles. Already they have worked this out.

In the workshop, Peter takes down a pipe from a shelf. He unrolls a piece of tinfoil and puts some marijuana in the pipe bowl and lights it. Briefly, Ann wonders where her father is and whether he will smell the marijuana. But it's so exhausting trying to hide things that she decides not to worry. Peter passes her the pipe after taking a long drag himself.

It's very pleasant in the tiny workshop. The light filters through cracks and small windows. All the tools hang from pegs, the wrenches in ascending order of size, the hammers grouped together, screwdrivers suspended by their handles between two nails. There are shiny nails in glass jars on clean shelves. Peter keeps his life so neat and tidy. Ann thinks if her own apartment had looked this orderly, Stanley would have been happier. During his visits, he frequently complained about the disorder. Stanley, however, has his own house with his own wife who, he once told Ann, waxes her kitchen floor once a week. Ann hardly ever waxes her kitchen floor but she does take a sponge to dirt spots occasionally. She gives her floors a lick and a promise, as Ada would say.

Stanley Horowitz had been Ann's lover for the past fourteen months until one morning, sometime between Thanksgiving and Christmas, Ann awoke and said to herself, I don't want to be the lover of a married man anymore. It was Easter, however, before she could bring herself to break it off.

"Why do you want to end a good thing?" Stanley asked over dinner at their favorite restaurant, Roscoe's House of Chicken & Waffles.

"Because I'm not happy."

"Couldn't it just be a mood?"

"You know it's not going anywhere."

"Give me until Memorial Day," Stanley pleaded.

She always got Memorial Day and Labor Day confused. She thought he was asking her to wait six more months, until the end of the summer.

"Too long," she said. "I'm going crazy here. It's not a good thing." She wanted to add she was having moral problems.

Stanley took her hand. "It is a good thing, baby," he insisted. "You know it is."

He never had called her baby. She didn't like it at all. "I

wish you would never call me that again."

"Boy, are you touchy," Stanley said. He withdrew his hand and began pushing the chicken bones on his plate around with the tip of his knife. "Just give me a little more time."

Ann, who was wearing her glasses instead of contacts because she'd spent the afternoon crying and her eyes were sore, lifted the frames away from her face and rubbed her fingers against the bridge of her nose. It gave her a pensive look, she knew. She wanted him to think she was thinking things over. But really there was no decision left to be made. Seeing Stanley had become a complex and unrewarding activity. Feelings can dry up, and hers had. The problem was that her feeling for just about everything had dried up along with her feelings for Stanley. She felt depressed. She was living a life that rattled around her. Days seemed brittle and nights were empty. When she moved around in her apartment alone she often heard sounds, like wind rattling dry corn husks. She had a hard time choosing what to wear in the morning and usually ended up putting on mismatched odds and ends and then felt out of it all day. Lacking an appetite, she couldn't eat properly, and when she did feel hungry, she found there was nothing in her fridge except a plastic lime and a few bottles of condiments—pickles, salsa, green olives—items whose surfaces were often covered by layers of soft mold.

Stanley worked at County Hospital where Ann was a medical recorder. He was a pale man with thick glasses who took his Jewishness seriously. (His wife, he reported to Ann, kept a kosher household.) "How can serious Jews have affairs?" she once asked him. "We're a very sensuous people," he said. Things like that sounded mocking and harmless at the time, but when she thought of them now, they made her angry. How could she have put up with that? How could he have acted so arrogant?

As a doctor, Stanley could explain his nighttime absences to his wife by claiming he had an emergency at the hospital. But instead of attending to some ailing, tube-riddled patient, he would sit in Ann's small, cluttered apartment, sipping wine and patting her firm thighs, which he found very attractive. Peasant legs, he called them, sturdy things. He had a happy nature and could deal with her moods, which no man had so successfully done before. They saw each other two nights a week, and at least once for lunch. He taught her to make a good tomato sauce, fixed her plumbing when it went bad, and made terrific chicken soup when she had colds. Not a morning went by that he didn't call and say, "Hello, Bubba-loo," having given her that pet name. It was very sweet having a pet name. Even though there were moral problems with the situation, Ann stuck to Stanley long after she began to think she shouldn't. To her friends who criticized her for putting up with his double life, she said, "He's exceedingly considerate."

Over dinner at Roscoe's, Ann realized it didn't matter whether Stanley wanted her to wait until Memorial Day or Labor Day. One more day was too long.

"I'm going now," she said, straightening her glasses on her face. "And I don't want a ride."

"Oh, Ann," Stanley sighed. "Please, please, Ann."

She shook her head. "Don't please me, please."

"I've always tried to."

"I mean, don't say please. Don't say anything."

"Think it over. It could be hard to get back together if you break it off this way. Do you want something irredeemable?" Stanley looked owlish and serious when he said this, as if it fell to him to give some terrible news to a patient.

"That's exactly what I want, something irredeemable." Ann stood up and walked quickly away from the table.

Stanley pursued her out onto the sidewalk. Across the street was a tarot-reading place. Next to that, a motel whose sign said, "XXXX-Rated Movies." He followed her to the bus stop. He said he couldn't, in good conscience, leave her alone in this neighborhood at this time of night.

"I like this neighborhood," she said. "It's got a certain *joie de vivre*." As she said this, she looked across the street. A prostitute was walking past the motel. She wore a colorful outfit and had on pretty—though impossibly high—heels. "There's a certain moral order here," she added.

"I won't leave you."

"Here's my bus," Ann said, and hurried to the curb. She hopped up the steps without checking its number to see where it was headed.

"It's good you came," Peter says to Ann, passing her the pipe. "I hope you didn't use up all your vacation."

"I'm glad we didn't go to Hawaii. This is much nicer."

"Tomorrow we'll take a drive. There's a road that winds through the mountains and comes out at Stewart's Point, right on the ocean. Then we can drive down the coast and stop and get some seafood in Jenner."

Ann nods. She feels nice and relaxed. Things look a little different now. Stanley is far, far away and Peter, the kindest brother in the world, is sharing his pleasant life with her.

"This is such a wonderful place," she says. "I would love to have a house up here."

"There's a house up the road we should look at later," Peter says. "Nobody has lived there for years. It looks like the owners abandoned it. Maybe they want to sell. They might only want fifteen or twenty thousand for it."

Ann has exactly twelve thousand dollars in savings. She's never thought of buying a house with that money. She's thought of taking a year off work and traveling to foreign countries, living for a while in Paris, Amsterdam, Valencia; seeing India, Yugoslavia, Australia; hiking the high route through the Alps and staying in mountain huts. She's imagined meeting men in foreign places and having quick, pleasant affairs. She's seen herself in the company of these foreign men with their different accents. (Maybe they don't speak English at all.) She's imagined herself learning languages and coming home and speaking Italian to Italian waiters like her friend Margo does. She has mentally packed suitcases with imaginary outfits for these voyages. But one thing she's never imagined herself doing, and that's buying a house. Houses were for couples, not single women.

Peter is saying something, and Ann, thinking of her money in the bank and the imaginary trips, has drifted far from the workshop where a smell, pleasant and familiar, like weeds burning on a ditch bank, hangs in the air.

"You don't have to keep hauling those rocks," he says. "If you're tired, just quit."

"But I like working in the garden," she says, "and you know Dad does. It's exactly how he wants to spend a vacation."

When Ann was little, her father worked for Kennecott Copper Company. For the fifth-grade science fair, Ann's project was entitled "The Many Uses of Copper." On a large piece of cardboard, she pasted samples of ore in various stages of refinement. She used copper tubing and pennies to illustrate the final product. In the center of the cardboard, Ann built a crude papier-mâché replica of the open-pit copper mine outside Salt Lake City where her father worked in a low wooden building marked "Personnel." The day her father took her to the mine to gather material for the science project, she got to wear a hard hat and ride in an ore train that descended, in ever-narrowing circles, to the bottom of the pit. "This is the largest open-pit copper mine in the world," her father said. "Over a mile across at the top. The largest man-made hole on earth," he added. Ann dutifully recorded these statistics, although they didn't impress her nearly as much as the way people treated her father. Everybody seemed to know him. They called him an old son-of-a-gun and patted his back or took his big brown hand and pumped it hard. It seemed to Ann that this was a kind of club where everybody had fun, got to work outdoors with big machines, and laughed a lot when they greeted each other. After the day in the mine, she thought of her father with more pride, because it seemed to her that he was someone important in the biggest hole on earth.

"Only one more hole to dig and then we'll have lunch," Peter says, looking past Ann to where the door of the workshop opens onto the garden.

"There's Pop," he adds, and puts the pipe back on the shelf.

Ann turns and looks at her father, who is struggling up the hillside, the wet clay giving way beneath his boots. Recently, he's lost the sight in one eye, the result of a blood clot. He has no depth perception, and she worries about him driving and climbing around on steep hills like this. When he reaches the string that's been tied to indicate a straight line for the posts, he stops and carefully steps over it. But something happens! For a moment, he loses his balance, and teetering, grabs for a nearby branch. It could go either way: Ann stops breathing, and sees her father falling, tumbling backward down the steep slope, his Stetson flying off, his neck contorting as he tumbles from ledge to ledge. But it doesn't happen that way. He catches the branch, and, steadying himself, pulls forward until both feet are on the other side of the string and he is safe, temporarily, balanced on the hillside.

"I read somewhere that kids who went to elementary school in Utah in the 1950s have very low scores on scholastic tests," Peter says, putting on his work gloves. "They think it was all the nerve-gas leaks and the atomic tests. Remember when all those sheep died from nerve gas?"

Ann remembers. There were pictures in the papers of fields of dead sheep, each looking like a harmless white boulder in a pretty pasture.

"Think of what it could have done to us," Peter says.

"You think we're damaged?"

"Who knows."

"It's such a lousy world," Ann says. "Chemical warfare, nuclear power plants, polluted air, water you can't drink, these shitty little wars that nobody wins." Ann is also thinking about AIDS, but she doesn't mention it. Three of Peter's friends have died from AIDS recently. The last time they talked about it, Peter said, "You don't expect to have to deal with the death of friends until you're much older. It's just not something you think will happen when you're in your thirties." Ann knew Tony, one of Peter's friends who died. He was twenty-two. At the very end, his father held him in his arms. His mother supported him as well. Peter was there, too, and Peter's friend, David. They sealed him in love, and when he was gone, finally, everybody was transformed.

Peter shifts from one foot to the other and shrugs his thin shoulders as if getting kinks out. "Well," he says, "back to work."

Ann's niece, Cindy, is getting married and Ada is making a scrapbook for her. She's been working on it since she arrived at Camp Rose. Ann finds Ada sitting at the kitchen table, filling in a page of the book, which has printed questions to be answered. What table manners did you teach your children? is the question Ada is answering when Ann looks over her shoulder. Ada has written, "Never talk with your mouth full."

She moves on to the next question. "What was your husband's favorite meal?" Ada writes, "Pinto beans. He liked them twice a week. He called them 'Arizona strawberries.'"

"This is a heck of a lot of work," Ada says. "I sure hope Cindy appreciates it."

On the table, lying open and face down, is one of Ada's romance novels. There's a picture of a doctor and a nurse on the cover.

"What's your father up to?"

"They're still digging post holes," Ann says. Ada has just written something under the heading "Household Tips." It's a formula for homemade window cleaner: "1 cup alcohol, 1 Tb. detergent, 1 tsp. vinegar, 1 tsp. ammonia. Put in gallon jar and finish filling with water."

Ann imagines making a gallon of window cleaner. She knows she'd never use it. In the three years she's lived in her present apartment, she's cleaned the windows once. There's such a difference between the way Ann lives now and the way she grew up. She was raised with seven brothers and sisters. Now she lives alone in three rooms. She'd never need a gallon of window cleaner.

Ada reaches up and puts her arm around Ann's hips and squeezes her. Ada is still pretty strong for seventy-four.

"How's my honey?" she asks her daughter, giving her a look which says, let's have a chat.

"Do you want the standard answer?" Ann asks.

"No, I want the truth."

"I'm fine," Ann says, giving her the standard answer.

"I sure love you," Ada says. "It's awfully sweet of you to take time out of your busy schedule to come be with us."

"I'm enjoying it," Ann says.

"I bet your father would like a drink of water. He's working too hard."

"I'll take him one."

While she's filling the glass, Ann remembers how her father used to stand outside in the garden and whistle for a glass of water. That whistle meant somebody better jump. He liked his water cold. There was always an old milk bottle full of ice water in the refrigerator. They never drank anything but water with meals. Sometimes when Ann would be out riding her horse, she would stop by the house for a drink of water. She'd ride up onto the lawn and whistle like her father. Ada would come to the door and say, "I'm not going to wait on you, I've got a million things to do. You can get down off there and get your own water." Then Ada would usually soften and bring Ann a glass of water, which she'd drink sitting on her horse, while her mother stroked the pale velvety flesh around the horse's nose, petting him shyly and tentatively, until Ann had finished and she could take the glass back inside.

She remembered her father dressed in dark clothes, just about to go by train to his work in the mines. When he came home, wordlessly he changed his clothes and went straight to the garden where, until called for dinner, he worked steadily among beds of tall roses, peonies, and brambly rows of raspberry bushes. His garden was his buffer between the world of the copper mine, which he came to hate, and the eight children and wife who waited at the table, about whom he had the most complicated feelings. "I never should have had eight children," he said to Ann when she was older. "I didn't have the temperament for it." He did have eight children, though, and between them and the mine, he was trapped, with only the earth and light of the garden to escape to in the hours between when the train brought him home and dinner was set out on the table.

Her father is resting on a shovel when she brings him the water.

"Thanks," he says, and drinks carefully from the rim of the glass, craning his neck and swallowing with audible gulps.

"That's delicious. What's your mother doing? Loafing? Reading those damned sex books?"

"She's working on Cindy's scrapbook."

"I give Cindy about three months in that marriage. Your mother gets upset when I say that but I don't see how anyone can put up with that kid." He nudges a stump with his foot. "This should come out. Get me a saw and we'll cut it off at ground level."

Ann finds a saw and climbs back up to her father and hands it to him.

"Did you ever think of cutting it yourself?" he asks.

Ann feels hurt. She gave him the saw because she thought he would like to cut the stump off himself.

"You're kind of a lazy kid, you know that?"

She looks out over the valley to the green ridge beyond the river. This was his idea of humor but it was humiliating to her. It had always been hard with him. When she was small, he used to kick her butt, just to get her attention he said. A soft kick, but shocking nonetheless. Sometimes he lifted her up slightly by the hair on the back of her neck and she would extend herself on her toes in an effort to relieve the tension. He didn't single her out, however; all the kids got the same treatment. But he had always accused her of being lazy. Once he'd written to her and said, "So how are you and your kinetically passive life-style doing?" She wrote back and said, "Where the hell did you get that one?" but it made her laugh and seemed like something someone would say about somebody living in southern California.

"With this bad eye, the doc says I can't lean over. I shouldn't be trying to cut that thing," he says. "Maybe you ought to just kill me off before I get to be a burden."

"You'll have to get somebody else to do it," Ann says. "I'm nonviolent."

"I think I could easily become a terrorist," her father says. "These damned utility companies and big corporations. They don't listen to anybody. Maybe somebody needs to stick a little dynamite under them once in a while. I'd be the perfect person to do it, don't you think? An old poot like myself, what have I got to lose? No, I tell you Ann, something's got to be done. Criminals are running the world. I know it's not a very Christian attitude. The Book says we're not supposed to kill. You know what Book I'm referring to? I don't know how familiar you've been with it lately so I have to check. What are you going to do when these people won't listen? We may have to fight fire with fire."

Ann remembers the last conversation like this. The manager of the condominium where her parents lived hadn't gotten their cable television hooked up when everyone else received the service. The cable company had refused to come back for six months. Her parents couldn't watch the basketball games or baseball or satellite movies. Ray was furious. He threatened to march down and blow up the cable-company office unless something was done. Fortunately, something was done.

Sometimes her father showed her the postcards he wrote to his state representatives, Orrin Hatch and Jake Garn, whom he referred to as "Roarin' Orrin" and "Jake the Fake." He wrote postcards instead of letters because he said more people could read his message that way—everybody from the postman to secretaries. He particularly liked postcards with pictures of pigs or jackasses on the front. His messages to Jake the Fake and Roarin' Orrin reflected the musings of a man tortured by the inequities of a system that favored the rich over the poor and fouled the earth for profit. In his rather mild, semi-terrorist language, he berated his representatives: "It's hard for me to tell who's the bigger jackass, you or the fellow on the front of the card," he wrote on one. The pig postcards suggested that sooner or later swine got sent to slaughter and compared the hog on the front to a gluttonous consumer economy. "What about the rest of the world?" he wrote. "Don't they deserve a spot at the trough?" Ann felt her father would make a pretty pallid terrorist with all those bucolic references to farm animals. He called heavily on his boyhood days on a ranch in Arizona for his imagery, but the sentiments were those formed by the train ride to the mines, all the mean resentment of a poorly paid and unrecognized worker, the harried breadwinner for a family of ten.

"I really can't see you as a terrorist," Ann says.

"No?" Ray says, and winks at her with his good eye. "I might just surprise you one of these days."

Ann and Peter make lunch for their parents and spread the food out on a table in the shade of the oaks. Plates of bright red tomatoes and steaming corn on the cob sit next to potato salad and cold chicken. The food looks pretty in the dappled light. A sense of serenity prevails as Ada bows her head and says a long, slow blessing, which includes a plea for peace in the world and good health for them all. The morning of work has left everyone feeling tired and hungry, but also satisfied.

After lunch, Peter asks Ann if she wants to walk up the road and look at the house he thinks might be for sale. As they climb the stairs leading past the workshop, Ann can feel the effects of carrying heavy rocks all morning. Her legs seem weighty and stiff, as if pounds have been added to them, but Peter bounds up the stairs ahead of her, as light and quick as a frisky dog.

The house Peter shows her is almost hidden from sight. The green roof is level with the narrow dirt road.

"You didn't tell me you could drive onto the roof," Ann says.

She has worrisome visions of cars missing the curve in the night and landing on the house.

A steep wooden stairway, overgrown with willows, leads down to a deck surrounding the house. Both the stairway and the deck are rickety, and Peter goes first, cautioning Ann to watch her step. They have to fight their way through the tender, pliable willows blocking their path.

"I think this place has been empty for years," Peter says, holding back a branch. "The next-door neighbor told me a judge used to live here. When he died, it was sold at auction. The people who bought it have never lived here. They're just letting it fall apart."

Steps are missing. Part of the wooden railing has been eaten through by termites, and when Ann touches it, it crumbles into a fine powder. Still, the moment she stands on the deck and looks at the house, she feels excited. She wants it. Some part of herself rushes ahead into the future to claim it for herself. Her heart goes out to this red-shingled structure.

Peter leads her to the railing at the rear of the deck. It's like standing at the edge of a cliff. The two-story house hugs the side of a steep hill. Below them, the Russian River is a smooth band of green water flowing west through a misty valley toward a horizon of pale blue hills. Vineyards are visible in the distance.

"Quite a view, isn't it?" Peter says. "Much better than the one from Camp Rose."

Ann, who is already thinking the view is hers, could always be hers, simply nods. She thinks she could almost buy the house outright and have a rent-free future.

They climb down the steep hillside, through the weeds and willows, to find there's a lower porch with wooden pillars and a low ceiling. On the porch is a mattress on a wooden box, a small stool, and a clothesline.

"A sleeping porch," Peter says. "The judge must have slept out here in the summer."

Ann tries the door at the end of the porch and finds it opens. Inside, cobwebs brush her face as she steps into a utility room. There's a bathroom and two small bedrooms. Everything looks long abandoned. The furniture is skeletal; beds without bedding, a dresser with its drawers partly open, a rug rolled up in a corner. Ann, who believes in ghosts, feels a presence in the house.

Ann leads the way up narrow stairs to the second floor. They come into a living room with a flagstone fireplace. A big green chair, covered in worn leather, sits facing the fireplace. The judge's chair, thinks Ann, who decides she will keep it.

"Here's the problem," Peter says, pointing to the floor. The floor slopes badly toward the windows facing the river. In fact, the whole house feels like it's pulling way from the hillside, leaning out at a precarious angle, and when Ann walks to the far end of the living room and looks straight down from the windows, she feels for a moment as if her weight could cause the whole house to topple over.

"Come in here," Peter calls from another room. He's standing by a dresser with a telegram in his hand. The date on the telegram is 1948, the year Ann was born. It's obviously from the judge to his wife, telling her what time his train will arrive. "Coming home," it concludes. Sitting on the dresser is a picture of men in army uniforms, lined up and smiling for the camera. What strikes Ann about the photograph is the fact that all the men looked middle-aged. They are not young soldiers. They're all smiling. Each face is handsome, farm-fresh, open. No wonder the English liked the American soldiers so much. These men all look like such nice guys. Ann wonders if one of the soldiers is the judge. The date on the picture is 1944, and suddenly Ann realizes why all the men look older. By 1944, all the young men had been drafted and the older ones were being called up. At least, she thinks, the judge survived the war. He came back and lived here and took trips and sent his wife telegrams telling her when he'd return and sat in the green leather chair before a fire, slept out in the cool damp air in the summer, stayed on, in other words, until the end of his life.

Walking back toward Camp Rose, Ann is quiet. The house seems too much to hope for, but still, she has these hopes. It's old and decaying and Peter has said he doesn't know whether it can be saved. It might be too far gone. Yet Ann is sure she could fix it up, little by little. She draws a deep breath, looks up at an illuminated canopy of leaves, and thinks how nice it is here.

"I'm so lazy," Ada says when they walk through the door. "I haven't done a darned thing since I arrived." She's reading one of her novels.

"That's what you're supposed to do, Mom," Peter says. "This is your vacation."

"Still, I should have done something."

Ray is lying on the couch, his hands folded above his head. He looks peaceful, yet frighteningly still, the way people are said to look in death. Ann knows he's listening, awake, yet he doesn't move when they come in.

She notices her mother's book. This one is called *Tomorrow's Never Far Away*. Ann ponders the title and tries to imagine what it means, what the story is about. The title's so imprecise and stupid. She retitles it to *Tomorrow's Never More Than Twenty-four Hours Away*. Of course, it would never sell that way. She thinks she knows, somehow, what the title means, what the story is about. You're having a bad time. Time becomes important because it's moving so slowly. It's a bear, a ball of fur, a thick and sad thing lying before you, a dark hole you're sinking gracelessly into, powerless to believe, your faith dimmed, all but lost. Then something comes to your mind, like the feeling that this will pass, and then time seems like the bearer of glad tidings, if only it would move a little faster, hurry its step, kick the dark and slumbering animal until it rouses itself and, having felt its unwantedness, moves on. The story, she concludes, must be about somebody having a hard time, waiting, hoping for something good to come along. Because it is a romance novel, that good thing must be a man. But it could just as easily, Ann thinks, be a house, or even a trip.

• •

The next day, after a morning of yard work, they drive out into the countryside in the afternoon. Ada sits in front with Peter, who drives, and Ann is in the back with her father. After a while Peter turns left and heads west toward the ocean along a narrow road that climbs through the hills. The road is windy and Ann begins to feel carsick, but she doesn't say anything because, short of asking to change places, there's nothing she can do about it. They stop at a turnout that overlooks a reservoir under construction. Brackish water lies still in the bottom of a narrow valley, the oily green surface extending like a flat tarpaulin between the hills. Ann stands on a picnic table and takes a picture of her family lined up against a railing. Then she hands the camera to some people from Canada who have also stopped at the turnout and asks them to take a picture so she can be in it. Peter puts his arm around her. By the time the Canadian has taken the picture, Ann has tried several different facial expressions—smiling and showing her teeth, smiling without showing her teeth, smiling less and looking up at Peter, not smiling at all and staring straight at the camera. It takes so long for the Canadian to finally release the shutter that Ann is caught with her mouth open in the middle of asking a question and feels a pang of foolishness come over her, as if it's silly to line up for these kinds of pictures in the first place.

They are driving south along a narrow highway overlooking the ocean, having stopped at a general store to buy candy and soda pop.

"M&M?" says Ada, thrusting a package toward the back seat. "Have some pop, too. I've had enough and it's getting warm. Drink it up, Father. Finish it off."

"I don't know what we're going to do about the Mexican problem," Ann's father says, taking the Pepsi from Ada. "What do we do? Just let them stream across the border? The thing is, we need them. The farmers can't get by without the wetbacks."

"Do you have to call them wetbacks?" Ann asks.

"Oh, excuse me," Ray says, with more irony than remorse.

"It *is* kind of racist, Pop," Peter says.

"I see," Ray says. "It's a good thing I've got my children to set me straight on these things." He's being very smart, Ann thinks, but she can't help laughing.

"You're some liberal," she says.

"Well, what are we going to do, gal? What happens when over fifty percent of the population of California doesn't speak English? Do we just say, sure, come and get it. We'll educate your children and let you take the jobs away from American citizens. It's a real problem, Ann. How can we absorb all these people? Who pays for them?" Ray has gotten serious. He's really troubled by this.

"They work the jobs nobody else wants," Ann says.

"Yes, and they're exploited," Ray says. "They're underpaid. They work in sweatshops and are treated terribly."

Now which side of the argument was he on? He seemed to be throwing his sympathy suddenly on the side of the Mexican workers, as if he were more worried about them than the American Way of Life.

"I don't think there ought to be borders in the world. People should be able to go where they want to," says Ann.

"Hell, if that were the case we'd have half the population of Mexico up here. The system just can't take it. It could bring this country down."

Ann is about to say, Well, this was all their land a hundred years ago, and who's to say that this isn't the way things are going to get equalized in the world, the rich countries are going to have to absorb some of the problems of the poorer ones, when Ada suddenly speaks up: "It's a wonder those cows don't fall off into the ocean."

The cows she's referring to are grazing on the sloping meadows that top the cliffs, which drop hundreds of feet before meeting the ocean. It seems as if the cows would be battered to death by the constant sea winds and the cold fog, tortured by the elements on the treeless bluffs. But in fact, they look sleek and shiny and fat.

"No, I think we've got real problems with this immigration thing," Ray says.

"I just can't get used to seeing cows so close to the ocean," Ada says. "I guess I think of them as range animals. Look, there are sheep, too."

"Sheep are kind of stupid," Peter says. "They probably could walk right over a cliff."

Ray goes on now about the current legislation to control immigration, which the House will vote on soon. He's already expressed his views on postcards to Roarin' Orrin and Jake the Fake.

Ann drifts far from this conversation. It seems futile to talk politics with her father, although she always does. It's their irresistible subject, the way in which they disagree without having to disagree on anything important, or personal. When they agree, which they often do, it's their means of bonding, of being true daughter and true parent, heirs of spirit as well as flesh and blood. Usually when they talk politics, even if they start out with contrary views, they hammer the thing out, expressing their feelings, until they're so much in accord it seems they've solved the problem together and need not talk anymore. They have the answer. But really, what happens is they find the center they've always wanted to occupy together, that moment of harmony, like the day they descended into the mine together.

But today Ann doesn't want to wrestle the immigration problem into accord and, rude as it seems, she just stops talking. She looks far down the coast at the beautifully curving surf and imagines herself accomplishing the impossible feat of swimming out through jagged black rocks to where the sea takes on the vivid green of plants. The chair in the judge's house is almost this exact shade of green.

All the time Ann was having the affair with Stanley, she kept thinking that one day it might work out for them to live together in their own house. The days of secrecy would end. He would no longer sneak in and out of her apartment at odd hours.

She wouldn't have to wait for his wife to go off and visit relatives in order to see Stanley overnight. They would have common ground, a house of their own. All the utensils in the kitchen would be theirs. Together they would put pictures on the walls, plant a garden, choose fabric for a chair. Their books would mingle on shelves, their clothes in the closet. But it never happened. Instead they had split apart, halving their lives like cells dividing to go off and make other cells. The day that Stanley stopped by Ann's apartment to pick up some things he'd left, she had stacked all his belongings near the door so he wouldn't hang around too long or feel like he could go through her apartment reclaiming the vestiges of his life. The things in the pile included his vegetable steamer and his colander, both of which were in better condition than her own, a wooden pasta utensil, volumes of Turgenev, Sterne, and a novel by Paul Bowles, a lamp, a rice cooker, two sweaters, and a beach blanket—little remnants of their mock domesticity. Stanley, long-faced, stood by the door and said, "It's going to leave a big hole in my heart without you." He clasped some of his goods to his chest as if stopping the flow of blood from his punctured heart. She found she felt disgusted, and wondered how she could ever have loved a man who would say something like that. After he left, Ann sat stroking her cat until a pile of loose hair had built up in her lap and thought about a lot of things, including how she could have been so immoral as to love a married man.

Clouds scud across the sky. Some fierce wind must be blowing up there, Ann thinks. Down here on the ground, the leaves stand still on the trees. Today is their last day at Camp Rose, and Ada and Ray are inside packing up their suitcases. Ann wants one last look at the judge's house. She takes her camera, thinking she will take some pictures, but the house is difficult to photograph. She can only get a part of it into the viewfinder, no matter how she turns the camera. She snaps a picture of the upstairs window, where inside she knows the judge's telegram and the army photograph lie on the bureau.

Then she goes down and takes a picture of the view from the sleeping porch. She wants to take a picture of the porch itself but her light meter tells her it's too dark to get anything. Finally, she sits on the chair and puts her feet up on the wooden railing and takes one last photograph, which includes a tiny part of the railing, her own feet, and a lot of blue sky.

Upstairs at Camp Rose, Ada and Ray sit at the table playing one last game of cards. Peter is gathering up all the dirty laundry around Camp Rose and stuffing it into a large wicker basket. He puts this on his shoulder and carries it downstairs to the kitchen were Ann is on the phone, getting directions to the county assessor's office in Santa Rosa, so that on the way back to the city they can stop and look up the name of the people who own the judge's house. Ann plans on writing to them as soon as she gets back to Los Angeles.

Peter stands with his back to her, takes his clothes off, puts them into the wicker basket. Where his back meets his buttocks, there are two patches of fine black hair, curving in beautiful whorls, so neat they could have been recently combed into place. He turns and gives her one of his beautiful smiles, an invitation into a conspiracy of well-being, and Ann smiles back at him.

Later, Peter is dressed and sitting across from her at the table downstairs. His hair is combed perfectly. His face shines. He's wearing his brown bus driver's uniform because as soon as they get back to the city, he's got to be at work. Peter just got his ten-year award from MUNI, the San Francisco municipal bus system. Ten years of good driving and public service. They gave him a nice belt buckle. At first, the older drivers, most of whom are black, hadn't accepted him into their ranks. Now, all that's changed. It would be pretty hard for anybody to resist Peter's kindness. The funny thing is, when Ann sees Peter in his uniform, she thinks of their father dressed for work, about to take the train to Salt Lake City and his job in the mine. Peter even has some of Ray's looks, the dark wavy hair receding just a little, the domed forehead with strong, sculpted temples, the finely shaped nose. Suddenly she sees her dad there in Peter. It's lucky people have families, Ann realizes, because no matter what you think, they always go on.

Just before they leave Camp Rose, Ann goes down to look at her rocks lined up around the flower bed. The great oaks make large shaded areas and walking through them, the ground feels air-conditioned, but coming out into the sun, the light falls on her with a bright heat. A smell of decay rises from the earth. She admires her wall, and then moves two rocks to improve the symmetry. When she stands up, her father is there beside her.

"We sure fixed up this place, didn't we?" he says.

Ann agrees that they got a lot of work done on the yard.

"I don't believe I've ever seen anybody work harder than that brother of yours," he says.

She looks up at her father. For the first time, she sees how his blind eye is growing smaller.

He feels her stare and, wordlessly, turns and walks slowly up the dirt path.

When Ann gets back to Los Angeles, the heat in the city is terrible. On her block, children are restless and bored and the adults can't get up the energy to take them to the beach. There's lots of bickering in her apartment building, kids crying, and televisions go all day long. Even the Flores family next door, who never have a cent to spare, invest in a fan and a plastic kiddie pool in the shape of a frog, which they set in the dirt lot and fill by carrying buckets of water from their kitchen down three flights of stairs. Most of the water is splashed out of the pool in the first hour, and what remains is muddied by the dirty feet of children climbing in and out. No one can find a key for the outside faucet. Mrs. Flores gets tired of carrying buckets of water. Pretty soon, the pool develops a tear in the plastic where children have pushed against the sides, and then the frog is split in half and the children go back to the television.

The first thing Ann does when she gets home is write to the owners of the judge's house, whose name, she has discovered, is Petrie. She tells the Petries of her interest in their house. She would like to buy it. Would they be kind enough to answer her letter promptly? Then she settles in and waits for an answer, with ten days left of vacation time. She's decided to use all her vacation. She has no interest in returning to the hospital yet, where she is sure to run into Stanley.

In the evening hours, when a small breeze rises up and stirs the palms, Ann puts a chair on the fire escape and drinks a gin and tonic and watches the activity in the Alpha Beta Supermarket parking lot directly below her. One night she gets an urge to call Stanley, and actually dials his number. His wife answers. Ann, although she has absolutely not planned on doing this, suddenly says, "Did you order a pizza?"

"Nobody here ordered a pizza," Stanley's wife says in a high and very nasal voice. This is a voice you could listen to for about a minute before it would drive you crazy. She's glad to hear this voice of Stanley's wife. It satisfies some curiosity she's harbored for many months, and she wants to keep her on the phone.

"I've got an order here," Ann says, "but I can't read the address, only the phone number."

"We didn't order any pizza."

We, Ann thinks. That "we" held her Stanley in his place.

"Too bad," Ann says. "This pizza's just going to go to waste." She feels delightfully anonymous. "I could send it out if you think you might want it. But it's got anchovies on it, I should tell you."

"I'm sorry," Stanley's wife says, "but you don't have the right party."

"Oh, it's OK," Ann says. "It's not your fault." She hangs up and feels that she'll never have to call that number again.

A week after she sends the letter to the Petries, she receives a reply. It comes on a day when Ann is feeling as if she could be getting a cold, even though it's still more than a hundred degrees in the city. The handwriting on the envelope reminds her of Ada's; it has the same shaky appearance. For a moment her hopes are raised. The Petries are old, she thinks, and they'll see no future for themselves in the house. But the letter says they have no plans for selling the place, which they call their Fitch Mountain home. For the time being, the letter says, they plan on keeping it.

The house is gone so fast, and the rent-free future with it. Like most things, Ann thinks, it was just an idea, it wasn't ever really there. She makes tea and thinks of getting into bed and being really, truly sick. But instead, after a while she gets up and goes to the market, returning with one small sack. There's a wonderful smell of ammonia as she begins mixing up a batch of Ada's window cleaner. It's like alchemy. She expects something remarkable, like a genie, to rise up out of the fumes. By the time the sun sets behind a row of billboards, the panes of glass are so transparent it's very hard to believe there is anything between herself and the shapes of things out in the world.

THE
JOAN CRAWFORD
LETTER

Alice Linder set herself tasks on her birthdays as a means of making them seem like ordinary days. One year she set off fogging bombs and rid the house of fleas; another time she cleaned out her dead husband's closet and sent the clothes off to her sister's son, an enormous boy with a glandular problem and the only person Alice could imagine filling up her husband's pants and shirts. Another year she indexed her recipes, transferring formulas such as "Aunt Nelva's Noodles" from the backs of torn envelopes to clean white cards.

This year on her birthday she was reorganizing the bookshelves in the living room when she found the letter. It was stuck inside a book called *My Way of Life* by Joan Crawford, and it was addressed to her husband. Alice was shocked at first, and then later she felt angry. She hadn't known Martin had ever received a letter from Joan Crawford. It read:

Martin dear,
It was such a great joy to see you on Friday. What a delightful way to start the New Year. A new friend! You were an angel to send your personal note and my favorite roses—"Tropicana" the color—the scent is pure heaven. I hope Miami wasn't too bad and that you were successful with the casting of the young prince. Do keep

in touch. You have my number. Happy New Year in spite of Miami.

Love, Joan

Alice kicked the dog off the couch and sat down amid piles of books and reread the letter. She looked at the envelope to see when the letter had been mailed and discovered it was sent a year before Martin's death.

It was just like Martin to visit Joan Crawford and never tell her about it! Martin had that cool ability to never tell all, to keep pieces of his life secreted away. It irritated her when he was alive and now it was irritating her when he was dead. Somehow Martin had gotten the notion that he could be a producer of plays, after years in the cast-iron business. He took a sizable portion of the family fortunes and dumped the money into ill-fated theatrical ventures and went gallivanting around, looking for stars. People were happy to talk to him, given his readiness to bankroll big productions. Worst of all, he didn't take Alice with him but once or twice. He roamed the world like Gulliver. His taste in plays was terrible. He backed an Indian sex saga called *Punjab Secrets* and tried to make a musical out of Admiral Byrd's account of a year spent alone in the Antarctic. All this happened within the two or three years that preceded his death of a heart attack at forty-eight. It seemed to Alice that Martin had just burned himself up with his new-found passion, and the man she found stone-cold dead beside her in bed one morning hardly resembled the man she had married, the Martin G. Linder III of the Linder Flag Pole Co., of Wynette, Virginia.

Alice didn't like the tone of the Joan Crawford letter. For one thing, it didn't seem very sincere. You didn't sign letters "love" when you'd just met somebody. And all those phrases like "great joy" and "delightful way to start the year" and the scent of roses being "pure heaven" sounded phony. Theatrical. "You were an angel . . . " Who talked that way except actresses?

Alice stared at the cover of *My Way of Life*, a picture of Joan Crawford holding two French poodles on her lap. She tried to imagine Martin sitting on that couch in that living room with that woman and her two poodles. Martin was so big he could break a couch if he sat down on it the wrong way, especially a spindly modern one like Joan Crawford's. She wished he had broken Joan Crawford's couch and upended her and the poodles. She was relishing the image of Joan Crawford sprawled on the floor with her dogs when the doorbell rang.

A United Parcel man was at the door. He asked Alice to sign on line sixteen, and as Alice took the clipboard from him, she caught him staring at the letter in her hand.

"Wow," he said, "is that really from Joan Crawford?"

Alice said that it was.

"That's incredible." The man tilted his head sideways to look at the letterhead. "I'm not reading what she wrote, I just wanted to see the stationery. I'm a paper collector so you gotta understand how much I appreciate something like this. I would love to see what her signature looks like."

Alice turned the letter over and showed him the signature. "What's a paper collector?" she asked, taking notice of him for the first time. He was older than she'd first thought, not a delivery boy but a middle-aged man, rather slight and tall and pink-complexioned, with very nice blue eyes.

"Anybody who collects paper goods. It can be posters, autographs, letters, anything printed on paper that's got some value and is collectible. This is definitely collectible. It's probably worth about five hundred dollars, maybe more."

"It's not worth anything to me," Alice said. "I just found it in a book. It was written to my husband. I didn't even know he knew Joan Crawford."

The man thought he sensed in her voice a bitterness, perhaps some jealousy that bespoke infidelity on her husband's part. But that the other woman was Joan Crawford! That was almost an honor. He wondered if he could get her to sell the letter. Instantly he regretted mentioning how much it might be worth. If it meant nothing to her, maybe she would have even given it to him. The same old beast turned in him that had been there since he was a child, the beast of acquisition at any price, the lust for a signature or an image on a stamp or a cigarette card. What he wanted now was "Joan," scrawled on pale blue paper. He must move quickly, before she closed the door on him. He decided on the direct approach.

"Do you think your husband would be interested in selling the letter?"

"My husband is dead."

The man looked embarrassed and Alice felt sorry for him. He was so obviously interested in the letter. His sincerity was evident in those nice, blue eyes. Why look a gift horse in the mouth? Here was a personable man, perhaps her only visitor on this birthday. Why not prolong the occasion?

"So it's worth about five hundred?" she said.

"Joan Crawford's signature? Sure. She's been dead a while; that increases the value of something like this." He immediately regretted mentioning death again, thinking of her deceased husband.

"There's a date on the envelope," Alice said. "Do you want to come in and I'll show it to you?"

He followed her into a small room where the drapes were drawn against the light and almost tripped over a dog lying in the shadows. There were stacks of books everywhere, on the floor, couch, chairs, and a nice clean smell, like furniture polish, pervaded the room.

"So, you're a collector, too?"

"I don't get you," Alice said.

The man pointed to a shelf of porcelain dolls.

"I never thought of myself as such."

"It takes a certain kind of mentality to collect anything. Lots of people collect dolls. They've gotten real valuable."

"Are you from Wynette?" Alice asked.

"Greenville. I deliver in Wynette, Greenville, as far north as the sugar factory."

"My husband had a foundry near Greenville. Linder Flag Pole Company. Heard of it?"

"Oh, sure."

"He was in the cast-iron business, but later on in his life he also produced plays. That's how he came to meet people like Joan Crawford."

"Sounds very interesting." He wondered if she'd forgotten she was going to get the envelope. "What's your name?"

"Alice Linder."

"I'm Arnold Morris." He sat down on the sofa and crossed his legs and folded his hands in his lap.

"I've been collecting paper since I was a small boy. There was a theater in Greenville. The old Odeon, remember that movie house?"

"Oh, certainly. My mother used to take me there when my father was out of town. On Sycamore Street, wasn't it?"

"That's the place. I started going through the trash behind the Odeon, looking for movie posters they threw out. I got quite a collection of movie posters that way, some of them real valuable now. Later I collected stamps and cigarette cards, and then autographs." As Arnold spoke, some moral prompter told him he shouldn't try to weasel this letter out of Alice Linder, but offer her some price she'd consider fair.

"The envelope's stuck somewhere in here," Alice said, handing him *My Way of Life*.

Instead of the envelope, Arnold found two more letters. One was from Greer Garson, the other from the Prime Minister of Australia.

"My God," he said, "Greer Garson! Mrs. Miniver." He held up the embossed envelope and stared at the name.

Alice snatched the envelope from his hand. "Well," she said, "imagine that, these old letters turning up," and tried to sound calm. She sat down next to him on the couch and crossed her legs, which were straight and thin with almost no definition of a calf. He noticed her thick stockings were the color of the flesh on dolls, and the brown brogues on her feet seemed to add a dangerous amount of weight to her thin ankles.

Alice read the two letters. The one from Greer Garson said

much as she liked Martin's idea for the play, she didn't think she was right for it:

> It's all delightful fun, but I feel that the eye-filling designs and the music and comedy carry the show, and you really don't need me. Had we met earlier (ah!!!) you might have framed the show a little differently . . . but I must say I love it the way it is now.

The letter from the Prime Minister of Australia was a dry, short note thanking Martin for his contribution at the opening ceremonies of the Sydney Opera House. "Nice letters," Alice said weakly, looking up at Arnold.

Arnold pushed the lank hair away from his forehead and smiled at her. "Some people wouldn't find anything at all interesting about a signature. But I do. It's like an incarnation of a person. I think of the hand that held the pen."

Alice nodded as if she were listening more carefully than she was. What would have happened had Martin met Greer Garson earlier? Alice might have been out in the cold. How could she, who had failed to excel at anything in life except gardening, compete with a gorgeous and talented woman like Greer Garson? She consoled herself by thinking of the eye-filling designs of her own garden. Had Greer Garson ever produced hydrangeas of such a deep blue as to cause passersby to stop at her front gate and stare?

"Can I look at that Greer Garson letter? I wouldn't read it if you didn't want me to, just look at the signature."

"Oh, you can read it," Alice said. "I don't care." She handed the letter to Arnold, and then began nervously twisting her handkerchief in her hands, binding her fingers together as if attending to some suppurating wound.

"Well, that's the closest I'm ever going to get to Greer Garson," Arnold said after reading the letter. "Your husband must have wanted her to be in a play?"

Alice, who was still thinking about her shortcomings as a

person compared to Greer Garson, simply nodded. Arnold handed her the letter. Alice scanned it again and was struck by its gracious tone, so different from the false note Joan Crawford had struck.

It occurred to Arnold that there might be boxes of letters like this somewhere in this house. Hundreds of signatures of famous people, stashed away where no one could appreciate their worth and beauty. He could already imagine him and Alice becoming friendlier and friendlier until one day they would sit down together and go through her husband's old files (Boxes in the garage? A desk in his study?) and search for the signatures. He would help her understand the value of different letters and in exchange she would let him have his pick. They would both profit! He would leave her richer by showing her what she had in her possession!

"Did you ever have the opportunity to meet Greer Garson?" he asked.

"Oh, yes." The lie came out spontaneously. Once told, Alice felt the need to elaborate. "She was very imposing, you know, like Eleanor Roosevelt and with that same grand manner. Not uppity. Not stuck-up, if you know what I mean, but very—what do I want to say?—"

"Self-possessed?" Arnold offered.

"Yes, like that—confident, sure of herself, like she could handle any situation. She was rather sparkly, all the things I've wanted to be in my life and never was." Alice laughed.

Arnold regarded Alice with deep admiration. She was so self-effacing and humble, so nonchalant about her firsthand experience of celebrities.

"What about Joan Crawford? Ever meet her?"

"Uh, no, I never met Joan Crawford."

"She was good when she was young. Remember her in *Grand Hotel*? A sexy little minx. Later on she got stiff, acted like a zombie."

A silence lay between them, and then Arnold spoke up. "If you ever wanted to add to your doll collection, I know a woman who owns a shop in Roanoke with some good dolls at very fair prices and I wouldn't mind at all driving down there. There's a stamp store on the same street."

Roanoke was a hundred miles away! He was willing to drive from Wynette to Roanoke just to look at dolls and stamps. In an odd way, the idea appealed to Alice. They could stop at fruit stands on the way. She remembered a cousin in Marbleton; they could pay her a visit. In Roanoke they could eat at Green's Restaurant where she used to dine with her mother when they were in town to shop for school clothes.

She looked at the shelf of dolls. "I wouldn't mind adding another."

"I think you're a collector at heart." Arnold laughed.

Suddenly there was a loud clapping noise, which came from somewhere in the rooms off to Arnold's right and sounded as if something had broken or fallen closed, although Arnold couldn't have guessed what it was. Alice jumped up and stood frozen in the middle of the room, a slat of light intersecting her body, and then she brought the hankie she held to her mouth and said, "Oh, heaven help me, I got him." She took a few steps backward and eased herself down into the chair. "Oh, Lord," she said, "what do I do now?"

"What's the matter?"

"Oh, Lord," she said again. "I've got a rat. There's been a rat coming into my kitchen, eating anything left out. I tried poison and when that didn't work I set a trap this morning."

"That was the trap that just went off?"

Alice nodded.

Arnold smiled. He could see himself being helpful here. One good turn deserved another, and so on.

"Where's the trap?"

"On top of the refrigerator."

"Maybe we should go in and take a look—"

"No, wait a minute. I can't face it just yet."

"Look," Arnold said, standing up and smoothing the creases from the front of his uniform, "this isn't something a lady ought to have to take care of. Lucky I was here, I say. Why don't you let me dispose of the rat?"

"No-o-o-o," Alice said, standing up. "It isn't your problem. Besides, I'm not really the squeamish sort, really I'm not. I just look that way."

"Not at all! I just don't see why you should be bothered with this when I can do it for you. Just point me to the kitchen and get me a paper sack or something."

"The paper collector needs a paper sack!" Alice said, impressed by his gallantry. She really was very glad he was here, but she wasn't going to let him take over her responsibility.

"I tell you what, Mr.—?"

"Morris."

"Mr. Morris, we'll do this together. A little camaraderie in the face of the enemy, eh? You come with me and we'll just dispose of Mr. Rat together, unless I'm keeping you too long from your work."

"Oh, no, that's no problem. On my job, I'm my own boss. Besides, I don't have much left to do today." Already he was thinking she might invite him to stay for dinner. There was nothing in his fridge except boiled potatoes and kielbasa, his meal for the past two nights. No wife or children awaited him, only a cat who was fairly indifferent to his presence except at mealtime, when it rubbed his leg and went yow-yow-yow. There was no reason to rush home tonight. He would be willing to miss the special on TV he'd planned to watch. The thought of those letters made him wildly happy, as if life was made for adventures like this, for the company of a nice woman and the prospect of unearthing treasures.

"Just don't look at it," Arnold advised Alice as they headed for the kitchen. "Let me handle it."

"Still as a mouse in here, isn't it?" Alice giggled.

In the doorway of the kitchen, Alice let out a scream and backed into Arnold, who was standing right behind her. He couldn't see what she was screaming about until he took hold of her shoulders and moved her to one side. There was the rat, a few feet away, crawling toward them across the kitchen floor, leaving a trail of bright red blood. The rat's progress was slow; he lurched like an unsteady baby taking its first steps. He looked up with bright beady eyes and let out a terrible squeak, and then began convulsing.

Alice couldn't bear it. As repulsive as the rat was, all she could think about was putting it out of its misery.

"We've got to kill it, now!" she said. But Arnold didn't move. He just stared at the place near the rat's neck that shuddered and heaved rhythmically as if responding to a musical beat. He thought he might be sick.

Alice grabbed a broom by the door and brushed the rat across the floor toward the door that led to the backyard. It wasn't like sweeping dirt: a feeling of life came up through the broom handle as the rat rolled over and over, squeaking and bleeding. Again and again she made eye contact with the rat and felt some ferocious connection with him. A living thing, a mammal like herself! He seemed so solid and heavy against the broom.

Arnold froze. He wanted to say, Here! Let me do it, but he couldn't move. The blood horrified him. There was a thin trail of blood down the front of the refrigerator, and one leading across the floor. It wasn't dark blood, but pale and watery, a bright and festive pink.

Alice called, "Get the door," but Arnold didn't move.

"The door," she said. "Hold it open for me."

Finally he crossed the room and opened the door. Alice batted the rat over the threshold and onto the lawn and with a red hoe, pounded its head until it lay lifeless. Then she got a plastic bag from the kitchen and, using the hoe, pushed the rat into the bag and carried it to the trash.

Arnold felt foolish. He had been no help at all. Alice got out rubber gloves and a yellow pail that she filled with water and detergent and wiped up the blood, first from the floor and then from the refrigerator, using a stepladder to reach the top. She talked to him as she worked: "How he got out of the trap, I don't know. I don't even see the trap, it must have fallen down here behind the fridge. Well, it can just stay there. I've had enough for today, haven't you? Those traps don't kill, they just maim. Poor thing! Rats have such a bad name, don't they? And yet, they're not much different than squirrels. Squirrels carry disease, too, but we don't kill them. I think it must be the tail, that awfully ugly tail rats have. Well, that's done." She pulled off the rubber gloves and rinsed out the pail and put it back beneath the counter. Arnold watched her, grateful for her sensibleness, her matter-of-fact attitude.

"I feel like I could use a drink. How about you, Mr. Morris? Join me in a Scotch?"

Arnold nodded. He felt badly shaken up, like the time in the war when he'd come upon a corpse with a pig rooting in its body cavity. He broke down and was sent home. He didn't have good nerves anymore, couldn't take the sight of blood. He hadn't expected there would be any blood with the rat.

They sat in the living room, the letters lying on the table between them. Alice had color in her cheeks that hadn't been there when Arnold first arrived. Her hands were steady. The handkerchief was tucked into place in the sleeve of her dress. Wisps of hair had come loose from the bun at the nape of her neck and curled softly around her face. Arnold hadn't found her attractive until this moment. She chattered. He was very grateful for her chatter. Slowly, he began to recover.

"I'm certainly glad you were here, Mr. Morris." She felt like he had turned up fortuitously, like that young prince Joan Crawford had mentioned in her letter, the one Martin had been seeking in Miami.

"You did it all," Arnold said. "To tell you the truth, it made me a little sick. I know I wasn't much help."

"Oh no-no-no, that's not true. Why, I would have had a terrible time without you here. Moral support, Mr. Morris, that's what you provided. Camaraderie in the face of the enemy!"

They had a second Scotch. It felt quite like a birthday then, and Alice lifted her glass. "It's my birthday today. I propose a toast. Not to me, but to you, Mr. Morris, for showing up at the right time, and for your . . . steadfastness!"

"I couldn't really drink to my steadfastness. Let's drink to your birthday."

Alice sipped her Scotch primly. Arnold tipped his glass until the ice cubes collided and drink spilled down his shirt. Alice offered him her handkerchief and had to resist the temptation to wipe the front of his shirt for him.

"Would you like this letter?" She held out the Joan Crawford letter to him. "I'd like you to have it, since you're the paper collector. You can appreciate it. To me, it's just a reminder of . . . of the husband I lost."

Arnold took the letter, feeling humble. "Thank you very much, thank you," he said.

"And the envelope," she said. "It's here somewhere."

While she thumbed through *My Way of Life,* looking for the envelope embossed with the name of the mythical movie queen, Arnold said, "There's a real good special on TV tonight on whales."

"Oh really?" Alice said, distracted.

"If you like we could watch it together and I could take you out for a birthday dinner."

"But—" Alice started to say, and Arnold thought, She's going to say, but I've got plans. Of course she would have plans, someone like Alice, somebody who'd met Greer Garson.

"But I've got pork chops I've already thawed," Alice said. "We could eat here."

Arnold bought champagne at the Wynette Liquor Store and finished his deliveries while Alice started the preparations for dinner. As she waited for Arnold to return, quite suddenly, and with what seemed like a dangerous amount of abandon, she decided to change out of her thick stockings and everyday shoes, and her cotton shirtwaist dress, and after canvassing her closet, she put on something quite different and altogether more daring.

GOING OUT
TO SEA

The baby was very sick and the doctor didn't think it had six months without an operation, which could not be performed in their hometown. It couldn't even be performed in their state. The doctor mentioned three possibilities to them: Minnesota, Texas, and Massachusetts. Take your choice, he said. Since Dale, the baby's dad, was also looking for a place to go to college, they chose Minnesota, where he was accepted at the university, and even given a tuition scholarship.

It was the first time either one of them had left their home state of Utah for anything but a vacation, and they had never been east of the Rockies for any reason. Preparations for the move took several weeks. At the last minute, they decided to take the dog rather than leave him with friends. Fortunately, he was a good traveler and would pose no problems on the cross-country trip.

They drove to Minnesota, stopping at night to put up a large tent in campgrounds along the way. Every morning they awoke to a day more humid than the one before. The farther east they went, the heavier the air became. The night they spent on the banks of a river in Iowa, the baby cried and kept people in nearby tents awake. In the morning, while Dale took down the tent and packed the car, Marva carried the baby to the restrooms and gave him a bath in the sink. One of the campers, an older woman who had been kept awake by the baby's cries, complained to Marva.

"That baby kept me awake all night."

"He doesn't feel well," Marva said.

"You should stay in a motel then. I don't come camping to hear a baby howl all night."

Marva felt her face burning. She dried off the baby's feet. Each toenail had a bluish cast, as did the baby's fingernails and lips. If it weren't for the fingernails and toenails and lips, it would be difficult to tell there was anything wrong with the baby. Except he was awfully small. He was about half the size he should be for his age. And he was thin, too, which made his head seem oversized. Sometimes the baby made her think of pictures she'd seen of children in concentration camps. His eyes were the biggest thing about him.

She felt injured by the woman's remarks. She couldn't shake off the bad feelings. In fact, it made her mad this woman lacked any understanding of the situation. She stood at the sink with angry words forming in her mind. Why don't you stay at a motel? What's the big deal about a baby crying? Again, she wanted to say, He doesn't feel well, don't you see? But she couldn't say anything. Things were so stuck inside her when it came to the baby that she felt if she said one thing, a whole bunch of stuff might come out. Anyway, the woman turned and left. As the door slammed shut, the baby blinked, startled by the noise.

"What a good boy," she said. She lifted the baby up to the light and dried his bottom. Dozens of moths, trapped against the windowpanes, flapped and made a hum like electricity coursing through wires. The baby responded to the sight of the buzzing moths by waving his arms.

"Oh boy," she said. "Oh boy."

"I'm starving," she said to her husband. "Can't we get off the freeway and get something to eat?"

"Sure," he said, but it was miles before they saw an exit ramp that looked promising. She could see a McDonald's and a Wendy's and a Burger King, all clustered together just off the freeway, near some service stations.

"Let's just eat in the car," she said. "I don't want to wake him." She looked at the baby sleeping in a plastic carrier on the back seat.

"It'd be nice to go inside and get out of the heat."

"He'd just start fussing if I woke him and I couldn't enjoy my food."

"We could leave him in the car. We can roll down the windows and park where we could watch the car."

"We can't leave him in the car," she said.

"No, I guess we can't."

"It's just so hot, isn't it?" She stuck to the seat. Her legs prickled from sweating and she felt like she wanted to scratch all over. "Jeez-Louise. I just want to get cool."

"You and me both."

"I wish they had an Arctic Circle," she said. She liked their burgers. She especially liked the sauce they gave you, a combination of catsup and mayonnaise all mixed together to make a smooth coral paste.

"I haven't seen an Arctic Circle since we left Utah," he said. "Maybe they don't have them out here. So what's it going to be? McDonald's or Burger King?"

"Burger King, I guess."

While he went for the burgers, she flipped through a copy of *Western Horseman* she found beneath the front seat. Something had spilled on the magazine and pages were stuck together. It opened to an article on teaching your horse to accept the correct lead.

Before leaving Utah, they'd sold their horses and a horse trailer that was practically new. There wouldn't be any place for horses in Minnesota, of that they were pretty sure. But it bothered her that she didn't know what their lives would be like. Where would they live? Would they find a house to rent or live in an apartment building? Would they be right in the city or outside of it? Would little Roy be perfectly normal after the operation? She didn't have any idea what they were getting into. It was like driving off into a void, leaving everything behind without knowing what was at the other end, like a pioneer or a space traveler. It made her sad to think of the horses belonging to somebody else, but what else could they do? Roy needed the operation, they had to go someplace. There's nothing you can't go back to, she told herself. If we don't like Minnesota, we don't have to stay there. Once Roy was fixed, they could go anywhere they wanted. She turned to look at the baby and noticed he'd opened his eyes.

"What are you looking at with those big black eyes?" she asked him. It was more humid today than yesterday, and the heat felt worse. The dog was curled up on the seat beside the baby's carrier. He was panting hard and every once in a while, drops of saliva fell from his tongue and splashed on the seat. The girl couldn't have imagined air could feel so wet without it raining. Holding the magazine above the baby's head, she fanned him, but it seemed to irritate him, and he started to cry. She played peekaboo with a clean diaper until he stopped. She watched her husband come out of the restaurant and look both ways before crossing the parking lot.

"I got some Tater Tots and a couple of cherry pies," he said. "Also, some milk for the bruiser."

"He doesn't seem to have any appetite."

"Who does in this heat?"

"Me for one." But when she looked at the hamburger, it didn't look at all appetizing. The meat was thin and dry and had been pressed into an unnatural-looking square, and it was corrugated, like cardboard.

"You make a mistake," he said, "if you look at this stuff too closely before you eat it."

"You can say that again." She fed the burger to the dog, who ate it in one gulp, and then she took a cherry pie and broke it in half.

"Now what are you doing?" he asked.

"Somebody did research and found out they only put about two cherries in these things," she said.

"Don't worry about it."

"Gah-wah," the baby said, reaching for the dog. Everything was gah-wah to the baby.

"Did it feel like this when you went in the navy?" she asked.

"Did it feel like what?"

"Like you were headed for the most unfamiliar place on earth?"

"Sort of," he said. "I guess you could say it felt like that. No matter how much you imagine a place before you get there, it isn't anything like what you think it's going to be. Nobody could've told me what it was going to feel like to be on a ship in the middle of the ocean."

"Was it better or worse than you thought?"

"Just different. For one thing, at night when you're standing on deck and you look out at the horizon, it feels like you're higher than the stars. You're actually looking down on some of those stars. It feels like the earth curves more out there on the water. Want any more of these Tater Tots?"

"No, you finish them. Tell me more about what it was like in the navy."

At sea, he said, everything was quite different. Many times, toward evening, there were thunderstorms and the water glistened in the distance like a lizard's underbelly. Later, the moon was hidden by ragged patches of cloud, which the wind blew into zigzags, crosses, and triangles. These shapes were lit up as if from within. The water was more monotonous than the land; after a while, jut a little change in the shape of the swells seemed remarkable. She listened to him with appreciation of how the navy had made him much more knowledgeable of the world than she was.

"Sounds nice," she said. "But who knows what Minnesota will be like."

"Land of lakes," he said. "I hear there's water everywhere, hundreds of lakes, some right in the city. Everything's green. It's supposed to be beautiful."

"I guess it's better than Texas."

During the last days of the trip, the baby got much worse, and the first thing they did when they arrived in the Twin Cities was to ask directions to the hospital. There, in the emergency room, the baby was undressed and placed on a table where he was examined by several doctors. A nurse took the girl into another room and asked her lots of questions about the baby's medical history, while the boy stayed with the baby. These were questions she'd answered so many times they no longer seemed to refer to anything real but were like stories she'd memorized in school. They hardly applied to the baby or her at all. They always asked what religion you were, and she always said, latter-day Saint. They always asked if anybody in her family died of cancer or was diabetic. They wanted to know if there'd been any problems with the pregnancy, but the truth, which was she'd had terrible morning sickness and taken a variety of pills to try and cure it, didn't seem to interest them at all. But that was the thing that worried her. Had she done something to cause the baby's problems?

When she'd finished answering the questions, she joined her husband and the doctors. The baby was breathing hard and seemed feverish. His stomach was swollen and his chest, naked and bluish under the harsh lights, bulged on the left side where, beneath his ribs, his heart labored to squeeze blood through its malformed chambers. Someone had put a mark in blue ink on his stomach. Her husband said the doctor had done it to mark the position of the baby's liver.

"His liver's depressed. He's in heart failure. He's running a high fever," he said to her, summarizing the situation.

The doctor said the first thing was to bring the baby's fever down, and then treat the congestive failure. To get the fever down, the baby was placed in a small plastic tub of water. Ice cubes were added to the water, and one by one they melted, just as they did when she added them to Jell-O to make it set up faster. It must be unpleasant for him, she thought, lying in icy water, but after the initial shock he didn't cry, just said gah-wah a few times and reached for her hair when she bent over him. By early morning Roy's temperature had dropped and he was taken to the pediatrics ward on the second floor and placed in a room with an oxygen tent covering his bed.

The doctor took them aside and explained the situation to them. The surgeon they'd been told to contact would see the baby the next afternoon, but it was clear that surgery was out of the question until the baby was stronger. The doctor felt it might take several weeks, perhaps a month, of hospital care before surgery could be attempted, but only the surgeon could determine this. Meanwhile, the doctor, regarding them kindly, said, "You should get some rest, you look like you need it." The doctor's kindness threatened her more than the camper's rudeness had. She felt herself very vulnerable before such kindness and, taking her husband's arm, she pulled him toward the elevators.

After leaving the hospital, they drove until they came to the first motel, the Paul Bunyan Inn on Snelling Avenue, and they took a room and began unloading their things from the car. The dog, who had been cooped up overnight, trotted around the parking lot on stiff legs and looked happy to be loose. Dale threw a ball for him, and the dog skidded after it. After a while, Dale poured some food out of a Friskies bag into a metal bowl and set it down near the curb. While the dog ate, he sat on the curb and occasionally stroked his back. Watching her husband and the dog from inside the motel room, Marva felt the absence of the baby as something strangely light and exhilarating. She looked beyond the parking lot at some stores and empty fields. So far, it didn't look like they were anywhere new. It just looked like everywhere else. From a machine near the motel office, she bought a Coke and some peanut-butter-and-cheese crackers. Then she drew the thick drapes to block out the daylight and got into bed, and, lying in the dark, she ate her crackers, finished the Coke, and fell asleep, full and with a sweet taste in her mouth.

It was luck that took over after they arrived in Minnesota. They met some people in church named Pingree who were also from Utah, and the Pingrees offered them a place to stay rent-free for three months. Dr. Pingree was going to Brigham Young University as a visiting lecturer for the summer. They moved from the Paul Bunyan Inn into the Pingrees' house exactly a week after they arrived in Minnesota.

The Pingrees had a very nice house. As soon as they moved in, Marva began worrying about the dog. The carpets in the house were almost white and she worried about the dog peeing on the carpet. She worried about dirt, too, and she made a rule that they wouldn't wear shoes on the carpet. The furniture in the house looked very expensive. The first time the dog got up on the couch, she scolded him. Then he tried a chair and she chained him outside, until his sorrowful looks caused her to relent and she let him come inside again. "Stay off the furniture!" she said to him.

Everything in the house matched. The drapes matched the bedspreads, the chairs matched the couch, the towels matched the wallpaper. Just like in decorator magazines. Things were so nice it made her nervous. She felt responsible. Whenever she went out walking the dog, she made certain to wipe his feet off with an old towel before she let him inside again.

The house was a block from a lake. The Pingrees had left them a canoe, beach balls, a raft, and even snorkeling equipment. Use the private beach reserved for homeowners, they had said. They had also introduced them to Bert and Effie, their affable neighbors, who lived in a two-story house at the entrance to the private beach.

One night, shortly after they moved in, they paddled across to a monastery on the far side of the lake. Remembering her husband's words, she looked for clouds scudding across the moon, shaped by the winds into zigzags, crosses, and triangles. But the clouds were dark and thick. From time to time, however, a reddish fragment of moon could be glimpsed through the smoky apparitions, as it appeared, disappeared, and reappeared, like a warning lantern drifting across the sky.

They left the canoe on the beach and walked to a thicket of woods and sat down on a stone bench. Sounds came to them on the warm night air: a rustling of some creature in the woods, water lapping at the sand, voices drifting from the houses that hugged the shore.

"It's like we're on vacation," he said.

"Or like we became rich overnight."

Before leaving Utah, they'd lived in a house that cost forty dollars a month. The baby slept on an enclosed porch near the washer and dryer. In the winter, Vizqueen was tacked over windows to help keep the cold out, but it blurred the world and gave it a filmy whiteness, and still snow as fine as dandruff crept under doors and scudded along the floors, driven by drafts from room to room. Now they were in a two-story house and had a canoe to take out on the lake whenever they wanted.

They talked about the baby for a while.

"I think everything's going to be OK," he said. He added, "I think the operation will be OK."

"Oh, I know it will," she said.

She went to the hospital every day to be with little Roy, and he went to his classes at the university, which was not far from the hospital. Both places overlooked the Mississippi River, a slow, murky channel of water that wasn't nearly so wide at this point as it was a little farther south. Every day before she left the house she placed chairs at the entrance to the living room, creating a barricade to prevent the dog from getting onto the carpet. She did the same thing with the dining room. She closed the doors to the bedrooms so he couldn't get up on the beds. She put stacks of books on the couch in the TV room to keep him from climbing onto the cushions. At night, she put chairs against every door that led outside so he wouldn't scratch the molding like he did when he wanted to go out. The dog still wasn't used to not being able to roam at night like he had before they moved to Minnesota, and they were often kept awake by his pacing.

One night, watching her make these preparations, her husband asked her if this was really necessary.

"I don't want anything to happen," she said. "We're responsible if it does." She pushed another chair against the door.

"But this seems a little excessive to me," he said.

Later, in bed, he said, "Come here."

She got close to him and yet, when he tried to make love, she stopped him. She said she was thinking about the baby.

"I thought it was going to be different," he said.

"I did too," she said, "but it isn't."

"I thought it would be over with by now."

"And we're still waiting."

"Still waiting," he repeated.

"I went to the beach today," she said. "Effie was there so I talked to her for a while. She had some oxtail soup in a thermos. All her kids were with her. They were having a picnic at the beach. So I had some soup with them."

"I've seen her kids jumping on a trampoline. How many kids does she have?"

"Seven, I think. I've got the recipe for the soup," she said. "I thought I'd make some."

It was hard waiting for the operation, but it would have been harder if they hadn't had the canoe, the screened-in porch to barbecue on at night, the nice neighborhood where they walked the dog along streets that wound up and down past expensive houses with large lawns and beautiful trees. The Pingrees had a pool table downstairs and they played pool and watched TV. They got to know Effie and her husband, Bert. Effie and Bert invited them to dinner, and they in turn asked them for a barbecue one Friday. But early on, she said to him, "Let's not tell Effie and Bert about the baby."

"Why not?"

"I get tired of sympathy," she said. What she meant was, Effie and the lake were immutably connected in her mind as a place to go to be free of thinking about Roy and the hospital visits and the upcoming operation. She didn't want Effie talking to her about these things. The lake was just beginning to feel like the one pure place in the world, a true escape from problems.

The baby didn't improve as quickly as everyone had hoped, but neither did he get worse. He seemed lethargic, although not in much pain. He lay in his plastic tent, day after day listening to the soft hiss of the oxygen while a mist as fine as spindrift collected in droplets on his hair. She knew what it felt like inside the tent. She often sat on a chair beside the bed, with her head and shoulders inside the plastic, talking to the baby, holding toys up for his inspection, turning the pages of little books, whose covers gradually warped from the moisture. It was like being back in Utah in the house with Vizqueen over the windows. Everything muted, milky, and soft. When she thought of this, she laughed and said aloud to little Roy, "We've spent half our lives behind plastic."

Roy was smart, she could tell. But he refused to learn how to talk. In this he was behind other children.

In an effort to get as many credits as possible, he began taking classes at night. At first she minded being left alone several nights a week, but then it just became part of the routine that constituted their lives. She became addicted to the sitcoms that played on the nights he was gone. With so much more free time, she decided to learn how to cook better, and when he came home from classes, she surprised him with new meals.

One night, when she set the food on the table, he said, "What's this?"

"Onion-cheese sandwich," she said. "It's Effie's recipe."

He took a bite and chewed the food a long time.

"How did you make this?"

"It's very easy. You just take bread and put mayonnaise on the inside. Then you put on cheese and a thick slice of onion and put the sandwich together. Then you butter the outside of the sandwich and fry it on high until the cheese melts all over the onion and it's brown on the outside."

"I see."

"Maybe it got a little burned on the outside."

"I think it did."

"The cheese should have melted more."

"All I can taste is onion. It's like eating a slab of onion on two pieces of bread. Burned bread."

"Win some, lose some. Don't eat it if you don't like it."

"Is there anything else?"

"I think there's a little chicken left in the fridge."

He got up and began removing plates and bottles of food from the refrigerator. It didn't seem to matter how hard you tried to make something come out right, she thought. Either it did, or it didn't. Was this luck or timing or what? So many things were uncontrollable, even when you thought you had control. Outside, fireflies moved along the hedge, their lights going on and off like car blinkers. Even at this distance, she could hear the frogs down at the lake, and she suddenly wanted to be skimming the black waters, riding the canoe, dipping her paddle first on one side, then the other.

He came back to the table with a piece of chicken in his hand, a thigh and a leg. Where the thigh had been wrenched from the torso, the pink socket glistened like a piece of pretty plastic jewelry.

"There's something I want to tell you," he said. "I've met somebody at school. I want you to know right now that it isn't sexual. I mean, I haven't slept with her. It's not like that. But I'm getting a lot of emotional support from her. She's a psychology student. She listens to me when I need to talk."

She wondered, at first, if the frogs had suddenly, for inexplicable reasons, gotten much louder, or whether the silence in the room was simply so intense that she'd pulled all the noise in closer to her, just to fill her mind. She went over what he'd said, as if his words were like a passage in a book that was particularly elusive and required a second reading. There was somebody else. A girl at the university, a psychology student, whom he hadn't slept with, but who gave him emotional support. He could talk to her, she listened. They talked, presumably when they met on campus. She tried to fit these two people into a context. Yes, they must meet at the university. Fellow students. A realm she'd never entered.

He had told her these things, but why? What did he expect from her? Acceptance? If the girl was just a friend then nothing mattered, but if he was drifting into a love affair, what made him think that she, his wife, would want to drift into it with him? Wouldn't it be much better not to know?

"I don't want to know," she said.

"I felt like I needed to tell you. I didn't want to feel like I was hiding something."

She said nothing.

"I could have used you, you know," he added. "Several times lately I really could have used you. I needed you, Marva. But it didn't feel like you were there."

She knew what he was talking about. People make cases out of these things, for or against the wife or husband. But whose fault was it that you didn't have sex? When it stopped, it was a very hard thing to get going again. To bring things within the range of sex again, it seemed like they would have to start over, and how do you start over when you're already there? It would be like taking a trip to Hong Kong, getting to Hong Kong, feeling bad and wanting to go back and start all over again. You can't afford it. You're already in Hong Kong. The only thing you can do then is stay in Hong Kong and try to make the best of it. This idea made so much sense to her, it seemed to explain so much of what was happening to them, that she told him word for word what she had just been thinking.

"I don't know where you get all this crap about Hong Kong," he said.

Truthfully, at that moment, neither did she. As soon as she said it, it sounded all wrong, like crazy talk.

She started laughing. "I guess we're not in Hong Kong. We're in the Twin Cities, aren't we?"

"I'm telling you something here," he said wearily.

"And I'm listening."

"I want so much for things to work out but I'm hanging by a thread these days emotionally. She helps me and I don't want to have to give her up. I don't want to feel bad about it either. So that's why I told you."

After a while, she said, "What's her name?"

"Bobbin," he said.

"Bobbin?"

"Yes, Bobbin."

"Bobbin?" she screamed. "That's a goddamned sewing machine part!" She ran out of the kitchen. When she got to the master bedroom, she closed the door and threw herself across the bed. She thought, I would like to shuffle off this mortal coil. That was her father's phrase. Shuffle off the mortal coil. See the wires holding you break away so you can ascend some place, free, unfettered. Shuffle off. To Buffalo, to Hong Kong, the mortal coil. Unwinding in one great looping length, it trails behind you, falling away, a ribbon in space. These words, Buffalo, Hong Kong, mortal coil, and something ineffable and quite wonderful behind them, calmed her, soothing her until she felt enclosed, as if by a blanket of warm air, and fell asleep.

Sometime in the night she was awakened by a small scratching sound. The dog! She'd forgotten to put the chairs by the door and the dog, seeking an escape, had put thin, deep grooves in the woodwork. She turned on the hall light and stood staring at the damage. "Bad dog!" she said, and the animal slumped on his haunches. His ears flattened. He looked broken and sad, his spirit depressed. When he ventured to look up at her, it was if he peered out from under a thick ledge that both threatened and protected him. All he needed to be released from his frozen condition of remorse was for her to say, in a tone low and warm, "Come here." Those were the redemptive words. She was so moved by his sorrowful looks that she knelt down and spoke to him. "Come here," she said. The dog, instantly relieved and light again, came to her and settled his head against her chest. She led him into the living room where it was softer on the white carpet and spoke to him, telling him it was all right.

He gave her all his attention and devotion and seemed eager for her stroking, for when she hesitated, and her hand rested lightly, inert on his head, he jerked his nose in the air, as if to say, Don't stop. As she sat with the dog, the name came back to her: Bobbin. So curiously cute and alive, a whirring little spinning part, feeding the thread that was caught by the needle. I'm hanging on by a thread, he had said, but now he was caught up by this whirring, spinning little object, growing stronger and thicker, the layers building around the bright and shiny spool. She imagined the thread stacking up with precision, row after row, adding up with mechanical beauty, going on endlessly.

The baby celebrated his second birthday in the hospital. Not much was done to mark the occasion, except they spent the entire afternoon on the children's ward, which meant he missed his daytime classes at the university, and she arrived later than usual, having spent the morning shopping for presents. They met at noon in the baby's room. They gave him a wheelchair ride up and down the hallway, visited with the women at the nursing station, and stopped in the game room.

The seasons had changed. Dr. Pingree, who had gotten an extension of his visiting professorship, had written to ask, Did they mind staying on in the house through December? It was now October, and the leaves on the trees outside the baby's window quivered red and gold in the breeze.

On the afternoon of his birthday, a light snow fell. The storm raised everyone's spirits. The hospital was more active than usual. The weather was something to be studied from windows, commented on, wondrously noted. The first snow! A festive spirit settled on the ward, and in the game room, the children, excited by the snow, were unusually restless and sometimes exuberant. They turned their fierce energy on each other and small battles erupted. The boy with leukemia, who was easily bruised, had to be taken back to his room after his mother exchanged sharp words with the parents of a mongoloid girl who'd begun throwing blocks. Nobody thought much of the argument. It was quickly forgotten. Everyone knew that on the children's ward emotions always ran high.

The snow continued to fall. The world outside looked harsh and bright with the added layer of white. Tires left ribbons of black on the street. Everything was dusted over. Only the river took the snow, devoured it, and made it nothing.

Late in the day, they saw Dr. Montoya, the surgeon.

"Maybe he's going to come talk to us."

She said, "Maybe so." Any chance to talk to the surgeon was welcomed, since it relieved the silent anticipation. When would Roy be operated on? Each time they spoke with Dr. Montoya, his words made a concrete impression on an otherwise unbroken landscape of waiting, like footsteps in snow, and engendered a feeling that someone wise and better-informed was leading the way.

But Dr. Montoya didn't come. They sat on their chairs, awaiting his visit, playing with Roy, watching the TV mounted on the wall. The day changed to night. All along the river, lights appeared in buildings and houses. Still, he didn't come. Finally Dale said he was going to the library to study. Marva didn't believe him. She just assumed he was going to meet Bobbin. But she said nothing.

Almost as soon as he'd left, Dr. Montoya appeared in the room. Usually he arrived with an entourage of attendants—residents and interns who accompanied him on his rounds. Tonight he was alone.

Dr. Montoya was from Nicaragua. Each time she'd spoken with him, she felt his kindness. This kindness unsettled her. Usually she had felt a patronizing attitude or a thinly veiled indifference from the doctors who had attended to Roy. It was as if the families of patients were a nuisance to them, people best dealt with abruptly. Dr. Montoya was different. She felt he took a more intimate interest in everything around him. He was extremely alert. When he spoke, she felt something quick and sharp about him, which she assumed to be his superior intelligence. He was also very handsome and elegant. Beneath his white coat, his shirts bore the monogram FCM—for Ferdinand Carlos Montoya—appearing in beautiful script on the pocket. He wore delicate tortoise-shell glasses. The nurses liked him for his easy humor.

"What's this sitting in the dark?" he said to her as he entered the room.

She smiled and got up to turn on the lights.

"I came to see Roy earlier today," he said. "I've come to the conclusion that we should operate. That doesn't mean I'm happy about it. We have no choice. It's a very tough situation. You know that, don't you?"

She nodded.

"It's lousy, in fact, if you don't mind my saying so. He has simply gotten to the point where he's not getting stronger. In fact, we see a certain decline. I wish I could be more optimistic, but I wouldn't be telling the truth. We should operate rather than wait any longer. The situation has peaked, so to say. He has improved to the maximum point."

She nodded. She imagined this peak, which at first took the form of a perfectly symmetrical mountain, like Fuji, and then changed to a graphlike chart, such as those used in geography books to indicate rainfall or population patterns.

She waited, though she had the feeling he expected her to say something now. He was looking at her, watching her closely.

He said, "You're from Utah?"

"Yes."

"There's excellent skiing there, I believe. I went to Alta last year. I almost broke my poor scrawny neck on those treacherous slopes."

"I love skiing," she said. "I miss it."

"You are probably what we would call an expert, right?"

"Well, I'm all right. Back home I used to ski whenever I could. I started young."

"Ah, so you are good, just as I thought."

He took out his stethoscope, and bent over Roy, who was

sleeping. She watched him move it gingerly from point to point on the baby's chest. When he'd finished, he pulled the baby's shirt down and touched him lightly on the stomach. He let his hand lie on the boy for a few moments and gazed steadily at him.

Then he sat down opposite her.

"Do you mind me asking you something personal?"

"No."

"How old are you?"

"Eighteen," she said. Something made her ask, "How old are you?" and she saw he was caught by surprise.

"Thirty-seven," he said.

"I don't think you look that old."

"You're a very generous person," he said, smiling, and added that he didn't think she looked as old as she was either.

"My husband's twenty-three," she said.

"You're very young to have a two-year-old child, especially young to have to deal with these problems."

The girl felt unaccountably embarrassed and wanted to dismiss her age. "Well," she said, "where I come from everybody gets married pretty young. I guess it isn't that way around here. Was it that way where you grew up?"

"No, it wasn't," he said. Then he hesitated, as if he wished to give a fully honest answer, and added that it wasn't this way among his friends, at any rate.

"My best girlfriend, Roxie Wimmer, got married when she was fifteen. I waited until I was at least out of eleventh grade. I would've waited longer if it hadn't been for him." She pointed to the baby. "Some things you just don't plan for.

"Some things you do plan for," she went on quickly, feeling more and more talkative now. "But they don't happen like you think they will either. So I figure it's all luck. Only I've begun thinking lately that it's more like timing than luck. Maybe there isn't any difference between the two but I think I can see a little. When people say a person is lucky or unlucky, it makes you feel like you either got a good spell cast on you or a bad one, and if it's a bad one, you wonder why, and maybe you feel bitter and worry that it's never going to change. But with timing, you just bump into things that are already out there. Not a thing you can do about it, it's all about being in a certain place at a certain time. You don't earn good fortune by being born under lucky stars or anything. You just happen to be there when it arrives. That's my theory, anyway."

"Yes," Dr. Montoya said. He got up and went to the window. For a long time he stood looking out into the blackness. Then he turned and sat on the windowsill and looked at her. She expected him to speak, but he didn't. He simply looked at her with abundant kindness in his eyes. "I think you're right," he finally said, then he crossed to where she sat and put his hand on her face, very lightly, just for a moment.

As he was leaving the room, he said, "Maybe, if the storms continue we'll have an early winter and we'll be able to go skiing soon."

"Maybe," she said.

"Early the day after tomorrow," he said. "We'll start very early."

As soon as Dr. Montoya had gone, she left the hospital. Instead of going to her car, she crossed the street and began walking north along a path that bordered the river. It ran along a bluff about fifty feet above the water, and there was no protection from the wind. For the first time, she felt the force of winter coming on. Snow, hard and fine as grains of sand, stung her face. The earth was warmer than the air now and the snow melted as it landed. Thick platters of mud built up on the soles of her shoes and weighted every step. She felt exhilarated by the weather, by the hardness of the snow and the sharp, cold air. She lowered her head against the wind and walked faster. Then she remembered the scarf in her pocket and tied it around her head to keep her hair from whipping across her face. The chill got to her and she dropped down over the edge of the embankment to get out of the wind. She moved carefully so as not to slide in the mud and finally reached a clump of trees whose branches had formed a protective roof over a bed of semidry leaves, and she sat down to rest, watching the river not five feet away slipping quietly past her. Later, she knew that if she didn't move her legs would turn numb and cramp with the cold, so she struggled back up the embankment, grasping branches and pulling herself forward. Now, added to the mud caked on her shoes, were leaves whose shapes created feathery forms that stuck out from the soles. Soon she was close enough to see the lights of the university buildings. Her hands were cold and she blew on them, leaving small black marks around her mouth where her fingers, soiled by wet bark, had touched her face. The path ran closer to the street and every time a car passed she stepped back, hoping to avoid the spray of slush from tires. Her panty hose clung to her legs, and at times she felt little clumps of slush sliding down her ankles. Early day after tomorrow, she kept thinking. Soon she reached the campus and stopped some students coming out of a building. She asked directions to the library. They told her it was across from the administration building and walked away quickly, but she had no idea where the administration building was. She asked again, and this time a girl in a bright blue parka took the time to point the way, telling her where to turn and what to look for. Classes must be letting out, the girl thought. Suddenly there were more students, hurrying in small groups or moving singly in a purposeful and animated way through the storm. Their assurance seemed stunning to her. Could learning do that? Girls her age looked as beautiful as women in movies. They were erect and poised. The boys were out of magazines. They didn't seem to have a normal walk but sprang off the balls of their feet like they'd just been excited by good news. They all shielded their stomachs with clutched books, or else wore backpacks and used their arms to carve great gestures out of the air. They shoved their hands deep in their pockets and formed loops for other arms. She was the same age as these students but she felt immutably alien. She was looking at another species of humans.

At a corner, she stopped and tried to clean some of the mud from her shoes with a stick.

"Step in something?"

When she looked up at the boy who'd spoken, his face changed. His smile disappeared and he looked away and hurried on. Her looks could wither. She felt a fierce separateness that she suddenly wanted to nourish.

Inside the library, she removed her coat and shook the water off it and put it back on. There were several rooms. She started with the largest, and when she didn't see him, moved on to the next. He wasn't there either, and she began to think she had missed him or he had never been there to begin with. Then she spotted him. He was sitting at a long table, next to a woman with dark hair. The way he tipped back in his chair, his hands clasped behind his neck, it reminded her of the way her father sat after dinner, when he was his most amiable and relaxed. The girl next to him wore a yellow scarf at her throat. From time to time, she reached up and ran a finger under it, like a man does when his collar's too tight. Otherwise, her hands rested in her lap, one on top of the other, palms turned up. The only time she'd seen somebody hold their hands like that was the one summer during high school when she worked at Vern Bushman Photographic Studios. Mr. Bushman posed the brides that way.

Taking care not to be seen, she moved down an aisle, her fingers bumping over spines of books. For a long while she stood and watched them in conversation, noticing things about her husband that seemed brand-new. For instance, he was developing a roll around his middle. His neck, thickened by years of school wrestling, seemed a thoroughly inadequate spacer for his head and body. He was wearing a pair of shoes she didn't remember seeing before. These things struck her as comical, and also as proof of estrangement. Suddenly he laughed, his mouth opening wide to reveal his white teeth. It was the laughter that propelled her forward, sent her right up to the edge of the table.

"Marva," he said, with such wonderment in his voice it was as if he'd never spoken her name before.

"Marva, what are you doing here? What happened? Where have you been that you look like this?"

"I came here to tell you something."

She looked at the girl in the yellow scarf and then back at her husband.

"This is Marva, my wife. This is Bobbin James."

"Pleased to meet you," Bobbin James said.

"You've got to be kidding." She stared hard at Bobbin James. "You and Bobbin just cramming for finals?"

"I don't know what's happened, Marva, but maybe you can just sit down."

"I've got to be leaving anyway," Bobbin James said, and started to get up.

"Sit down before I smack your head off," she said.

"Dale," Bobbin said, appealing to him for help, "I don't need this."

"That's exactly what I told him, I don't need this. That's pretty funny."

"You never told me that."

"Didn't I? Maybe I just thought it. Anyway, I didn't need it. I didn't need this thing that's happening between the two of you. Didn't you think I had enough to handle, Dale?"

"Why don't you and I talk about this and leave Bobbin out of it?"

"Want to know what I came to tell you? The baby's going to be operated on this week. Day after tomorrow. I came here to tell you that."

"OK."

"He says, OK. Boy, I don't know what to say to him anymore. Maybe you can talk some to him, Bobbin. He says you're a real good listener. Maybe you're a good talker, too. Are you a good talker?"

"You've got a lot of hostility and I think it's misplaced if you direct it toward me."

"Yeah, and I think you're a whore."

"You need a therapist."

"You need a dose of real life. Doesn't she, Dale?"

"You've got everybody in this place looking at us, Marva. If you don't care what people think, I do."

"I don't care what people think, do you, Bobbin? I don't think you do. If you did, I don't think you'd be doing what you are, because what if people found out? Wouldn't that make you look bad?"

"I don't know what you think we've done."

"He says you haven't slept with him. Is that true? It seems an awful waste. I wish you had. Then maybe at least I could tell myself it was serious, that it was something that really matters. You might as well make it worth the grief. I hate to be screwed emotionally for something that isn't even real. I really do."

Bobbin stood up. "Your wife is crazy," she said to Dale, and left.

"Just remember," Marva yelled after her, "just remember that anybody finds out and you're going to look bad. They're going to think very badly of you!"

They had to take the bus to get back to the car in the hospital parking lot. Every time she tried to look out the window, she saw their reflections instead.

"I know you slept with her already," she ventured one time, without getting any response.

Her own person looked more disheveled than she ever remembered. She wished somebody would turn off the lights in the bus so that her face would be buried in darkness instead of appearing like an admonishing image reflected in the glass. She really did feel she was looking back at herself sorrowfully, as if this other self regretted knowing her, or worse, pitied her. But turning away from the window meant looking at him, and she couldn't do that.

Another time, she said, "I guess making a scene doesn't bother me so much. It's just like what happened this afternoon in the playroom when the kid threw blocks. No matter what happens, everybody forgets."

He said, "Words are different. They're difficult to take back."

That was the only thing he said during the bus ride. He was quiet in the car, too. She didn't care. The silence felt good. Who had anything to say, anyway?

Roy was operated on, and he survived. In the days following the surgery, she existed only for the moments she could visit him in Intensive Care. She rarely left the hospital, except at night. She ate sandwiches that had been heated in the micro-wave while still in their plastic wrap, sitting at a counter in the hospital's snack bar. She looked at magazines without reading a word, studying only the pictures, the clothes, the spring fash-ions and the model houses. She watched the hospital personnel come and go, people whose faces were familiar now. Once, in Intensive Care, Roy opened his eyes and said, "Mom," and im-mediately closed them again. After two weeks he was taken off the critical list.

And then she had two dreams, one of them good, and one that was terrible.

But they weren't only dreams. Life occasionally prefigures itself, suggesting through an antecedent image the shape of something to come. In the good dream, she had sex with a man who told her he was from New York. He wore a very good suit, which he folded carefully as he removed each piece. In the mid-dle of the dream, she awoke to find herself coupled with her husband. They were actually making love.

In the bad dream, a child called for help, but she couldn't reach it. It was sliding wildly down a chute, like a long slippery passage, and calling for someone to catch it. Though she ran and ran, instead of coming closer to the child the ground be-tween them widened until the child was a speck in the distance whose screams, nonetheless, could still clearly be heard.

The day after the good dream her husband put his head in

her lap while they sat in the car, confessed to adultery, and said he was sorry.

The day after the bad dream, a child in the crib next to Roy stood up and looked at her. She was sitting on the opposite side of the room. Suddenly, the child pulled himself up and threw himself over the top of the protective railing. He'd just had kidney surgery and was still attached to plastic tubing stitched into his side. The tubing did nothing to break his fall. It tore loose from his flesh during the descent. She ran to him. Her screams brought the nurses. He was rushed back to surgery. Nobody could believe the child had been able to climb over the railing. Nobody understood how his restraints had come untied in the first place.

And no one really thought about her, what she felt after the accident. In the pandemonium, she was forgotten. For a while she stayed by her own child's bed, watching him. But her heart raced and she could barely breathe. Suddenly her chin jerked repeatedly, and she could do nothing to stop it. Then the spasms subsided. When Roy finally fell asleep, she got up and tried to act calm as she left.

She drove home at a ferocious speed. Several times cars honked at her recklessness. Loose objects rattled around in the backseat and the tires squealed as she took curves. Yet she drove with a feeling of being absolutely safe, as if protected, with no doubt about getting home.

When she walked into the house she sensed immediately that something was wrong. The chairs had been breached, the barricade broken, and in the living room, near the far end of the couch, a golden stain formed an irregular circle on the white carpet. The dog sat in the corner, facing her. In his unflinching gaze, there was neither remorse nor guilt. She went to him and her fists struck his hard muscle, which yielded nothing, not even an inch, to her blows.

Down by the lake, the snow on the beach was undisturbed. The canoe had been turned over to keep it from filling with leaves. The sky, which was opaque at the horizon, then a sickly yellow farther up and blue at its highest point. The last clouds of the day were in the process of scattering. The water had not yet frozen, but there were crystals at the edge of the lake, sharp slivers of ice. She paddled out to the middle of the lake. She had an expertise with the canoe after months of practice. Drag a paddle and you turn. Shift your weight and watch the subtle result. Water-skeeters, those graceful bugs she pursued as a child, didn't move across the surface of water any more smoothly than she did in her canoe. The bells of the monastery rang out the hour. As the light dropped, the trees became feeble shadows. The shoddy, provisional fragility of chance brought her here, kept her here, made all things possible, resulted in the terrible as well as the good. Roy had survived. And the child who threw himself over the side of his crib? Would he survive? Let them all live, she thought. Let all the kids on the children's ward go home. The stars took shape and filled the bowl of the sky. A little while before, they hadn't even been there. Now they congealed in immutable form, set for clockwork rotation throughout the night. If she overturned, she wouldn't last long in these waters. But she wouldn't overturn. She was absolutely certain, finally, of one thing, and that was she would not overturn. She would paddle, paddle, paddle toward the lights of Effie's house, hugging the shore for guidance, and she would knock on the door, she would accept a cup of coffee from Effie, she would sit down among the noisy exuberant family members, and she would ask, Do you know any tricks for getting urine stains out of carpet?

CLEARFIELD

When a fire destroyed the canning plant in Clearfield, where I'd worked for ten months, firemen were subjected to a bombardment of exploding cans of beets, peas, string beans, and apricots. People stood outside the burning plant, watching the fire fighters and listening to the explosions, which broke out windows and sent streams of stewed fruit and vegetables into the air. I was there, too, standing next to Henry Drisdom, our foreman. All I could think was, There goes my job.

We knew the plant wouldn't be rebuilt right away, if ever. It could very well have been arson that set the whole thing to burning in the first place. Equipment was outdated, profits were down, the entire place needed modernizing. Firemen came staggering away from the blaze with whole tomatoes sliding down their yellow slickers, apricots caught in the brims of their hats, string beans mashed on their shoes. A great inferno of food had erupted. Days later perfect purple beets were found hundreds of feet away from the wrecked plant, lying like parts to a game in the fields that bristled with golden weeds.

Years earlier I had gotten married, had a child, gone away, lived elsewhere, divorced, and finally come back home because I didn't know where else to go. I had no training, no money, and a five-year-old who had been sick most of his life and whom I needed some help with. So I turned to my parents, who said

OK, you can come back here and live with us for a hundred dollars a month. When my father said I'd have to pay a hundred dollars a month to live in their house, I thought, Why don't they just let us live there free since they have empty rooms, but I suspected, without even asking, that it was The Principle of the Thing. In other words, he was teaching me that you don't get anything for free, trying to make me learn that I'd have to take responsibility for myself. If I'd ever told him, I can't pay that hundred dollars, he would have caved right in. But I didn't, because I had my pride, too. So instead, as soon as I returned home, I began looking for work until I found the job at the Clearfield cannery.

My mother was very religious, and so was my father. Like all the people who surrounded me, the Mormon faith extended backward in their lives, through their own personal histories to their births, and then back through their parents' lives and their grandparents', so the faith was ancestral and deep, and it claimed them as completely as the religious forefathers had claimed the Great Salt Lake Basin in which we lived as the new promised land for their people. When I brought my boy home to live with them again, I had to adapt to their ways. I saw no problem, although I was no longer active in the church. It just meant keeping my opinions to myself, going with the flow, so to speak.

Nightly we prayed. Family prayers came before dinner, when everything was ready to go. Steaming pots were turned off and left covered with lids while we knelt down together. We were three generations . . . me, my son Roy, and my parents, who were getting old. There wasn't anybody else at home. Sometimes we prayed around their bed, kneeling on the carpeted floor, sometimes we knelt in the living room, where the fabric on the couch, left over from the fifties, had a harsh surface of tight little knots.

Clearfield was just a little row of businesses built up along a crescent bend in the highway. Irrigated alfalfa fields and acres of forage cropland crowded the highway and pressed close to the business district. The cannery sat at the end of one of the dirt roads that branched off to residences. It provided summer jobs for many of the town's younger women, and a few year-round jobs for older people. But most of the activity happened in the summer, when tomatoes and other vegetables and fruits were packed not later than one day after picking. The tomatoes, for instance, were mechanically washed, then fell onto an inspection belt, from which those showing mold or decay were discarded. Jets of live steam played upon them in a scalder, until, by a slight finger pressure, the skin slipped from the fruit. Girls cored and peeled them by hand, and they were placed in an automatic filling machine, which filled each can with the specified amount of juice and tomatoes. Labeling and casing were done by machines, and the labels were customarily put on upside down, so the housewife could have a shiny, dust-free top to open. My own particular job was inspecting the tomatoes for any mold or decay. I worked with a woman named Ilene, who sat across from me on the other side of the conveyor belt, and who cracked a lot of jokes. From the first day on the job, I knew I was going to like it there. This may sound improbable, but in some ways it was like going into a big kitchen each day and cooking up something with friends.

Henry Drisdom, our foreman, never treated Ilene and me as if we were just his workers. There was repect in that plant. I liked the way the machines didn't rush you; the conveyor belt moved slowly, giving us plenty of time to look over the tomatoes, sizing up their perceptible flaws, their imperfections, before deciding whether to discard them or not. Often we brought our lunch and ate outside, sitting at a picnic table Henry had brought from home, with a view of flat dusky fields stretching toward the Great Salt Lake, and talked about men and women, our children, and the prospects of love.

Because Roy had been so sick much of his life, my parents had a special feeling for him. When I came home from the cannery in the afternoons, I found him calmly sitting on my mother's lap, watching game shows on TV with her, or following my father around the yard, assisting him in some project by holding a can of nails or the end of a sheet he was bringing from the clothesline. My father was retired. My mother worked part-time in a department store. Roy quickly became the focus of their lives. They didn't exactly spoil him, but they enfolded him in love, which was just what he needed to still the nightmare of needles and the unsteadiness the divorce had brought on. Only once did I see my mother lose her temper with Roy. They'd gone to the dairy for milk. On the way home, Roy, who was in the backseat of the car, tried to lift the big gallon container of milk from the floor and was told to leave it alone. He tried again, and this time the lid came off and most of the milk spilled out onto the carpet, just as they were pulling into the driveway. My mother yelled at him when she saw what he'd done and tried to smack him on the fanny, but Roy ran into the house and hid under a bed, making it impossible for her to reach him. For weeks after that we had to leave the windows down on the car, and still, a sour stench hit you every time you got in. The smell never really came out of the carpet, an odor that was acrid and unpleasant like a person's sickness.

After the accident at the cannery, I didn't know what to do. I'd been happy there, and I was so sick of changes in my life I didn't want another. Fortunately, my sister came through. She had an idea that changed the course of things.

"You going to live at home forever?" she said to me one morning when I stopped by her place.

"It's not so bad."

She was quick and small and moved around her kitchen like she was in high gear. Her daughter had recently married, her son was on a mission in Japan. She missed them and had filled her life with other things in order to diminish her loneliness. She was president of the Young Women's MIA—Mutual Improvement Association—the church group for teens, she took aerobics, she acted as the accompanist for the choir, she belonged to the Daughters of the Utah Pioneers, she golfed, she jogged, she volunteered for Meals on Wheels, she traveled to conventions in foreign countries with her husband who was, that year, president of an insurance adjusters' group.

"You're not going to meet any men living at home," she said.

"Maybe I don't want to meet any men."

"What are you, queer?" she said, and we both laughed. She's got a good sense of humor. She says whatever comes into her head.

"I don't want to meet any men *or* women," I said. "I just want to get on with my life. Right now I can't do anything until I get another job."

"What kind of job would you really like?"

"I don't know. Something that would pay well. Something that's interesting to me."

My sister looked at me funny. "What?" she said. "What kind of job is that?"

"I don't know."

"Don't you need to go to school?"

"I think I probably do," I said.

The phone rang, and my sister answered it, leaving me to think about what I'd just said. What if I really did go to school?

A picture of her son, Rowan, was sitting on the sideboard. Rowan, I remembered, was planning for his mission while he was still a little boy. He used to stand up in church and sing, "I want to be a mish—on—ary . . ." He once said he hoped the church didn't send him to Japan because he'd heard all the missionaries got to eat over there was birdseed and Kool-Aid. When he turned eighteen and got his mission call, sure enough the church had decided to send him to Japan. Sometimes I thought of writing him and saying, Hey, Rowan, how's the birdseed and Kool-Aid over there?

My sister was really laughing over something. She held the phone so tight I could see her knuckles turning pale, and when she laughed, she bent over and almost brought her nose to her knees. She had so many friends that her phone was always ringing. If you wanted to call her up, you'd better do it early in the morning or late at night. Otherwise, the line would either be busy or she'd be out somewhere. Aside from Ilene and Henry and a few others from the cannery, I didn't really have any friends, and these were not people who ever called me up at night to talk or with whom I ever made plans to do anything.

When my sister got off the phone, she said, "Going to school wouldn't be such a bad idea. I bet you'd meet some men." She sure couldn't see me leading the single life. She wouldn't rest until I'd attached myself to a man again.

"What would you study, though?" she asked, rearranging the magnets on her fridge. Each magnet was a piece of fruit. There was one odd magnet—a cute gray kitten. She lined up the banana, cherry, watermelon, lime, and strawberry, and then she put the kitten right below. It looked as if the kitten were getting ideas about fruit, imagining things like in cartoon bubbles.

What would I study? Business administration, I was going to say. Political science. Psychology? None of these seemed right. I couldn't see myself caring anything about those subjects, or sitting through classes.

"I'd have to look into it," I said.

"You know," she said, "there's an apartment opening up at The Ralphonso." The Ralphonso was the name of some apartments my sister and her husband, Marty, owned. "We could let you have it for what you're paying at Mom and Dad's, just to help you get going. Then you'd only be two blocks from the college. You could check into financial aid. Marlene Dunkley got into a program for women returning to the work force and didn't have to pay a dime for getting trained as a CPA until two years after she graduated from college. You could call her up and ask her how it works. But you ought to get out of Mom and Dad's and get your own life going again."

"I like it there," I said to her.

"But you ought to be on your own."

"Why?"

"Because they deserve not to have any responsibility at this point in their lives. They need their privacy, too. Don't take this wrong, but it's a burden having your kid at home, especially having a five-year-old around."

Well, I felt a little hurt by that. But I knew she was right. I probably was imposing on them.

The Ralphonso was a fourteen-unit apartment building, located at the south end of town. It was named after Marty's father, Ralph, who had suffered a stroke and now lay immobilized in a nursing home in Kaysville. Ralph had once owned many acres of land but, after the stroke, the land had to be sold bit by bit in order to pay medical costs and to keep him in the convalescent home, until the last and largest piece was finally bought by a big developer and became the site of a large shopping mall. The only property the family kept was the site of the apartment building, which was constructed in the style of a mock-Italian villa and located across the street from the mall. They wanted to honor Marty's father by naming the apartments after him, and were delighted to find that his name, Ralph, converted so easily from English to Italian.

One day in the fall, Marty and my sister brought a truck and we moved everything belonging to Roy and me to the two-bedroom, split-level unit in The Ralphonso. My sister had put balloons on the ceiling. They were supposed to make me feel good, I know, but instead, I felt depressed. The apartment seemed astonishingly vacant, even though Marty and my sister had lent me a few pieces of furniture. I was especially depressed by the dining-room area, where, beneath a globe of bumpy orange glass, a card table had been centered, with two folding chairs placed opposite each other, chairs that looked bleak and expectant. They seemed too small for me and too large for Roy, as if people of an intermediate size, like adult midgets, were supposed to occupy them.

Mabel Ridges accepted Roy into her Progressive Tots Preschool. My classes started a week later. A counselor helped me prepare a list of courses that could eventually be applied to an all-purpose degree. Surprisingly, the first semester I got good grades, excelling in every subject except one—Earth Sciences. I applied myself seriously to the course work. I wasn't distracted by dating, sororities, or extracurricular activities, like some of my classmates. It amazed me I took to school the way I did, since I'd never been a good student before. But it seemed to me that encoded in the materials for my courses was an explanation for things that had already happened to me, help in understanding my own life, and also the beginning of wisdom about the future. I found beauty, and a logic to experience that had thus far eluded me. No wonder they called different studies "disciplines": there was order here. I didn't know how I would use all this information I was getting. Occasionally, I thought of becoming a teacher, and I realized what attracted me to this idea was a quality of surety I'd observed in some of my own professors. I thought, I'd like to have some of that. Still, it seemed to me that I was old to be going to school, but it could have been worse, I could have been forty like Joyce Slater, who was in my Earth Sciences class. One afternoon, when I was having a particularly hard time comprehending something, I turned to her and said, "What do you think we're doing this for, Joyce?" And she said, "So we'll have a place in the world."

The Earth Sciences class turned out to be my favorite course that semester. I loved learning about weather patterns, currents in the oceans, the names of faraway capitals, the age of the earth and the guesses people made about what its core was made of, and looking at the ragged edges of continents to see how they might have once fit together before breaking apart into arbitrary shapes, like a cookie snapped in two. But I didn't do well on the tests. The best I could pull down was a C minus. It brought my whole grade point average down. I failed the final and, consequently, the whole course. I didn't seem to have a scientific sensibility.

I decided to take the course again and see if I couldn't do better, but I had to wait until fall. During the summer, I worked for Wolthius Dairy, selling milk from a small store adjacent to the pasteurizing plant. Sometimes Roy came to work with me and played with Betty Wolthius's children, a boy and a girl who were sweet and sharing. I still felt protective about him, but gradually the impulse to shadow him constantly, ready to catch him midfall or keep him from taking risks, subsided, and I saw him becoming a normal little boy, whose legs were strong enough to carry him when he ran and who found balance and more and more strength. That was the summer I let go of him in some way that's hard to describe. I said to myself, Let him go so's he can be healthy. I stopped making Roy take naps. I stopped making him do a lot of things. I felt like he ought to start making his own pace in the world, and it worked. I stood inside the store that summer and watched him conquer things, one right after the other—slippery slides, wagons, trees, the tying of his shoes. A new fierceness rose in him when other kids tried to take what he thought was his, whereas before he had surrendered and run to me for comfort. I thought, Why do parents ever worry when their kids start pulling away, drawing themselves into a shape that's their own? To me, it seemed that Roy was helping make us both free. His hair bleached out. He got a healthy color of pink, totally different from the shades of blue (before the operation) and white (after the operation) he'd been most of his life. He grew astonishingly rosy and his flesh became full and firm and, more and more, when I looked at him, I felt the marvel of a creation that was in part mine.

Money was very short for us since I was trying to put some away for the winter months and school. Sometimes I stole food from FoodKing, steaks or pork shops or small roasts, items outside our budget, developing a system so smooth it seemed, after a while, very unlikely that I'd ever be caught. I would pick up the steaks or chops, then grab a few other items—milk, bread, Oreos, lettuce, things we could afford—and put them in a plastic carry basket. Then, before going to the checkout, I would stop at the little snack-bar fountain in the corner of the store, where there was a counter and a few stools, and order ice cream cones for me and Roy. Sometime during the eating of the ice cream cones, I'd reach down and look for something in my bag and at the same time, take the steaks out of the basket and slip them inside my purse. I always carried a big purse. I always sat at the corner of the counter, near the wall, where I was partially hidden from view. And I always felt this combination of emotions—guilt, an exhilaration derived from danger, and something that seemed to me like passion, simply an overwhelming passion for living—just at the moment when the meat was being transferred to my purse.

Snow came early that fall. By the time school started in September, Ben Lomond and Mount Ogden and the ridges in between were white all the way down to the cliff face. The leaves on the oakbrush were just coloring and their fierce reds and oranges burned through the lighter dustings of snow. My father had a seizure and swallowed his tongue. He bit my mother, who was in the process of saving him. He was all right after the seizure, but her hand looked as if she'd been attacked by an animal. His jaws had been viselike in their rigidity, unresponsive to pleas or screams. She had to work against his teeth, which bit into her as she struggled to find a hold on his slippery tongue, clawing the fluted ridges of his mouth, and the slick, somehow slightly indecent-feeling walls of his throat. For minutes they were locked in this struggle. She straddled him on the floor of the den, and fought to keep him alive. There was no way to free her hand, no possibility of leaving him long enough to make a phone call. She had to stay with him, joined in a sort of panic and combat, and save him from himself. Later she admitted that she thought he was a goner. They joked about it afterward, but I sensed in them a new wariness, as if they feared it would happen again.

Roy started first grade and was now in school all day. With the help of a student loan, I signed up for eighteen hours of classes, my heaviest load yet. Once again, I did well, with the exception of Earth Sciences, which seemed no easier this time around than it had before. Until I met Darcy, that is.

I noticed him the first day of class, not because he was one of those people who purposefully brought attention to himself, but for just the opposite reason. He was quiet, withdrawn, very serious. He was a few years younger than me. I later learned he'd just returned from a mission to Tahiti. That figured. He had a wholesomeness about him. But what made him different from the other returned missionaries—and there were a lot of them in my classes—was his absolute serenity, a quiet composure, a depth I sensed in him that made me feel that if he was a believer, the church couldn't ever begin to contain all those beliefs. I felt they must have spread out beneath the surface of him in many different directions, creating a person more complex, and more questioning, than the average returned missionary, who usually thought of one thing: getting a girlfriend who could turn into a wife.

This is what I guessed, but I had to wait to find out if I was right or wrong.

What I did know was this. Every time he spoke up in class— and he usually only did so when the professor called on him, when no one else had been able to answer a particular question—Darcy quietly delivered a few sentences that were so lucid and clear it became obvious to me that he already knew everything this class was trying to teach him. Moreover, the way he said it made everything more comprehensible to me. He could explain things better than Dr. Blankenship, the professor, could. It seemed to me he had the knowledge I wanted, about a subject I loved but that continued to elude me, and I began thinking that if I approached him, he might help me.

One day, before class, I waited for him outside the social sciences building until I saw him coming up the walk. He was pleasant-looking in some ways, but he wore the top button of his shirt done up and it made him appear old-fashioned. His pale blond hair was cut so that it was left long on top and flopped over his eyes, but was almost shaved on the sides above his ears. He wore small round glasses that looked too little for his full face. His body was square and muscular. You might have thought he worked out at a gym, but I later learned his strength came from working on his father's farm. His eyes were a blue that was undisturbed by traces of any other color. His skin was very creamy in color and texture. His cheeks were mottled pink, like a child who'd been out in the cold.

When he got close enough to hear, I said, "Darcy?"

"Yes?" He looked at me very seriously.

Beyond him, way over on the other side of the valley that stretched below us, I could see the Great Salt Lake, lying like a sheet of tin between brown hills.

I reminded him I was in his Earth Sciences class and introduced myself. I told him what I wanted, that I was having difficulty understanding some things, and I wondered if he could spend a study period with me.

He didn't say yes or no. He said, "When?"

"Maybe this evening?" I said.

"I've got to baby-sit," he said.

"Tomorrow, then?"

"I have to baby-sit then, too."

Was it that he didn't want to help me? And what was a grown man doing baby-sitting, anyway? Whose babies were these?

"I could do it Friday," he offered. "Sometime in the afternoon."

I said that would be great. That's the word I used, great. We agreed to meet in the Student Union at a certain time, and parted. Not once had he smiled. His seriousness, rather than appearing offensive, struck me as a quality I could deal with. Also, I suspected, just from the way he had spoken to me, that he was a very gentle person.

"What's the thing that's giving you the most trouble?" he asked.

We were sitting on a sofa outside the cafeteria, on the second floor of the Student Union. A smell of overcooked food, like boiled canned peas, came from the next room.

I said, "Trying to determine latitude from the day of the year and the angle of the sun above the horizon." This had been a problem I'd been struggling with all week.

He opened his book onto his knees. Where his trousers pulled over his thighs, I could see an outline of his Mormon garments underneath. He wore a short-sleeved white shirt and a tie that looked as if it could have come from his time in the mission field in Tahiti. It was maroon with yellow bananas that appeared hand-painted. I could also see the outline of his garments beneath his shirt.

"You understand," he said, "that the sun never moves farther north than the tropic of Cancer, or farther south than the tropic of Capricorn, in terms of being directly overhead. Of course, its light reaches to the poles." On a map, he pointed these out to me, the tropical lines, the poles. The world was encased in a very symmetrical grid whose lines were ever-bending toward the finite points of the poles, which were not true magnetic spots but hypothetical locales. The equator, of course, was the great circle of the earth that was everywhere equidistant from the two poles and divided the earth's surface into the northern and southern hemispheres.

He discussed the concept of solstice and equinox, the seasonal migration of the sun, and related this to the equator, the poles, the tropical lines. Now came, for me, the difficult part—comprehending the mathematical equation I needed to solve the problem presented by Dr. Blankenship. For the next hour, Darcy set up hypothetical situations: It's December 21. You wake up in the morning on a boat in the Pacific. With your sextant, you can measure how far the sun is above the horizon line at exactly twelve noon. What is your latitude? Or, You're on board a ship. You've been out of port two days. It's June 21. You wake up with the sun already overhead . . . high in the sky . . .

I tried to pay attention, but I kept thinking of Roy's father, who had been a navigator in the navy and had, time after time, in response to my requests, described for me the way the ocean appeared from the deck of a ship.

I didn't do too well that first tutorial session, but we met again the next week, and the one following that. We didn't talk about ourselves, only the class assignments that were hardest for me. He had a lot of patience. Sometimes I just looked at him, thinking I would never get this. And then he would begin explaining it again, in a different way.

The third meeting, I said to him, "Darcy's a funny name. Where did it come from?"

I thought he would tell me a story of some kind, but he only said, "I don't know." He seemed to be blushing slightly.

"I should have said it was different, not funny, I guess."

"I've never liked it," he said.

"Where do you live?"

"Clearfield," he said. "West of the old cannery."

I didn't tell him I used to work at the cannery. Nor had I said anything about being married before, or about Roy. He seemed to me to be so much younger than I was, so much more . . . what? Inexperienced? Purer? And yet I couldn't help it. More and more, I began wishing that we had more time together, and that we could do something besides just study.

Out of the blue, he stopped me one day after class and asked me if I'd go to the Gold and Green Ball with him. The Gold and Green Ball was put on every year by different wards in the church. It was a dance for everybody, for old people, young people, all ages. I hadn't been to one since I was in junior high school. The Gold and Green Ball? Couldn't he have asked me to do something else? But I said yes, I would go. The dance, it turned out, was six weeks away. I couldn't believe it! Did he think somebody else was going to ask me and he had to get to me early? Wouldn't it be awkward now, being together, with this date looming in our future?

In truth, nothing changed. He continued to help me, showing me kindness in what seemed a rather formal way, but it may have only been his nature to be so reserved and serious.

Many mornings when I woke up in my bedroom in The Ralphonso, I wished Roy and I were back in my parents' house. I didn't feel I could begin to fill up the rooms in the townhouse with what was needed for us to be comfortable. I don't mean furniture or anything like that. I mean a sense of living, of family. We didn't go anywhere. TV bound us up like the glue in our lives, attaching afternoons to evenings, evenings to bedtimes, sometimes even mornings to evenings. Everything around us was new, the carpeting, the drapes that seemed like melted glass spun into fiber, the cabinets in the kitchen that caught dust in their ornately carved surfaces. And yet, small worrisome accidents began happening: The toilet paper holder, a gilded thing hinged to a burnished plate, fell off the wall. Formica began separating from the counter in the kitchen. A light fixture in the bathroom pulled out of the ceiling when I tried to change a bulb. Carpeting on the stairs came loose and began curling up like wood shavings. All these new things were falling apart around us, and each time I had to tell my sister about some new mishap, I felt she blamed me for not caring enough about what had been entrusted to me. The other tenants of The Ralphonso were young, childless couples, or else retirees. There was no one for Roy to play with, and he was constantly underfoot. I felt we were both becoming bored and more anxious. We ate junk food. We slept a lot. I even began missing a few classes, because I began thinking, What's the point of this? I was three years away from a degree, and what would I do with it when I got it?

"Give her another waffle," my mother said.
"I really don't want it."
"It isn't cold."
"I didn't say it was cold. I'm just not hungry."
"If you'd set it upright like this," my father said, tipping the waffle so that it rested on the table, leaning against the plate.

"If she'd only tip it up like this it wouldn't get soggy. It wouldn't sweat," he added.

He was right. Where the waffle had been lying on the plate, there was a perfect outline of its shape in the form of humid, steamy droplets.

"Nobody wants to eat soggy waffles," my father said.

"I'll eat it," my mother said defiantly. She sat down at the table with us and snatched the waffle up. "If it's not good enough for the two of you, I guess it'll just have to be good enough for me. That's all right. I'm not fussy."

"She means like some people," my father said.

"That's right. If the food around here isn't good enough for you, you should cook your own."

"I have to be real careful what I say these days," my father said, not being careful at all. "She's kinda touchy. I'd say she was going through her change if I didn't already know that everything's changed about as much as it's ever going to."

"What do you know?" she said. "I may have a lot of change left in me. I'm just not saying what I'm going to change, or when I'll change it."

They kidded each other like this a lot these days. I felt it had something to do with the seizure, that it had scared them and forced them to see that they might lose one another some day soon, and so they started shoving each other apart a little already. Sometimes it bothered me when they went at it, even in a joking way. I wanted to say, Hey, stop it you two. Don't hurt each other before the inevitable hurt that's going to come. But even when they were at each other, kidding on the square like that, I wanted to be at their house, where Roy and I could get caught up in their lives, rather than watching time go by according to the *TV Guide*.

Over the Christmas holidays, I got a job at ZCMI, the church-owned department store where my mother worked part-time in china shipping and receiving. School was out for three weeks. I figured I could make some badly needed money. I wanted to buy Roy a swing set, and it wasn't cheap.

My job was unpacking crystal and china and going over the packing slips to make sure everything itemized had been received. I worked with an older man named Hal, as well as my mother and a woman named Adele, and also Frances, who later joined the WACs and sent me an ashtray from Turkey. Hal was concerned with his retirement, my mother with my father's health, Adele with simply adding up a column of figures correctly or mastering the tax chart, and Frances, the only person close to my age, had only one thing on her mind and that was joining the military. Something happened over the holidays. My sense of estrangement became complete. I huddled over cardboard boxes, opening them with my Exacto knife, sheltered by rows and rows of plates and glasses, candy dishes and Hummel figurines, and listened to distant conversations about birthday clubs, social security allowances, training programs in the Women's Army Corps, and the easiest way to figure six percent. What was I doing here, back in this town, starting where I began? Sometimes, kneeling over my work, I became obsessed with remembering something and disturbed when I couldn't. One day, for instance, I was thinking about a kid in high school whose father had been the school janitor. Carl was the boy's name, but I couldn't remember his last name. I felt annoyed. Carl . . . ? Mr . . . ? Everybody thought Carl was poor and felt embarrassed for him because his father was the janitor. But both he and his father had a dignity and everybody ended up liking them both very much. A Swedish name . . .? For hours I tried to remember the name, and during that time, it felt as if I were terribly dislocated and could only become oriented again if I discovered the name. Finally I remembered it: Gunderson. And it was with great relief. These things seemed so important to me, but at the same time, Carl Gunderson and his father and the high school were distant from me. I never ran into anybody from school. I might as well have been living in a town I didn't grow up in, except there it was around me, like a memory I was confusing with reality.

"Do you feel OK, honey?" my mother said to me one afternoon. I told her I was fine. I told her this in a voice that said she needn't have asked. Later in the week I got angry with my sister. We were having a conversation about kids. I said, "Nobody realizes what it's like being a single parent. Somebody ought to help us," I said. "Thousands, hundreds of thousands of women all over the country are trying to do it alone, and nobody is giving them any help." All my sister said was, "You've got to remember, nobody made you get married, nobody made you get divorced, and nobody's saying you can't get married again if you want to. You just have to get up off your duff and find a man, that's all." That's when I yelled at her. I told her, Maybe some women didn't want to get married again, maybe they just wanted a little goddamned help. And she said, "Don't swear like that in my house," which was when I left.

Another thing happened. One day I was having my lunch in the restaurant on the second floor of ZCMI. I was sitting at the counter, when one of the store's security guards came and sat next to me. I'd noticed him before. He seemed cocky to me, macho, as if he thought he was something special, and always seemed to be on the make. He seemed like that to me when he sat down next to me. Predatory. He started talking to me, asking which department I worked in, that kind of thing. I gave him short shrift. He tried to entertain me by telling me about what he did during his off hours. He roped with a bunch of guys down at the Coliseum. They could rope even in the winter, because the place was heated. He kept two horses at the Coliseum, an Appaloosa and a quarter horse. I knew the Coliseum. I'd ice-skated there as a kid. I could have talked to him about that, but I didn't say anything. I wasn't exactly rude, but I didn't say but one or two words.

After a while, he said to me, "What have you got to be nervous about?"

That got my attention. I said, "What do you mean?"

"What are you upset about? Is there something you're trying to hide?"

"I don't know what you mean," I said coolly. But I was feeling nervous. There was the matter of his uniform, his police getup, the badge, and though I hadn't taken anything from ZCMI, there were all those groceries slipped into my bag at FoodKing that I couldn't help thinking about.

He reached over and turned my thumb between his fingers. "Somebody bites their cuticles like that, it means they're feeling real nervous. I get curious. I want to know, what are they nervous about? Have they done something wrong?"

"Go to hell," I said, and got up to leave, but it took me a second to gather up my junk, and he said to me, smiling in a thin-lipped way, "I think I'll be watching you."

Christmas was dismal. On New Year's, I went over to my sister's and played crazy eights and shot pool with Marty, her husband, who kissed me like he really meant it at midnight, and I almost wanted to thank him for that little bit of affection, except I knew it was nothing I should fool around with, not even kidding. Guy Lombardo said, "Everybody have a wonderful, wonderful New Year," and I thought, You bet. I was having terrible thoughts like that all the time now, things I couldn't control coming into my head.

Gunderson. Carl Gunderson. Mr. Gunderson, the janitor. Where were they now? Did Carl Gunderson grow up to be as nice as old Mr. Gunderson? Did he smile as shyly, as sweetly, as his father had, and have a face as honest as the day was long, so that to look upon him was to see a pure human soul?

I got an offer to work full-time at ZCMI. They needed somebody in the cosmetics department. I could make six-fifty a month. I seriously considered it. School no longer seemed like such a hot option. I began thinking about all the things I could spend my money on—a new car, trips to places like . . . well, I didn't know because there was no place I really wanted to go at the moment, but anyway, new clothes, eating out more often, things for Roy and me. I hadn't yet made up my mind when it happened. I got caught shoplifting at the FoodKing.

His hands were warm on my back. I'd worn this dress to make it harder for him. Where to put them, I imagined him thinking? What could he do with his hand when the dress was cut so low in back? He rested it demurely on my waist, where there was some cloth. But it also meant his fingers had to feel my hips moving, how the swell of my buttocks rose and fell as he guided me through a dance.

Refreshment! Good idea. Punch and cookies. We ate them hoping not to set off an avalanche of crumbs with each bite and muss up our nice clothes. I was feeling bad. I didn't want to be bad to him, but I could see it coming.

"You're religious, aren't you?" I asked when we started dancing again.

"Yes," he said, as even as ever. He didn't say, Are you? like I expected him to.

"I've been married before," I said. "There isn't much to say about it," I added, although he hadn't asked me to say anything. Then I told him all about Roy's father, which took two more dances. How he got involved with another woman. How the woman had a trust fund. How she was named Bobbin, like the sewing machine part. How we got into fights, made up, fought again. How we tried for two years to put things back together. How he now lives in Brainerd, Minnesota, where it's fifty degrees below zero at night in the winter, with his new wife, who makes thirty-two thousand a year as a lawyer. He did not, I told him, marry Bobbin after all. Darcy just looked at me. But when I finished talking, he said, "Do you want to keep dancing?"

"What else have you got in mind?" I asked, trying to throw him. And it seemed like I did. His eyebrows furrowed. But then he just took me up again, and we were off dancing to "For Once in My Life."

He was holding me closer.

"I used to be a Mormon," I said. "But I'm not anymore."

"I've always thought you were what you were born, like being Jewish."

I've always kind of thought this, too, but I didn't tell him that. I said, "Not really. You can also just be nothing."

⋅ ⋅

The Gold and Green Ball was so gay I couldn't stand it. Everybody was so nice, it was just too much. I started to think I was going to erupt. We'd dance, stop, and then start dancing again. People around us had a dewy-eyed happiness—old people, young people, the entire wholesome lot. I had dressed to be daring, red lipstick, a blue dress with a low back, more eye makeup than I ever wore, but when I caught sight of myself in a darkened window, I thought, Boy, do I look awful.

"Can we leave?" I asked.

His pickup had no heat. I was shivering, aching with the cold as we drove away from the dance.

"So much for the Gold and Green Ball," I said.

"Do you want to go out and get something to eat?"

"I want to go home," I said.

He stopped in front of The Ralphonso.

"See you later, alligator," I said, and jumped out quickly, without bothering to look at him.

In bed, between the cold sheets, I thought, What a joke. He's a kid. Mr. Polite. He's too young. Been two-and-a-half years in Tahiti, totally celibate. Probably never done anything in his life. Doesn't even try to kiss me. (Be fair, you didn't give him a chance.) Too good, too good to be true. You should have told him about FoodKing. You should have said, Guess what happened to me this week.

But the truth was, he was the only one since Roy's father, the only one I felt anything for at all.

The checker said, "Could we look in your bag, please?"

I said, "What?" and held my purse closed, thinking, Oh no, please no.

The manager, when he came over, had a face badly scarred from acne. His face was very severe. He pressed his lips tightly together. He shook his head when he looked at me. He said, "The question is, do we call the police?"

• •

"The test will be multiple choice," Darcy said, "except for the mathematical problems. Do you think you've got those formulas in your mind, now?"

"You mean the formulas for locating yourself, for finding latitude?"

He nodded.

"I think so," I said. He gave me a problem, and I solved it, just to test my comprehension.

"The rest should be easy for you," he said. "It's the part you like, names of places, highest mountains and longest rivers, major ocean currents, patterns of weather."

"Right," I said.

We were sitting on the same old sofa, outside the cafeteria in the Student Union. Hopelessly young-looking girls with thin, white legs that ended in shoes with thick, wavy soles, and boys who spoke loudly and laughed among themselves, were waiting in a food line.

"I'm sorry for the other night," I said. "I haven't been feeling myself."

A boy in a toga walked past. He must be going to a costume party, I thought.

"I've been very depressed," I said. I'd never said it out loud. I didn't seem to care anymore that someone should hear what I was thinking. Also, I wanted to set something straight. I didn't see any point in being mean to him again.

"I have a little boy who will be six next month. I'm thinking of quitting school and getting a full-time job. It's too hard keeping things going this way. I've slept with a lot of different men. I don't believe in anything anymore. Sorry, these are all true things. And I'm sure things are going to be all right for you. I like you, but I don't want to go out with you again."

He looked at me as if he were going to speak, but when he didn't, I added, "I also just got busted for shoplifting some steaks from FoodKing. They didn't call the police, but they gave me a lecture in front of the whole store. My little boy was there, too."

"My car battery's dead," he said, like that was the most logical extension of what I'd been saying. "I've got some jumper cables but I need somebody to give me a start. I'm in the upper parking lot. Do you have time to help me?"

I don't know how it started. I don't know exactly who did what, but it seems like, as I remember it, we were bending over the battery, each looking into the dark well filled with looping rubber hoses and grease-blackened objects, when he put his lips on my hair. I turned my head. He moved his hands to my shoulders. We got in the car. We lay down on the seat. His garments felt like a woman's slip. Afterward he said, "Don't quit school. You don't need to do that."

Roy got pneumonia. Everyone said he would recover, and he did, but there were weeks of worry. When he was finally better, I began looking for another place to live. I found something not far from the little house where I was born, on Maple Street. When my father saw it, he said, "I hope it doesn't fall in on you with the next snowstorm." It came with a chicken coop, which my mother said was hardly distinguishable from the house.

The test was a cinch. The only question I didn't get was, Burkina Faso is the new name for what African country? Otherwise, the answers came to me as if I'd always known them. Personal adornment and ritual mutilation began at about the same time as the development of cave painting and sculpture, around forty thousand years ago, during the Upper Paleolithic era. Cirrus clouds form in air above the freezing level. There are four kinds of precipitation—rain, glaze, dry snow, and hail. Frontal systems develop between the polar and tropical air masses. Mountains are found in the bottom of the oceans and form an extensive worldwide system. The Grand Canyon has been developing for twenty-one million years. The earth today, moving in a stable orbit, has an equable temperature and oxygen-rich atmosphere, so that it alone of all the planets in the solar system is suitable for life.

And so on and so forth.

I finished the course with an A.

Sometimes in the evening Roy and I walked along the street where I had lived until I was nine and my parents moved to a different neighborhood. The houses were small and varied, each different in architecture from the next. The neighborhood was so old things had had a chance to grow in. There were trees, bushes, flowering shrubs I remembered from childhood, and if I tried, I could remember how they looked to me then and compare it to how they seemed now. For instance, the Wangsgards had had a wonderful walnut tree. The Wangsgards were gone, but the tree was still there. Roy and I, cautiously edging up the driveway, sometimes picked up walnuts that had dropped to the ground. We found grapes buried in the vines growing over a fence near the corner of Tenth Street. Roy spat out the coarse seeds, I ate mine, and when I did, there between my teeth was my childhood. One time on one of our walks, I headed for a vegetable garden owned by an old woman, who seemed magically to produce the biggest tomatoes, the most beautiful squash, the finest peppers on a small plot of land just outside the chainlink fence surrounding her house. I never spoke to her, but I came to look at her garden. This day, from a ways off, I spotted potatoes that had just been turned from the earth. "Look, Roy," I said. "Potatoes!" I'd never seen them growing in the neighborhood. But there they were, red potatoes, looking beautiful lying on top of the rich loamy earth. As I got closer, however, I saw that they weren't potatoes at all, but windfall apples, dumped onto an empty plot and left to rot and enrich next year's soil.

I told Darcy the story about the apples I'd mistaken for potatoes. Those were the kinds of stories he liked, instances of mistaken perception, times when one thing was transmuted into another in the twinkling of an eye, anything that was harmless, like a joke told on oneself. We were standing in his parents' kitchen and he was cradling his youngest brother in his arms. Darcy had twelve brothers and sisters, and he was the oldest.

His parents were in Brigham City visiting relatives and he was baby-sitting again. The boy in his arms said he was hungry. "Do you want a peanut butter sandwich?" Darcy asked. He put the child on the floor, got a dull knife out, and a slice of bread, as well as the jars of jam and peanut butter, and placed everything on the floor beside the boy. "You'll have fun making it yourself," he said. The floor, I noticed, was pretty dirty.

Roy was watching TV with five or six of Darcy's brothers and sisters, who were stacked up on the couch. They all had blond hair. He blended right in with them. "Watch things for a minute," Darcy said to his sister Lulu, who was fourteen. "We're just going to step outside."

"What are we doing this for?" I said as we walked out into the night, although I thought I knew. But I was wrong. He only wanted to look at the sky. He had pretty much decided his field, while I was still uncertain. He was going to be a geographer, with a specialty in cartography—or to be even more specific, satellite mapping. We searched the sky for things that moved, and things that stayed still, trying to distinguish stars from satellites. That's how far we've come as a species, I thought, we've filled the heavens with man-made objects. His eyes were better than mine, so he spotted more satellites. But it wasn't at all difficult to see. It was a clear night and we were surrounded by farmland—dark, silent fields—so the sky really looked alive with a million-zillion stars. Suddenly, for reasons I didn't understand, I thought about all that had happened to me, how far I'd come, how I wanted things to work out, and how it seemed to me they had.

FOR THE BEST IN PAPERBACKS, LOOK FOR THE

In every corner of the world, on every subject under the sun, Penguin represents quality and variety—the very best in publishing today.

For complete information about books available from Penguin—including Pelicans, Puffins, Peregrines, and Penguin Classics—and how to order them, write to us at the appropriate address below. Please note that for copyright reasons the selection of books varies from country to country.

In the United Kingdom: For a complete list of books available from Penguin in the U.K., please write to *Dept E.P., Penguin Books Ltd, Harmondsworth, Middlesex, UB7 0DA.*

In the United States: For a complete list of books available from Penguin in the U.S., please write to *Dept BA, Penguin*, Box 120, Bergenfield, New Jersey 07621-0120.

In Canada: For a complete list of books available from Penguin in Canada, please write to *Penguin Books Ltd, 2801 John Street, Markham, Ontario L3R 1B4.*

In Australia: For a complete list of books available from Penguin in Australia, please write to the *Marketing Department, Penguin Books Ltd, P.O. Box 257, Ringwood, Victoria 3134.*

In New Zealand: For a complete list of books available from Penguin in New Zealand, please write to the *Marketing Department, Penguin Books (NZ) Ltd, Private Bag, Takapuna, Auckland 9.*

In India: For a complete list of books available from Penguin, please write to *Penguin Overseas Ltd, 706 Eros Apartments, 56 Nehru Place, New Delhi, 110019.*

In Holland: For a complete list of books available from Penguin in Holland, please write to *Penguin Books Nederland B.V., Postbus 195, NL-1380AD Weesp, Netherlands.*

In Germany: For a complete list of books available from Penguin, please write to *Penguin Books Ltd, Friedrichstrasse 10-12, D-6000 Frankfurt Main I, Federal Republic of Germany.*

In Spain: For a complete list of books available from Penguin in Spain, please write to *Longman, Penguin España, Calle San Nicolas 15, E-28013 Madrid, Spain.*

In Japan: For a complete list of books available from Penguin in Japan, please write to *Longman Penguin Japan Co Ltd, Yamaguchi Building, 2-12-9 Kanda Jimbocho, Chiyoda-Ku, Tokyo 101, Japan.*